Secrets of the Asylum

Secrets of the Asylum

Linda Hughes

Linda Hughes

Deeds Publishing

Published by Deeds Publishing in Athens, GA
www.deedspublishing.com

Printed in The United States of America

Cover design and text layout by Mark Babcock

Library of Congress Cataloging-in-Publications data is available upon request.

ISBN 978-1-944193-99-7

Books are available in quantity for promotional or premium use. For information, email info@deedspublishing.com.

First Edition, 2017

10 9 8 7 6 5 4 3 2 1

In memory of Elizabeth "Liz" Champlin, who loved nothing more than a good story. Her undying support, wicked wit, and writing advice will live on forever in *Secrets of the Asylum*.

1

Elizabeth Antoinette Wolcott Sullivan stood as still as Venus de Milo, looking out over the vast body of water before her. From her shaded vantage point high atop a hill in the white gazebo with its blue gingerbread trim, she became mesmerized by the glisten of sunshine on the bay. The whitecaps appeared to be dancing a merry jig. She stored the pleasing image in her memory for a future painting.

Emerging from her fugue, she looked around, trying to decide which way to go next. Seeing that it was a pleasantly warm day, her outdoor options seemed boundless.

A breeze caught a lock of her silky black hair, disengaging it from the hastily coiled bun on top of her head, allowing the runaway strands to tickle the side of her face. She reached back to pull out hairpins, carelessly tossing them aside, allowing her long mane to swirl about her shoulders. That felt much better but didn't solve the quandary about how to spend her morning.

Elizabeth turned her head. A lazy lace-trimmed hammock stretched from column to column beside her across a corner of the gazebo. It seemed to beckon her to snuggle in for a while. She knew from experience that would allow her mind to float as freely as her suspended body and could easily eat up the rest of the morning.

She took a quick gander behind her. Yes, there was the house. Actually, all she could see from here were steeply-pitched gables with blue gingerbread trim, as another hill between this spot and the enormous Victorian structure cut off full view. She knew it was there all the same. She always knew. How could she forget? Her stalwart husband reminded her daily of her household duties as the wife of the most prominent and wealthy businessman in the entire northern half of Michigan's lower peninsula.

He also liked to remind her of her duties as a mother. But her child, a three-year-old girl, remained in that house with her nanny, whom she seemed to prefer over her own mother. That was fine with Elizabeth, seeing that the mother-child bond expected at birth had entirely eluded her. She'd heard other mothers talk about this bond as reverently as if it came as naturally as their own heartbeat. Elizabeth supposed she should believe she was missing something essential to life, but the truth was, she did not. In fact, she felt nothing other than relief that her daughter and the nanny adored each other. She was glad little Meg had motherly love from somewhere; as long as she didn't have to do it.

Margaret Ann, that was the girl's name. Elizabeth liked to call her Meg, but "he" insisted upon using her full first name, as she'd been named after his mother who, from Elizabeth's point of view, would never have allowed her stuffy, arrogant, pretentious self to be called by a nickname. Thank God the old biddy had croaked the year before and Herbert's father had been dead since long before his young bride arrived, so Elizabeth didn't have any pesky in-laws to cater to. But still there was, naturally, Herbert.

"He" insists upon a lot of things, which is how I came to this, she thought, placing her hand on her pregnant belly. As if having to suffer through the throes of childbirth once hadn't been enough.

Suddenly she knew what she wanted to do. She suspected she'd known all along and didn't know why she so often went through this charade of pretending she might consider going back to that house.

With no one to see; as the mighty Sullivan property stretched for two miles on each land side and down the side of the hill, across a shifting sand dune, and over the beautiful white sand beach to the shore; she shucked her shoes, pulled up her taffeta morning skirt, gathered up her pristine white petticoat, pulled up the bottom of her knee-length drawers, and yanked off the garter that surrounded each thigh to secure her stockings. Tossing those little ribboned annoyances aside, she went for her stockings next, rolling the translucent silk down to each ankle, and then one-by-one sliding them off and dropping them on the spot. Next up was her white cotton shirtwaist, a casual garment donned solely for this opportunity. Impatiently, she worked the tiny ivory top buttons until she could yank the thing off over her head and get rid of it, too. Thank goodness society's strict rules didn't call for a pregnant woman to wear a corset when in private, so she was glad she didn't have to fuss with that stupid torture chamber. Off came her skirt and petticoat. Standing now in nothing more than a shockingly indecent sleeveless camisole and calf-exposing drawers, she finally felt like she could breathe.

Elizabeth Sullivan, only twenty years old, breathtakingly beautiful, and jailed in an unwanted marriage to an older man, spread her arms and let the air grace her sensuous, bare skin. She closed her eyes, breathing deeply. *Ah-h-h....* This was what life was meant to be like. Not mind-numbing dinner parties, not scolding church sermons, not yippy women's social clubs, not having a big old man poke her in the night, not even taking care of children.

With a yelp of joy, she leapt down the steps of the gazebo and gleefully galloped down the side of the dune, sand playfully squishing up between her toes as she went. Arms swinging, legs sprinting, and hair flying, it took only minutes for her to reach her destination on a grassy knoll halfway down the dune: The Cottage. Once a tumbledown shack left from before her husband's father bought the land and built the big house, she'd begged her spouse to let her fix it up and use it as a retreat for painting her pictures. A newlywed at the time, he'd agreed in order to keep her, his beautiful young bride, happy. Elizabeth knew he'd expected her to tire of her "little amusement" once they had children, and he'd even confessed to her that at that time he'd have the place torn down.

Little did he know that cottage would become her sanctuary. Since then, he'd argued with Elizabeth that she'd become too attached to the place and had become obsessed with her leisure pursuit. When she'd told him she had to paint to live, he'd looked as stricken as if she'd slapped him across the face, standing there as he had in his crisp black suit with a Waterford crystal whiskey glass with two fingers of Walker's Old Highland held suspended motionless in the air. She'd known then that he was sorry he'd ever married her. But he was also smart enough to know that if he did away with her cottage she had the gumption to do away with their marriage. She knew he'd never let that happen. That was too much of a scandal for a man like Herbert Ambrose Sullivan, Jr., to imagine.

So, he let her have her "silly painting shed" and left her alone there in the hope that someday she would come to her senses and take on a wife's responsibilities. In the meantime, as he'd told her many times, what could she possibly do out there all by herself that would lead to mischief anyway? She liked to paint pretty pictures. So be it. He'd never even gone down there.

As long as she showed up for aperitifs before dinner, dressed in fine silk and jewels, with her hair in a proper chignon, what she did during the day didn't affect him. They had a large staff of servants to take care of the house, including a tidy head housekeeper, efficient upstairs and downstairs maids, and a gifted cook. They had a nanny for taking care of children. They had a stable master and livery driver. They had groundskeepers. Herbert didn't believe Elizabeth could possibly do anything improper in what she called her painting cottage that would embarrass him while he spent his days at his office in town.

Or so he thinks, Elizabeth thought, smiling as she unlatched the timeworn wooden door and reveled in its cranky creak as she entered her haven. She went straight to her latest canvas, a half-finished water scene with vibrant blues and greens and white emanating from its surface, propped up on an easel. Running a finger over the dry oil paint, a tingle ran up her spine in response

LINDA HUGHES

to its effervescence, the hues radiating off the flat canvas to waltz
the picture to life.

Rushing to the windows on the bay side of the cottage, she
thrust them open and let the humid fresh air swash over the
room, the sheer white curtains she'd put up herself billowing ro-
mantically in the breeze. She pulled them aside for an unfettered
view of her subject. Then she opened the windows on the front,
the land side, allowing the breeze to enter in one side and depart
out the other.

Nothing would ever be held captive here.

She went back to a bayside window and spread her hands out
to rest on the sill. She'd had the windows put in, three on the land
side and three on the bay side. The foundation of the building was
a log cabin that had harbored only two small windows. At some
point during the long life of the place, plaster walls inside and a
clapboard exterior had been added right over the logs and mortar
to give it a homey, cottage feel. So, the walls were extra thick,
allowing for window sills large enough to sit on.

She skootched her fanny up on the sill and looked east to
scan the scene before her. The west arm of Grand Traverse Bay
sprawled out below, with the land arm of Old Mission Peninsula
across the water directly in front of her. To the south, in the distance where the bay curved to turn back into that peninsula, the
water abutted the town of Traverse City, where Herbert had his
office. She quickly turned away from that view and looked north,
where the bay disappeared over the horizon, leaving it to blind
belief that it mingled with mammoth Lake Michigan.

As a young girl in school, she'd learned that the Great Lakes
had been carved out by behemoth melting glaciers thousands of

6

years earlier, reshaping the land as they crawled south from the Arctic Circle and northern Canada. They'd done a spectacular job here.

How she loved her bay. Born and raised in Chicago of one-time wealthy, high-society parents who lost it all during something called the Long Depression of 1873-1878, before she was even born, her parents had hung on enough to keep up appearances until their daughter reached a suitable age to sell her off to the highest bidder. Of course Elizabeth knew they hadn't actually done that, but it had been clear to her throughout her teen years that she was expected to marry well in order to keep them afloat. And so she had.

Herbert, eighteen years her senior, had been an easy mark. A very lonely but very rich man, he'd been smitten the moment he saw her four years earlier at the Traverse City dock, where she, along with her parents, had landed for the weekend after sailing up Lake Michigan from Chicago with friends on their small sailboat. Herbert had been at the dock doing business of some kind and as soon as her parents ascertained his status in the community, they had been more than willing to facilitate an introduction to their supposedly sweet and obedient daughter. Elizabeth had always known, however, they had been happy to get rid of their recalcitrant child. Now her parents kept their distance in a respectable townhouse in a posh area of the Windy City. She hadn't seen them since her wedding day.

Good riddance. I did my duty there. Now I'm done with them.

She didn't intend to ever set foot in Chicago again and seldom gave her parents one iota of thought, knowing Herbert religiously sent them a monthly check, but today it made her laugh out loud as she had a fleeting notion they'd think her insane if they could see her cottage. There were canvases painted with outdoor landscapes and wild animals and birds all over the place, stacked on the floor, hanging on the walls, and propped up on logs of driftwood she'd dragged up from the shore. There was a plump chaise lounge upholstered in flowered chintz and scattered with fat pillows, facing the bay windows. A small table held a Blue Willow bone china tea set and a canister for tea, which was brewed in an iron pot over the small fieldstone fireplace on the side wall. A larger table held dozens of tubes of oil paints of every color and paintbrushes of all sizes, along with a can of turpentine and a glass jar with used brushes soaking in the pungent fluid for cleaning. A wooden stool sat in front of her easel.

She'd had everything delivered here by workmen and continued to have her paint supplies delivered on a regular basis. Herbert never said a word. He knew he didn't dare.

Elizabeth took in a long deep breath. Strong fresh air, mellow oil paint, and a hint of the turpentine: the smells of her world. Here she felt at home.

She took her yellow apron off the hook on the wall. Reaching under the untethered hair at the back of her neck, she fashioned a bow of the neck ties and then wrapped the waistband around to tie it in back. Picking up her paint palette, she stuck her left thumb through the hole and rested the palette on her flat palm. Taking a brush in her other hand and facing her work in progress, a sense of peace overcame her.

Finally, she could escape into her imaginary real world.

2

Meg fiddled with her dangly diamond and pearl earring.
Catching herself fidgeting, she stopped, demurely placing her
hand in her shiny fringed lap. Her other hand went to her champagne glass even though she didn't really want another drink.

Bored. That was the problem: She was bored stiff, a curious
development seeing that she sat at the head of a table at The 226
Club, one of the most titillating speakeasies out of hundreds of
speakeasies in Chicago. Surrounded by friends, with her dashing
fiancé at her side, they had gathered on this particular evening,
even though they gathered at one club or another on most eve-
nings, to celebrate the milestone of her twenty-first birthday.

She'd known as she dressed for the evening that she didn't
really care about going out. Usually meticulous about her appearance, pouring over the garments spilling out of her stuffed wardrobe, this time she'd donned the first chemise she spied, a black
and ivory chiffon Chanel with layers of glass straw beaded fringe.

9

Of course she'd thrown on her long triple strand of pearls and the earrings, but no bracelet as she'd speculated she'd be getting one as a birthday gift from her fiancé, which turned out to be a good guess. A sparkly diamond bauble encased her wrist. A carelessly tied black silk scarf circled her coif, serving as a headband, the ends of which reached to the middle of her back. Last year she'd sported a Clara Bow bob, the "It" girl's look being all the rage. But this year Meg had gone for a shorter cut, leaving her unruly black curls to fend for themselves. Tonight they chose to boink out in all directions around the scarf, giving the young woman who had just come of age an almost little girl appeal.

Feeling out-of-sorts for being bored in this place that she should enjoy, she sighed and looked around.

The snazzy jazz band with its Negro musicians playing a crooning clarinet, trombone, and saxophone offered up its usual repertoire of stimulating fare. The women club dancers had performed, kicking up their heels in the usual way, this night in flashy little red sequined costumes. Illegal booze, flagrantly ignoring prohibition, flowed freely. Smoke wound its way to the ceiling as young men partook of their usual cigarettes and young women flaunted their new-found freedom by puffing away, as well. Couples danced the one-step and the shimmy, with the exception of one couple who ignored the rhythm of the music and swayed cheek-to-cheek.

Earlier at Meg's table, steak dinners had been served. The crumbs of a white birthday cake sat in front of her, the confection itself having been devoured by her inebriated companions. Colorful paper streamers meandered every-which-way across their table in honor of her big day.

She should be having the time of her life.

Instead, the cacophony of blaring music, raucous laughter, and loud voices gave her a headache. She had to get out of this place.

Robert interrupted her thoughts. "Hey, baby, that's our song!" He grabbed her hand and yanked her out of her chair, dragging her to the center of the room. Shouting to be heard, he sang into her ear, "'Five foot two, eyes of blue, but oh! What those five foot could do, has anybody seen my gal?' That's you, baby!" He swung her around and broke into a lively one-step, then morphed into the shimmy. Feeling like an acquiescent sheep, Meg followed with a lackluster performance.

"Could she love, could she coo! Cootchie-cootchie-cootchie coo! Has anybody seen my gal?" Robert sang to no one in particular this time, appearing to pantomime, seeing that he could no longer be heard over the music. When he turned his attention to other dancers and they started competing to see who could kick the highest, a common practice with this crowd, Meg walked away.

Grabbing her sable coat off the back of her chair, she bolted toward the door. None of her friends even noticed her leaving, focused as they were on one particularly soused flapper on the dance floor who had shed her ostrich feather shrug and high-heeled shoes. When she started pulling up her lacy chemise as if to strip it off, the crowd went wild. Encouraging hooting and whistling reverberated off the walls, until a doorman nonchalantly picked up the dame, threw her over his shoulder, and carried her out the back. Boos rang out all over the room.

Meg fled through the entrance door on Wabash Avenue,

uncharacteristically rushing past that doorman without bidding him a courteous good night. Fresh night air thankfully filling her lungs the moment she alit outside. She thrust her arms into her coat and wrapped it tightly around her body against the brisk evening air of springtime, and stood there not knowing what she intended to do next. She'd left her gloves inside and didn't want to have to go back to retrieve them, so she stuffed her hands into the pockets of her coat. The gloves would undoubtedly be lost forever but it didn't matter; it wasn't as if she didn't have a dozen other pairs.

"Meg, what's wrong? Why'd you leave, baby? Aren't you feeling well?" Robert's voice behind her came as a surprise and Meg jumped.

"Oh! There you are, honey," she said, turning to face him. "No. I mean, yes, I feel fine." She looked up into his exquisitely handsome face. Robert, her intended, her love, her future husband, sounded more irritated than concerned. That irritated her. She couldn't stand the look of reproach in his eyes, their color so vividly green they looked like emeralds shining through seawater. She had to look away, choosing to set her sight instead on the five carat diamond rock on the ring finger of her left hand. She twisted it nervously.

"Well, what the hell? Why are you being such a wet blanket?" he admonished, tossing his cigarette onto the sidewalk and squashing with the toe of his dapper shoe. "Let's get back inside. This party is the cat's miaow tonight!" He took her arm and pulled toward the building. "It's your birthday we're celebrating, remember?"

"Oh, yes, believe me, I remember. That's why we need to talk,

Robert. The fact that it's my twenty-first birthday and I'm officially a grown-up now has made me know there's something I have to do. Really, Robert, let's go someplace quiet where we can talk. Please."

"And leave all our friends? Horsefeathers! No, I don't want to."

"Okay, go back in. I'll catch a taxi cab. Come to my house tomorrow so we can talk."

"Aw, rhatz, Meg. What a bunch of malarkey. You sure know how to spoil a party. Let me go get my coat. You can tell me about this mysterious 'thing' that's so urgent now that you're such an old lady." His sheepish grin didn't quite redeem him, but came close.

Meg smiled. "Thanks, honey. I'll wait here."

She watched him evaporate into The 226 Club and realized she hadn't given this any forethought or planning. What would she say? How could she possibly reveal what she had to say after lying to him for so long?

She didn't know how; she just knew she had to do it. This had been niggling on her mind for weeks as this birthday approached until it finally felt like it would drive her mad if she didn't get it out. If Robert was going to be her husband, he had to know about her mother. She loved him too much to let him marry her and then discover the truth. If their marriage couldn't be based on honesty, there shouldn't be a wedding.

Meg bit her lower lip. Brave thoughts to be sure, but how could she possibly translate them into words coming out of her mouth?

Robert appeared in his beaver coat, an open bottle of champagne in hand. He tipped his head back for a long draw and offered her some. "Here you go! Best toot juice in town. One more birthday drink!" She shook her head. "Holy hell, Meg, what's got into you?" he cast over his shoulder as he headed for his burgundy Pierce-Arrow roadster parked half a block down on the street. Meg followed but tagged behind, knowing full well what had got into her.

They drove to her townhouse, a neat flat in the classy Uptown section of the city, just off Lake Shore Drive. She'd inherited the house from her grandparents, her mother's parents, when they were killed in one of those horrible motorcar accidents a few years ago. They were people she'd never met and knew nothing about. She'd had no idea she would be a beneficiary but the timing turned out to be perfect for her to take up her own residence when she entered finishing school in the city after five years of living at an expensive girls' boarding school just outside of the city. Of course, he father insisted on house staff, so the three rooms in the servants' quarters on the third floor were occupied by a butler, a maid, and a cook. Even though the house made her feel independent, her father made certain she was never left alone.

Without a word, Robert drove, speeding his way down Wabash Avenue, going forty-five miles an hour and barely missing a horse and buggy as he passed them. The city now had more horseless carriages than horses and carriages but enough of the latter still existed that motorcar drivers had to be careful. Robert was not being careful, but Meg didn't admonish him, seeing that driving fast always made him happy. When he turned to follow the Chicago River to Lake Shore Drive she focused on the pretty view of the new electric city lights reflecting off the river and then when they turned the corner the gas lamps on boats reflecting off Lake Michigan. She loved this city and wondered if, after tonight, it would become her permanent home or if she'd feel the need to escape.

When they reached her townhouse and parked, Robert hopped over his door and ran to her side of the car, flamboyantly opening the door for her and extending his hand. "Beautiful miss, may I help you out?" His antics made evident his call for a truce. He'd accepted her wish to talk.

Meg took his hand and didn't let go until ringing the doorbell. Frederick, her butler, took so long to answer she'd begun searching her coat pocket for her key.

"I'm so sorry, Miss Sullivan," Frederick said as he opened the door. Meg had never seen the tall, thin, fossil of a man in anything but a black suit, causing her to wonder if he slept in the thing. He looked a bit like a fossil, but a calming one. She knew from the other servants he was a retired Chicago police officer, hired by her father to keep her safe more than to provide buterlery services. Even the big family home in Michigan didn't have a butler. Meg prided herself in never giving old Frederick a thing to worry about. She went to speakeasies until the wee hours of the morning but never overdrank like most of her friends, including Robert. She believed in chastity until marriage, so Robert had never been invited to spend the night. Sexual freedom might be normal now for people her age but it wasn't for her. Meg felt certain her butler's clandestine reports back to her father were as boring as beans. Still, her father's prying into her life aside, having an old police officer in her home made her feel safe and secure, and she was glad to have him. "You're home earlier than usual," Frederick said, "so I was up in my room. This being your birthday, we expected you to be out late."

She and Robert had entered, and Meg said, "That's okay, Frederick," as the man took their coats.

Robert addressed the butler, as well, explaining, "We came home early because Meg wants to 'talk.'" He rolled his eyes. The butler, probably out of habit due to his many years in law enforcement, did not respond.

"Frederick," Meg said. "Would you please have Anna bring tea to the parlor?"

"I don't want tea!" Robert insisted. "I've got this." He held up the champagne bottle.

"Well, I want tea," Meg said.

"Yes, Miss Sullivan, of course," Frederick said and disappeared.

Once in the parlor, Robert sat on the flowered chintz loveseat and patted the spot beside him. "Come on over here, my love, and tell me what's on your mind."

Meg went up and took the bottle out of his hand, setting it on a side table. She sat down and faced her fiancé.

"Oh, my, this is serious, I see," Robert said, crossing his legs and stacking his hands on his top knee. "Okay, I know what it is. You want to set a wedding date. You're unhappy we've been engaged for a year and haven't done that yet. Well, my love, I have a surprise for you. I was going to do that tonight, anyway. I'm ready whenever you are. So there." He grinned broadly, picked up her hand, and kissed it.

He could be a gallant charmer when he felt like it, a regular Rudolf Valentino, Meg thought. This promised to be more difficult than she'd expected. She cleared her throat.

"No, honey, that's not it. Although that's great! I want to set a date. But first I have to tell you about my mother."

The maid came in and placed a tea tray on the table in front of the loveseat.

"Thank you, Anna," Meg said as the stocky young woman left the room.

"I already know all about your mother. She's in a hospital for consumption. She'll probably never get out. I'm sorry for her, Meg, but that shouldn't stop us from getting married."

Meg poured a cup of tea for herself. Robert waved her off when she offered him a cup, opting to lean back and light a cigarette.

"No, Robert." She took a strong sip of tea for courage. "That's a lie. I should have told you a long time ago, but when we first met two years ago I didn't know we would ever be serious about each other, so a little lie of omission didn't seem to hurt anything. I didn't want to have to explain where my mother is really at. And then the time never seemed right. But you need to know the truth."

"Oh, god, is she living in sin with a sailor or something?" He puffed and grinned.

With a shaky hand, Meg put down her teacup and looked squarely at her husband-to-be, knowing this would determine if he truly loved her. "No, Robert, my mother has been in the Northern Michigan Asylum for the Insane for fifteen years."

"What? No, that can't be right. You don't mean 'the' asylum do you?"

She knew she didn't need to explain about the asylum; he knew good and well what it was. He'd even teased her when they first met about such an infamous place being in her home-town. He was especially aware of it because of the popularity of its Kirkbride architecture and being in the architecture business himself, the lavish Victorian style was well known in his field for having been used for asylums and hospitals around the country.

"Yes," Meg said, "my mother is mad. She'll never get out, from what I understand. My father had her committed when I was six years old and I haven't seen her since."

"Meg, you can't be serious. I know your father. He's an upstanding citizen and a very successful businessman. He wouldn't be married to someone who isn't playing with a full deck, for crying out loud. You must be mistaken. You haven't seen her in years; you don't really know. She must be in a hospital for consumption, tuberculosis. That has to be it."

"No, my father insists she's mad. But I've been wondering lately if that's true or if he just had her put away because she was too much of a free spirit for him, maybe even an embarrassment. Some men do that, you know."

"Yes, but either way! Hell, Meg, I can't marry a woman with a mother who is probably insane! In an asylum! What would people say? My family owns one of the biggest architecture firms in the city. It'll all be mine one day. I can't have a wife who could inherit insanity! My god, what if our children end up insane, too? No, this can't be right. You must be wrong. She must be in a hospital for consumption."

Robert had stood and paced faster and faster the more riled up he became, swiping his cigarette through the air. He stopped and looked at her, the ash from his cigarette falling to the plush Persian carpet below. Meg didn't move or say a word. Tears welled in her eyes.

"Oh, my god. It's true, isn't it?" Robert whispered, so discombobulated he forgot he held the cigarette and raked the fingertips of that hand through his hair. Dead ash fell onto his head.

"My father says it is." The tears spilled onto her cheeks.

"I, well, I see then," he stammered. "That changes things, doesn't it?" He confronted her, hands on hips.

"I suppose it does." She stood up and walked over to him, taking the diamond ring off her finger. Never so disappointed in anyone in her life, she said, "Here," and held the rock out to him.

"Oh, no, I'm never going to let anybody say I'm a cheapskate," he said, swishing his cigarette around as if to ward off the evidence that he'd ever been connected to this woman. "That's yours, Meg, even though our engagement has to be called off and we can't get married. You do understand, don't you?"

"Of course, I understand," she rasped, although she didn't. All she knew was that Robert didn't really love her. If he did, her mother's state of mind wouldn't matter to him, or at the very least he would have helped her find out the truth of the matter before calling it quits.

So that was that.

Robert, now her unintended, flew out the front door as if he walked barefoot on hot coals.

Meg stood in the middle of her fancy parlor, sobbing as she heard his fancy roadster rev up and speed away.

3

TRAVERSE CITY, MICHIGAN, 1921

Home.

The girl was coming home.

Abequa Crane, "All-Seeing Abby," the local Chippewa Indian fortune teller, had no other messages coming through tonight as that one clamored through so strongly, shoving any others aside. Margaret Ann Sullivan, "Meg," would be returning home soon. Perhaps within the week.

Abby figured there could only be one of two reasons for this message from her ancestor spirit guides to pound out so fervently, like the beating of powwow drums. Its vibrational energy permeated the thin veil between this plane and the next with a bang rather than the usual tap-tap.

The first reason was that Meg coming back to her hometown foretold a momentous event that would change the young woman's life and the lives of those around her forever. Perhaps even change the town of Traverse City itself forever.

The second reason, or perhaps an additional one, sat before her. Truth was, the girl sitting in front of her was so insipid and namby-pamby the spirits most likely were as bored with her as was Abby. The seer tried to focus her attention on the wan, skinny, young woman. Nope, nothing came through from the spirit guides. They were either so much more interested in the Meg message they didn't care about this unfortunate girl's future or the Meg message proved too strong for any other missive to slip by. In either case, the situation called for a measure this clairvoyant had seldom had to resort to in over twenty years of offering readings. She was going to have to act her way out of this one.

She cleared her throat, took a deep breath, and straightened her spine as she sat in her chair. She once read about that in a *Photoplay Magazine* she found blowing down the street, most likely left behind by a tourist in a silly bathing costume lolling around on one of the area's many white-sand beaches. Whether driving in their motorcars or taking the train up north to this part of Michigan from Detroit and Chicago, Abby would consider the intruders to be a nuisance except for the fact they reveled in partaking of what they saw as the occult, something they might not do unless on vacation. And that fattened the pot for All-Seeing Abby. The magazine that had probably been cast aside by one of the tourists had an article describing how entertainers prepared to go on stage for the Ziegfeld Follies on Broadway by standing tall and breathing deeply, all the way to their diaphragms. This might not be New York City but this performance promised to be just as challenging as far as Abby was concerned.

Norma... Was that the girl's name? Oh lordy, she was so dull Abby couldn't even remember. Obviously a vacationer from a wealthy city family, she wore a yellow suit with matching mid-calf skirt and knee-length cape. Brown fabric with a zig-zag pattern edged the cape and made up the belt at her waist. A white shirtwaist blouse and silky brown scarf tied in a bow at her neck added to the ensemble, and a brown short-brimmed felt hat topped it off, leaving only an inch or two of blond, tightly waved hair escaping into view. Abby thought it a ridiculous outfit for springtime. Well, for any time.

"All-Seeing Abby!" the girl exclaimed, embarrassingly breathless with anticipation. "You're so quiet. What do you see?"

Ah, Abby remembered her name just in time. "Nola, my child, I see…." She paused, needing to amend her thoughts quickly. "A tedious and mundane life" would never do. Better to out-and-out lie. "I see a happy life…." She paused again for effect, placing her hands over the crystal ball sitting in the center of the small table between them as she pretended to be glaring into the mysterious glass orb.

In truth, she didn't need a silly ball to receive messages from beyond. It could be a purple beet from her garden sitting there, for all that mattered. But Abby had learned years ago that her visitors were more likely to return if the scene fit their narrow conceptions of transcendence. Thus, they sat in her one-room log cabin, lit only by candles and a fire in the large fieldstone fireplace, with a filmy curtain mysteriously obscuring none other than her simple bed.

"I see a tall, dark, handsome man," Abby lied. Although, she assuaged her conscience by telling herself she had no idea what might ever happen to this painfully plain girl but anything was possible. Well, probably not, she admitted, but miracles did happen. Didn't they?

Nola's frail hand fluttered to her sunken chest. "Oh! All-Seeing Abby, that's wonderful! Will this tall, dark, handsome man fall in love with me?"

"Of course." Lying became easier as Abby hankered to get this person out of her cabin. Besides, it suddenly struck Abby that with the girl's apparent family fortune, there was no doubt some money-grubbing man would grab up this malleable female as his wife. "And that's all for this evening. The spirits are fluttering away in happiness for you."

"Thank you so much!" Nola picked up her handbag and stood. "Here!" She dug into her bag and came up with six one-dollar bills, three times the usual fee. "Here's extra for giving me such great news!" Reverently, she slid the bills across the table to place them next to what she considered to be the magical crystal ball.

Abby got up and ushered Nola to the door. "You are most welcome, my child. Now go in love." She opened the door and Nola stepped over the threshold, only to turn back.

"All-Seeing Abby, did the spirits by any chance tell you *when* I'll meet this man?"

"Um, soon. Very soon. That's all I know for now. Goodbye, my dear."

"Oh, okay. Goodbye." Nola offered a small wave and finally walked down the stone pathway to the black Ford Model-T Touring Car with a driver waiting for her on the dirt road that led through the woods to this cabin. Abby watched the motorcar turn around on the dirt patch out front and chug away down the road, its two front lights that looked like fish eyes shooting muted streams of illumination into the trees, as if spooky spirits frolicked in the foliage. Even though it was a short distance to the main road that connected town to the lighthouse on the peninsula, Abby knew her primitive, bumpy trail aptly added to the mystique for her guests. She loved it.

She watched as the lights turned when the motorcar came to the main road and disappeared. This was a ritual for Abby, especially at night like this, to make certain no one lingered on her property. And, she'd long ago admitted to herself, she liked to witness those fascinating sleek motorcars carry people to and fro. She'd been raised during the horse and buggy era, so being transported without the help of a big beast of an animal seemed amazing. Always trying to catch the names of the vehicles, she saw more Fords than anything, being in Michigan, after all. There were also Cadillacs, Dodges, and Chevrolets from this state, too. Once in a great while a Packard or Rolls Royce showed itself, traitors in the state where the automobile assembly line began with Henry Ford. Never had Abby had the pleasure of so much as touching, let alone riding in, one of the motorized carriages but she held out hope that day would come.

After removing the wood sign that said "All-Seeing Abby" from its nail on the outside of the door and placing it on the floor inside, she closed the heavy wood portal enough to leave it ajar and turned back to her room. Adeptly, she lit two kerosene lamps for more light, placing one on the table and taking the other outside with her, where she walked around the side of the cabin and into the woods to her outhouse. She knew it was popular to have indoor water closets but she'd never seen one and found the premise to be disgusting. That kind of business needed to be left to nature.

Gathering up her long skirt, she bid nature's call, ripping off a page of the Farmer's Almanac that hung from a nail on the wall to swipe herself clean. The owner of the garage where she did clairvoyant readings two days a week always gave her last year's almanac. Using it for this was so popular the publisher even provided a hole in the corner of the booklet for hanging on a nail. Abby found it wasteful that some people today spent money on prissy white "toilet paper" when all they had to do was use an outdated Sears Catalog or Farmer's Almanac. Even though she herself was half white, there were some things white people did that she would never understand.

On her way back to the house, she dipped her hands into her rain barrel and wiped them off on the rag nailed to the side, as was her habit. She paused for a moment to enjoy the smell of the lilacs along the side of the cabin. Once in the house, she closed the door with a satisfying thud, lowered the latch to lock it, and felt grateful to be left alone for the night.

Going to the wood shelf above the metal kitchen sink with its water pump, she took down a pottery dish, reached into a glass jar to extract a dried leaf of sage, and placed the leaf onto the dish. At the fireplace, she held the leaf to the flame just long enough to let the tip begin to smolder and dropped it back onto the dish. A tail of pleasant, pungent smoke wagged and wound its way towards the heavy wood beams of the ceiling. She plucked an eagle feather from the bouquet of feathers stuck in an old beer stein on the mantle, and carried the smoking dish around her cabin, using the feather to fan the smoke to clear the room of any lingering spirits that may have trailed in with her last visitor.

She did this with every visitor but this time it seemed especially important considering the prominent message her ancestor spirit guides sent this night. She wanted no interference. Ojibwas, more popularly known as Chippewas, always cleared a room or lodge or house—wherever it might be needed—to make certain evil spirits did not hunker down in the dark corners of the dwelling.

"Gichi-manidoo, aanikoobijigan manidoo, daga zhawenim wa'aw agaasate," she chanted as she circled the room, fanning the smoke. "Gichi-manidoo, aanikoobijigan manidoo, daga zhawenim wa'aw agaasate," she repeated two more times, three being the sacred number.

Then, just to be sure and out of respect for the other language she'd grown up with and the God of her mother's Methodist church, she repeated her chant three more times in English. "God almighty, please bless this small house."

Abby had no doubt her prayers were answered.

The room now fragrant with the scent of sage, she blew on the leaf to stifle its simmer and then placed the dish back on the shelf. She stuck the feather into the stein with its fellows on the mantle. Bowing in front of the fire, the giver of life, she said, "Miigwechiwi giinawaa. Thank you, dear spirits."

Abby sat down in her beloved rocking chair in front of the fire. This was where she could best communicate with her ancestor spirit guides.

First, however, as so often happened after performing a clearing in her father's native tongue, her mind wondered to thoughts of her parents, long dead. Her father, a proud Ojibwa medicine man whose freedom to fulfill his life's purpose had been strangled by white man's strange rules and laws, had died, she believed, of simple heartbreak over the oppression of his people even though they called it a heart attack. Her mother, on the other hand, a white farm girl who fell madly in love with a forbidden Indian and eloped with him when she became pregnant, had died of her own hand shortly after her husband died, her heart broken beyond repair. Abby's mother couldn't face the shame of her chosen "pagan" life without the subject of her ardor sheltering her from the fire of damnation hurled at her by her own kind.

Abby, Abequa, which meant "one who stays at home" in Ojibwa, had been fourteen years old when her parents died. Her mother's employer, Mr. Herbert Ambrose Sullivan, Sr., who hired Abby's mother to wash dishes and scrub floors in his opulent mansion on the hill, had visited the orphaned teenager to tell her he had long ago given the cottage and surrounding plot of land to her parents, so it was now hers. Legally, the plot sat on the edge of the many acres he'd purchased but seeing that her family had settled in these woods generations ago, he said, it seemed right that it remain theirs. She hadn't corrected him to say that her ancestors had dwelt in the area in spring, summer, and fall, but not winter.

The Ojibwa, proud of being one of many tribes of the large Algonquin family, had not been as ignorant as the white man. By the time brutal snow storms blew in from the northwest, they had built camps deep in the woods with stores of food to last through the winter. They knew better than to roam about in blizzards and get lost, like white men seemed to insist upon doing. After the thaw of the Moon of Snowblindness, what white men called the month of March, with the promise of spring, they moved their families to the maple groves and built a longhouse for everyone to share, so they could tap the trees and collect the precious maple syrup that provided a mainstay for the their diets throughout the year. Then they would move back to their rounded wigwams in small settlements like the one that had stood on this very property. There for the rest of spring and all of summer and fall they would plant and harvest, and hunt.

Some white men didn't seem to plan ahead so well, needing to spend money on food rather than planting and hunting it themselves. Most Ojibwa supposed white men couldn't help it that they were so weak. At least, these were the stories Abby's father had passed down to her when she was a child.

Ojibwa, Ojibway, Ojibwe: Abby had seen it spelled many ways and did not know which was most accurate. The people themselves used the word Anishinabe to describe themselves, but only with each other. That word, the meaning of which held stories of a history of the tribe beginning with the ancestors who came from the sky, was sacred. She mused at how her father had insisted upon being called Ojibwa rather than the term Chippewa that white people thrust upon them, mispronouncing Ojibwa. Ojibwa was the name given to their tribe by its enemies, so that was considered to be the more honorable word, seeing it indicated that the enemy, like the fierce Huron, recognized and thus feared them. But, frankly, the more fragile word Chippewa had become how Abby thought of herself because she used it to attract paying visitors.

She was, after all, a practical woman. Having to make a living with her clairvoyant gift and support herself since age fourteen made that necessary. She had indeed lived up to her name as the one who stays at home by often carrying on her business from her humble cabin.

Enough reminiscing! She decided. *On to the task at hand.*

Reaching back to drape her long, black braid over her shoulder, as was her habit, she gathered her skirt about her knees and wiggled her fanny back into her rocking chair to settle herself. Propping her moccasin-covered feet up on the hearth for warmth, she brought her palms together to rest on her belly, fingers pointed to the heavens. Eyes closed, she cherished the creak of her chair as she gently rocked back and forth.

"Dear ones," she said softly, "I heard you clearly tonight. I know she is coming. What else do I need to know?"

The ancestor spirit guides gifted her with much of what she wanted to know but left her in a quandary about what this would do to Lizzie. Elizabeth, Meg's mother, took heed of her own enigmatic guides and Abby dared not venture a guess as to what those epistles might entail.

All-Seeing Abby looked into the fire, with glints like starlight reflected in her earth brown eyes. Then she lifted her gaze to the beautiful painting sitting on her mantle, a peaceful springtime scene of the white birch trees in her forest and a spotted fawn peeking out from behind a fat trunk. She may not know everything, she realized, but did know without a doubt that whatever happened next she would need to stay close at hand to pick up the pieces.

4

Elizabeth stood back and studied her canvas. The lilacs might be too purple. She looked out the open window of her second-story studio at the blossoms gloriously gracing the view below and sending that wonderful lilac scent her way. No, she had them just right, she decided.

However, looking outside at the spring colors of lilac bushes, morning glories, and lush green grass, all awash in warm sunshine filtering through whimsical frail clouds, only served to call to her from out-of-doors. She had to be out there!

Sticking her paintbrushes into a jar of turpentine, she put her supplies aside and took off her orange apron. Glancing at herself in the full-length mirror, she appraised the gaily patterned silk lounging robe she wore, which she adored, but it wasn't appropriate for leaving her rooms. Undoing the gold buttons at her chest, she let the garment slip to the floor. It was decadent to demand such things of Herbert because it cost a pretty penny, but he had lots of pretty pennies so she didn't care. He'd certainly bellied up to get her two adjoining rooms in Cottage 23, a women's cottage, at the Northern Michigan Asylum, one room for living and one for painting. He'd sprung for draperies, Persian rugs, colorful pillows and blankets, a small chaise lounge, and a wardrobe for her collection of clothes. They were comfortable rooms, as she had no qualms whatsoever about asking that man for anything and everything she wanted. After what she'd gone through with him, she deserved it.

He still came to see her once a month, after all these years. His visits had become shorter over time, eventually dispensing of any pretense at idle chatter and being reduced to seeing if she needed anything. She spent all month in-between visits conjuring up items she "needed," like new clothes, which she liked now that styles were so much more relaxed than before, and new paint supplies. Her artistic endeavor had become so prolific she truly did need supplies on a regular basis. She even liked the housekeeper Herbert sent with the items, an attractive woman in her forties named Hannah.

Elizabeth wondered if Hannah and Herbert were lovers. She didn't mind. She thought everyone should have a lover, like she did, although she couldn't imagine any woman being sexually satisfied riding that horse.

Standing in front of the mirror, naked as a jay bird, she ran her hands over her luscious body. Thirty-eight years old, having given birth twice, her figure was still the stuff of men's dreams. Ha! Let them dream. There was only one lover who could truly satisfy her. Being in an asylum got her away from her husband and gave her the freedom she craved to pursue that love.

And to paint.

It was a good life.

Going through the door that joined her studio with her living quarters, she went to her wardrobe and threw on a plain cotton skirt and shirtwaist blouse like the ones worn by the other mad women here at the asylum. She grabbed her wide-brimmed straw hat and plopped it atop her black curls before going out and shutting the door behind her.

No one would question what she was doing. Being insane had its advantages, as everyone naturally always assumed she was nuts. That thought amused her, although she actually had "ground parole," meaning she was trusted to roam the grounds and work in the gardens as she pleased. She cherished her freedom and would insist on being released from this place if she didn't have it. Thank God, she'd often thought, she wasn't sequestered in one of the buildings with bars on the windows like the genuinely crazy people; that truly would drive her mad. Instead, she lived in a pretty "cottage," actually a huge house, which chambered about fifty women like her who were trusted to come and go during the day.

She started for the stairs at the end of the wide hallway but on impulse paused to knock on her neighbor's door. Jenny Pennington opened up and offered a weak smile. "Hello, Lizzie. How are you today?"

"I'm good, Jenny. In fact, I'm going for a walk. The weather is so nice. Would you like to join me?"

"Oh, my dear, that's so kind of you." The tall, angular woman sighed as she spoke. Lizzie liked Jenny. The mother, about her age, never bothered anyone and only once had complained to Lizzie that she wasn't crazy and shouldn't be in here. She wanted to get a divorce, and move to Grand Rapids where her sister had invited her and her four children to live with her. The trouble was that her husband was a brute who beat her repeatedly. When she finally went to the sheriff he'd sided with her husband to have her committed.

Elizabeth thought the way to settle that situation would have been for Jenny to shoot that son-of-a-bitch of a husband while he slept, bury his body in the vegetable garden for fertilizer, and live her life with her children as she pleased. Instead, the battered woman had sought justice, only to be jailed up because she was a woman. Had a man complained, no doubt he would have received privileged treatment. Men! Jenny wasn't the only woman in here who complained she'd been committed to get out of a husband's way so he could live as he pleased, control the children, have a mistress, or get away with all the family money. Or all of those things.

"No, dear, I'll stay in my room today. But thank you for the invitation." Jenny nodded and closed the door.

Elizabeth pitied Jenny her deep depression and promised herself she'd never let herself get depressed. She bounded down the decorative wooden staircase of Cottage 23 of the Northern Michigan Asylum for the Insane and out the front door. She knew, of course, that the place was now called the Traverse City State Hospital in deference to offending residents and their families. Nobody here was fooled, however; they weren't that crazy. They knew they were in a looney bin.

Once outside, she glanced briefly at Cottage 25 to the left. Twenty-five was becoming full of consumption patients and it was rumored that Dr. James Decker Munson, the superintendent of the asylum, wanted to reserve that cottage just for people afflicted with that disease, as he and other doctors believed it was contagious. They even called the disease tuberculosis these days. They wanted other residents to be protected from contamination. It had been common practice until now to put them wherever there was space among the other patients and there were still some scattered around the place.

She knew Herbert told people she resided in a ward for patients with the disease, in order to try to avoid embarrassment and gossip. Well, it was close, anyway, although she doubted that with the staff of this place being from town and the surrounding areas that there could be anybody left who didn't know she'd been declared to be bonkers. It made her laugh.

She knew her husband would have preferred to put her away someplace where no one would know her, and certainly not him. He'd brought her here in a panic but within a couple of months tried to convince her that the more private St. Joseph's Retreat in Dearborn, run by nuns, would better suit her needs. She'd thrown a vase of flowers at him. He never mentioned it again.

"Lizzie, my love, taking a little walk?"

She twirled to see Dr. Charles Whitmore behind her. He regularly met with residents to use the latest "Freudian techniques," as he called them, to try to talk them into being "well." With his wiry physique yet manly swagger, from the first moment she'd stepped into his office three years ago she'd known it would be easy to convince him to relinquish his psychoanalytical babble with her. It turned out that Dr. Whitmore's devotion to Freud's sexual theories got lost in translation as he readily succumbed to her conniving machinations.

"Yes, Charlie, I have to get some air! Want to join me?"

The look he threw her way telegraphed his desire. "Sorry, I have appointments with patients all afternoon. You're scheduled for tomorrow, correct?"

"Uh huh. See you then." She blew him a kiss and trotted away.

Strolling down Red Drive toward the farm, she savored the smells of springtime. Fresh grass, more lilacs, gladiolas, and lily of the valley sprinkled color along the lane, all mixed to give her a heady kind of intoxication. She loved the renewal inherent in this time of year.

Passing two dour nurses in their prim white uniforms, white stockings, white shoes, and little white starched caps perched on top of their heads, she nodded respectful greeting. "Beautiful day, isn't it, ladies?" she asked. One of them merely returned the nod and the other ignored her completely.

"Hello, Lizzie!" Rock the Hermit hollered in greeting from where he sat on a stool in front of one of the men's cottages. Born in Poland with his English never quite becoming clear, it came out like, "Ell-oh, Leezie!" But she understood Rock perfectly well and found him to be oddly interesting. Although everyone called him The Hermit, he'd once walked with her and told her the sad story of how he'd been a teacher and accidentally killed a student. He didn't go into detail about how the "accident" took place but she knew that was why he now resided in the asylum. Although the cause of that accident would probably never be clear to her, she knew the asylum staff wouldn't let him roam free if they felt he was a danger to anyone. Those who were a danger were locked up.

"Hello, my friend!" she called, waving back at Rock the Hermit.

Continuing on to the asylum farm, she took the narrow foot-bridge over Kids Creek, then followed the dirt road past the peach orchard, the raspberry patch, the cherry orchard, and the apple orchard. The fruit trees had just blossomed in a dramatic display of pink and white. Everybody here knew the story of how the farm came to be when Dr. Munson declared that "beauty is therapy, work is therapy." Any "resident," which is what Dr. Munson preferred that patients be called, who was willing and able to work, and who had ground parole, which depended on mental state, was given a job. She'd never been given a specific job, making her suspect employees were so pleased at having first dibs on her paintings they preferred to leave her free to roam about for creative inspiration. But many of the residents became farm workers, which wasn't new to a lot of them, and they reveled in getting out of their wards. The farm provided the vegetables, fruit, chickens, pork, beef, and dairy goods needed to feed its hungry inhabitants and staff. They even owned a milk cow champion, Traverse Colantha Walker.

"Hi, Traverse!" Elizabeth called and waved as she passed the pasture. "I'm going to paint you one day, you know!" The bovine damsel looked up, chewing on her cud, but didn't seem impressed. The fifty head of Holstein with her didn't even lift their noses from their juicy spring grass meal.

Elizabeth's intent had been to weed the vegetable garden, but suddenly she became struck with a suspicion that because it was such an agreeable day, her friend might be walking in the woods nearby. The asylum resident looked around. Although a dozen people worked the garden and a few men came and went from the barn, nobody paid any attention to her. So, she veered from her path and ducked into the apple grove. Passing the Spy apple trees, which she knew were great for baking tart pies, she went to the McIntosh trees, her favorite for eating raw. Being late spring, apple buds had poked their delicate white petals out all over the grove, nowhere near producing fruit yet.

She sidetracked into the apple cellar at the side of a small barn beside the grove. The wooden cellar door, slanted onto the ground beside the barn, sat open. Going down the dank steps, the coolness of the earthen storage room struck her as she descended. Stooping beneath the low ceiling, she let the dim light from outside guide her to the McIntosh bin, where she inspected two plump apples among the stash left from last fall's harvest. Finding them to be without worm holes, she put one in each of her skirt pockets. Then she went back out and ventured into the woods beyond.

Sunlight streamed through the large oak, maple, and jack pine trees of this part of the woods, causing dappled light to rollick upon her as she walked. Capturing lovely images in her mind for paintings, she wandered in the direction from which her friend usually came. And there she was, sitting on a log watching a baby squirrel.

"Abby! I'm so glad you're here! I didn't know for sure but hoped you would come."

The Indian looked up, smiled, and stood, taking long strides to meet her friend for a hug. "Lizzie! Of course, I'm here. How are you?"

Abby picked up a bag she'd brought and hung it from one arm while Elizabeth wound her arm through Abby's free arm. Out of habit, they turned toward an open patch where an old shed stood. A break in the trees allowed the ramshackle wood structure to bask in the sunlight.

"I'm good," Elizabeth said. "Isn't it a beautiful day? I've missed you! Did you get a ride with Mr. Hollis today?"

"Oh, yes, he's always so kind about bringing me into town and then letting me ride back with him in the afternoon."

"Do you think he'll ever give up on delivering his milk by horse and buggy?"

Abby chuckled. "Probably not."

They reached the shed, with only three walls remaining, but a surprisingly stable plank roof. The mortar in-between the planks of the walls long ago weathered away, giving the structure a cozy feel with light streaming through the slits on one side to draw delicate stripes on what remained of a plank floor. The women stepped onto the floor and under the shelter of the roof, and Elizabeth let go of Abby's arm to free herself to scrape the toe of her boot across the sun stripes on the floor, as if she might be able to make them move.

"How long has it been, my love, since we've seen each other?" Elizabeth asked, lifting her gaze to Abby. "You know how bad I am with time. It feels like forever."

"One month and two days. We had that nice spell of weather and then it got cold again. I've missed you, too. I can come more often now that the weather has turned.

"But today I came for a special reason. I have a message for you from my spirit guides."

Elizabeth stopped fussing with the floor and looked up. Abby turned to face her.

They knew they could not be more unlikely friends. Although both comely women of the same age, thirty-eight this year, one was pale faced and the other had tan skin. One had shoulder-length, black, curly hair and the other a glossy, black braid trailing down her back to her waist. One wore a simple ankle-length cotton skirt and plain shirtwaist blouse, but the drape of the fabric belied its expensive tailoring. The other wore a clean, hand-sewn, long skirt but a tattered leather jacket that looked as if it had been through a hundred years of wear. Elizabeth wore new work boots while Abby's footwear, although polished, still managed to look like it had miraculously survived the French and Indian War. In other words, they appeared to be the least likely of companions.

Yet, they had first befriended each other twenty years ago.

Consequently, they talked to each other as only old friends can do, with abbreviated sentences and a sense for what the other would say next.

"About the girl," Elizabeth said.

"Yes."

"She's coming."

"Yes."

"She may try to see me."

"That I don't know."

Elizabeth merely nodded. Without another word, Abby took a blanket out of the bag she carried, spread it on the floor, and proceeded to dole out a picnic lunch of dried venison strips, homemade bread, cheese, and carrots, as she'd done so many times before. Elizabeth contributed the two apples stowed in her pockets.

The two women ate in silence, the only sounds being the occasional hoot of an owl and the gentle rustling of the leaves in the surrounding forest trees. The sun shifted the stripes on their floor and only when the stripes disappeared altogether with the apparent gathering of clouds above did they decide it was time to leave their place of peace and quiet.

Outside the shed, they hugged one last time for this day and walked their separate ways.

5

Meg stared out the window of the train, torturing herself by looking back at Chicago, which sat in full view as the train rounded Lake Michigan just outside the city on its journey east and then north. The tall buildings, the sheltering private girls' school, the finishing school, her stylish flat, and the shops: Those were the places that had served as her primary home since the age of twelve. And more recently, she'd spent an inordinate amount of time in exciting speakeasies. As she looked back, one last tall church spire silhouetted against a cloudy gray sky faded from view and her city was gone. The sense of loss she felt, leaving her life as she knew it behind, seemed almost as bad as having lost Robert.

Of course, her father had always insisted that Traverse City was her real home. She'd returned there for holidays and summers until the age of eighteen, when she spent a year doing the continent, a tour of Europe. Since meeting Robert two years earlier, she'd only been home once for a brief stay, although her father came to Chicago to see her twice a year. She wasn't stupid;

she knew he also did business while there. She knew she should be glad of that, as his wise investments gave her a lifestyle most people could only dream about.

Her grandfather, an ambitious "shanty boy," a lumberjack, had eventually made a fortune as a lumber baron in the Traverse City area. Then he'd astutely invested in copper mining in the upper peninsula of Michigan, sawmills around the state, railroads throughout the northeast part of the country, and shipping on the Great Lakes. From there, especially when the forests started to become depleted and the lumber business waned, her father expanded the family holdings by investing in companies like Ford Motor, Firestone, and Edison. So, yes, Meg knew she was extremely privileged compared to most young women. Still, she'd always felt like something was missing.

That emptiness had started, she knew without a doubt, when she was six years old and her two-year-old brother, Harry, disappeared. His real name had been Henry, but even her father had relented in calling him Harry, it fit so well. She had loved her little brother dearly and his loss devastated her. He'd been her favorite playmate, too young to stop her from dressing him up in silly costumes and coercing him into playing the part of the hobo or pirate or cowboy in her pretend scenarios. He'd been a jolly little boy, a delight to be around.

And then one night he was gone, his little bed empty while his bedroom window ominously sat open. The panic that followed had terrified the six-year-old girl. It was then she realized that her family was different. Something was and always had been wrong, but she didn't know what.

Police, townspeople, the nanny and servants, church congregations, the Chippewas, everyone in the community spent days scouring the countryside, the lakeshore, old buildings, and the limestone caves that dotted the hillsides that led to Grand Traverse Bay. Her father spent days sitting by the new telephone in the house, waiting for a demand from kidnappers. None ever came.

Harry was never seen again.

It was then that Meg's mother was sent away to a hospital for consumption. Too young to understand what that meant, Meg only knew that her mother had become seriously sick when her brother disappeared and the maids whispered that the loss had been too much for her, and she would never get better.

Her father's despair became inconsolable. Meg remembered him pulling her onto his lap and hugging her so tightly she thought she'd pop. It had been as if he'd been afraid that she, too, would slip away from him.

Yet he'd sent her away at the tender age of twelve, away from everything she loved: her nanny, the cherry tree groves, the apple orchards, and the big lake with its shoreline just perfect for playing.

A flashback to that first time her father took her to Chicago on the train, the reverse trip of the one she made now, overwhelmed her with the knowledge that on that first day she'd felt as forlorn as now. It didn't seem to matter which way she went, there was no joy in the journey. But, of course, after overcoming her initial fear and loneliness, she'd settled into her new life in the city. After all, she had no choice.

Now she didn't know what her choices might be. When he heard about her broken engagement, her father insisted she come home for the summer. The flat in the city would remain under the care of the servants while Meg decided what she wanted to do.

The city of Chicago out of view now, she looked at Lake Michigan. Her lake. She supposed lots of people felt that way but it had always seemed to be there just for her to soothe her fears.

She thought back to the time she'd been home on holiday at age sixteen. A thin grin found its way to her lips at the thought. Quite rebellious for a young woman schooled in a protective environment, she'd confronted her father about why he'd sent her away. Five years later, she could picture the sadness in his eyes as if she were looking at him this very moment. He'd been working at his desk in his study when she'd lashed out at him, and he'd invited her to sit down on the divan and came out from behind his desk to sit beside her.

"You're old enough now to know, Margaret. I sent you away because life here for a teenager in your position would have been brutal, even at Holy Angels. It might be a private Catholic school, but not even the nuns can watch out for you all the time. I was trying to protect you. In the process, I punished myself because I missed you terribly. We're all we have left of family, Meg." She became moved by his sudden use of her nickname. "But things would not have been good for you here. When you're more grown-up you'll be able to handle it, but not yet."

"What things?" she stumbled over his words in an urgent need to know.

"It's your mother, dear. She's not well. She's not in a hospital for consumption. She is in the Northern Michigan Asylum. You know what that is, don't you?"

Meg had stared blankly at her father, although she knew what it was. "You mean… you mean, she's… mad?"

"Yes, that's what the doctors decided. She simply could not

cope with your brother's disappearance. I became afraid she would run away and get lost in the woods, or take a train and not know where she was, or something even worse. So, I took her to where I know she's safe. She has a beautiful room overlooking the park. She even has her own studio for painting. Do you remember how much she loved to paint? She still does. I know she's happier there. She doesn't have to worry about anything. Do you understand?"

"Yes, I guess so," Meg fibbed. Her mother had never spent much time with her, leaving her to the nanny. But still, she was her mother. Why had her mother so easily left her? That seemed too big a question to ask.

Her father patted her knee and put his arm around her shoulders for a side hug, something she knew was difficult for this proper man who'd never quite seemed to know exactly what to do with a teenaged daughter. "So," he continued, "I sent you to Chicago to avoid the gossip about your mother. Now seems like a good time to tell you about it, as you're getting old enough to understand. It's just gossip from people who don't have anything better to do. But, still, I wanted to take you away from the stigma of having a mother who's in an asylum. My hope is that someday, however, you'll want to come back home and live in Traverse City forever."

That was the last time Meg heard her father speak of her mother.

He had stood and offered her a hand, smiling down at her. She took his hand and rose off the divan. She didn't tell him she couldn't imagine coming back to this hodunk town to live forever.

But here she was on a train headed for that town, with no idea where it would lead.

6

Abby hadn't entered Lizzie's cottage since that fateful day fif-
teen years ago when Herbert Sullivan had his wife taken away.
The Indian woman remembered it all too well.

All those years ago she'd gone on one of her morning treks
to the big house to have tea with her friends, the cook and the
servants. On that morning, she'd taken the walk hesitantly, as the
night before while sitting in her rocking chair by the fire she'd
received a shady message from her spirit guides that something
momentous was about to happen at the big house. Her fear had
been that little Harry's body had been found. She approached the
kitchen door that day afraid of what she might learn.

But instead of news about Harry, the kitchen had been teem-
ing with the shocking revelation that the mistress of the house
had been taken away, kicking and screaming, in the middle of the
night, by big men in a big black carriage. Mr. Sullivan, they said,
insisted she had consumption and must be nursed at a hospital
but the cook, the cook's assistant, and the upstairs and downstairs
maids highly suspected it was something else.

They invited Abby in for tea and gossip, as usual, and she joined them at the long, plank kitchen table while they bantered about wild stories that Mrs. Sullivan had gone mad since young Harry disappeared only months earlier, or that maybe her husband had discovered she had a lover, or that Mr. Sullivan had tired of his spirited young wife and wanted to remove her to replace her with a more suitable companion. The most disturbing theory, however, was that Mr. Sullivan had been such a tortured man since their little son Harry went missing that *he'd* gone mad, having his wife taken away out of misplaced despair. It was anything, they insisted, but consumption.

Why, hadn't they heard her gaily singing *Always Leave Them Laughing When You Say Goodbye* just the day before? A person with consumption couldn't sing like that!

Abby had sat silently sipping her tea and picking at a biscuit to try to suppress the sickness she felt as her stomach tightened and twisted in anxiety. Her secret best friend, her Lizzie, was gone. When she could take no more of the gossip, she politely excused herself, took her basket of charitable goods, thanked her kitchen hosts, and left.

Fleeing to her cabin in the woods, she'd locked herself in for three days to grieve the loss of her friend.

Several years before that, when she'd first become aware that somebody had fixed up that old shed on a green knoll about halfway up a big hill near the south side of the Sullivan property, she'd initially been dismayed. She didn't want what she'd come to think of as her private beach to be disturbed. The Sullivans never came down here, except for the nanny and little girl during nice weather in the summer. Abby had no trouble avoiding them. And the servants certainly never came down. All her life since she'd been old enough to roam about alone, she'd walked that shore from the northern line of the Sullivan property where her cabin sat tucked into the woods and she'd always managed to do so in privacy. Walking along the bottom of the hills and dunes hid her from view from the big house. She couldn't see the house from there, so no one in the house could see her, either.

Later, Lizzie — Elizabeth to her husband and others in polite society, and Mrs. Sullivan to the servants — told Abby that the bayside rooms of the house had spectacular broad views of the water. However, the hills and dunes slanting down from the house were too steep to allow anyone to see where the bottom of the hill met the beach, where Abby always walked.

Before meeting Lizzie, Abby had heard, of course, that Mr. Sullivan, Jr., married a lively young woman, so she figured that was who would be in the cottage. Being mistress of a big, fancy house with a bigwig husband, Abby assumed she'd better steer clear of the elite, undoubtedly stuffy, woman.

Then one day she'd been walking her beach and spied a beautiful young woman with wild black hair, dressed in nothing more than her undergarments, her arms spread wide, standing on the edge of the knoll looking out over the bay. Abby howled with laughter, walked straight up the hill to the woman, introduced herself, and they'd been friends ever since.

Now, years later, her friend's grown daughter was coming home and might be curious about her mother's old cottage. Abby walked the same path toward that same cottage, memories flooding her mind. Reaching the spot where a path trickled up the hillside to the cottage, she stopped and looked up. She'd continued to walk the beach throughout the years but had never had the will to visit Lizzie's cottage without her there. It seemed like an intrusion, the invasion of a sacristy. Deep inside her soul, she suspected she'd been harboring a glimmer of hope that someday her friend would return.

Having seen Lizzie in the woods outside the asylum just that morning and knowing the girl, Meg, would be here soon, Abby had suddenly become obsessed with wanting to check out the cottage to see if there was anything there that would alarm or emotionally distress the girl, should she come snooping about. Abby also wanted to see if there was a clue as to the real reason Elizabeth had been committed to the asylum. The return of the girl had shaken her into finally wanting to face the truth.

Funny, how she could see the future for others, but could hardly handle the present in her own life. The irony did not escape her.

A light rain shower that afternoon had come and gone, leaving a fresh scent in the air, but the late afternoon sun had dried everything out enough that the path proved an easy climb with no slippery spots. The Chippewa in her made such walking easy, anyway, she reckoned.

Approaching the cottage from the bay side, she walked around the structure to get to the door, which sat on the land side. She was pleased to see that the place remained in decent shape, considering its abandonment for fifteen years. The windows were streaked with grimy sludge, but none were broken. The roof didn't appear to have any loose shingles, although they'd faded with some chipped at the edges. A pile of sand blown over from the dune had encroached on the fieldstone chimney, but it only reached up about five feet, doing no real harm. In fact, the chimney stood as stalwart as it always had, like a soldier refusing to give up his post. The clapboard siding was badly in need of paint, it's pale yellow that Lizzie had ordered done having chipped and mottled to dull shades of beige. The blue gingerbread trim that Lizzie had added to the eaves around the perimeter of the building hadn't fared too well, having a few spots where the open-lace woodwork had weathered away. The heavy wood door, however, remained in decent shape, having stood the test of time remarkably well.

Surely the door would be locked, Abby surmised, as Herbert would have had the place secured. Something, however, made her reach out to try the ornate brass knob, weathered to black. It felt sticky but she wrapped her fingers around it and turned.

She heard the latch release. She pushed. With a mournful creak worthy of an old haunted church, the thick wood door hobbled open.

Abby stepped inside.

"Holy Jesus, Mary Mother of God," she rasped, making the sign of the cross on her chest even though she wasn't Catholic.

Stale air assaulted her lungs. Stillness overwhelmed her senses. Her heart pounding, she gasped for air.

Now she knew why she'd not come before this, struck as she was with a vicious foreboding that in this place her spirit guides would tell her what had happened to that adorable little boy, Harry. This cottage, so silent, screamed of secrets and mystery. She'd always wanted to believe the child had been kidnapped by someone desperate for a son, someone who'd loved him and raised him to be a happy young man. That was most likely folly, she knew. The boy was most likely dead. Was that what she felt here? Death? Had some demented person taken him from here to brutally murder him? Or in her terror was she imagining things?

Breathing deeply, praying to both the Great Spirit and the Lord Jesus Christ, she looked around. Except for layers of dust—she wondered how that happened with the place closed-up—it looked as if Lizzie had stepped out of the cottage just yesterday.

Her colorful canvasses lay about. One, almost finished, sat on the easel. It portrayed the lovely white gazebo with the bay in the background. A woman in a plain, loose-fitting yellow dress lounged in the hammock in languid repose. The skirt of her dress trailed off the hammock and brushed the floor, while her arm dangled nonchalantly over the side, as well. A mass of blond hair could be seen, but her face turned away toward the deep blue water, leaving her features out of view. A strikingly restful scene, Abby's heartbeat relaxed at the mere sight of it and with the joy of seeing more of Lizzie's work again.

Abby had spent many an hour here, sitting on the chaise reading while Lizzie painted. They shared picnic lunches and drank tea. Sometimes Lizzie brought a bottle of wine from Herbert's cellar. Sometimes they talked up a storm and sometimes silence fit their mood. Always comfortable together, they'd never had pressing expectations of each other.

Lizzie's yellow apron, the one she always wore when she painted, streaked with paint every color of the rainbow, hung in its usual place from a nail on the wall. Abby fingered the fabric, now tattered with age.

She went to the chaise lounge and picked up an afghan carelessly thrown over the side. The flowered chintz fabric, underneath where the afghan had been, glared up at her in full color while the rest of it had faded. The afghan itself had been, she remembered, bright red but had morphed into an unpleasing dead rose.

At the windows, she ran her fingers down the frail sheer curtains, causing dust mites to filter through the air, catching what little light found its way through the dirty windows, making the dust specks look alive as they aimlessly wriggled about.

The Blue Willow tea set, covered in grime, sat on the small table, right where it had always been. The large table still held tubes of paint, dried up now, and other paint supplies. Herbert hadn't even bothered to have them taken to his wife; he'd just provided new ones.

His refusal to come here or to give orders for anyone else to come here to clean the place out struck Abby as telling. He'd avoided this cottage the same way she had.

Abby didn't touch the many paintings that were strewn about. *So lovely, what a waste to sit here unseen*, she thought.

Then, as if moved by an unseen hand, her head turned to notice, for the first time, a painting of a cemetery scene, sitting on a rug and propped up against the wall to the left of the fireplace. It would seem a morbid subject, yet she found it captivating, drawing the eye to dilapidated wooden crosses casting pale blue shadows over a blanket of white snow at sunset. She recognized it as the old Indian cemetery outside a deserted Methodist church a few miles up the peninsula, hailing from the days when many Chippewas had taken on that faith. The scene moved the Chippewa woman to tears and she gently touched one of the crosses.

The painting slipped and fell flat onto the floor with a loud whoosh, scrunching up the rug underneath it.

"Oh, damn it all to hell!" Abby let loose, then berated herself for using that particular phrase to swear at a religious scene. Bending to pick it up, she saw something on the floor, something that had been covered by the rug.

No longer interested in rescuing the painting, her eyes became glued to the floor. Using the side of her foot to push the painting away to get it completely off the rug, she pulled the rug all the way up and tossed it aside.

There, in the wood floor, sat a trapdoor. Without hesitation, Abby reached down and pulled on the heavy metal ring nailed to it. The door opened with a whisper of a whine. Peering inside, she could see a diagonal ladder with wide steps descending into what looked like a pitch dark cellar. Or a cave.

She straightened up and scanned the room. Grabbing a large candle and finding the box of matches in the same spot as always, she lit the candle and held it tightly as she went down the ladder.

When she reached the bottom and turned around to look about, Abby gasped. This, she realized, changed everything.

7

Elizabeth seldom thought about the past. Her marriage to Herbert, her children, and even her cottage by the bay did not often cross her mind.

But today for some reason her mind kept wandering back to more than fifteen years ago when she was still living with Herbert, with two young children to add to the package. Marriage had been a daunting enough task for her; raising children proved impossible.

She cocked her head to study the bonnet covering the features of the girl's face in her painting. Never liking to show the face when she painted a person, she always had to concoct a way to hide it. She loved the expressions on the faces of animals, so painted those in detail. But human facial features did nothing more than confound her; thus, she avoided them. In this instance, a big straw hat worked well, but it looked too yellow. Real straw had a more muted tone. She picked up the burnt umber tube of paint and spent the next fifteen minutes dabbing it onto the image.

"Ah, that looks just right. As natural as can be," she announced to herself, stepping back for a better view.

This painting of a preteen girl holding a pink baby pig had turned out to be delightful. Of course, the artist found all her work to be delightful.

Uninvited, an image of another painting all those years ago flashed through her mind. It had been of a woman in a yellow dress lounging in the hammock on the gazebo. Her face turned toward the water and away from the viewer. Elizabeth hadn't been able to finish that painting and wondered whatever happened to it.

Not that it mattered. She had plenty of others like this one.

It seemed curious, even to her, that she didn't miss her cottage at all. The place had meant so much to her. But then it became tainted with the obligations of marriage. Eventually she hated the cottage as much as she hated the house because the two became inextricably connected. Getting away from Herbert had meant giving up the cottage.

It was a small price to pay.

She had everything she needed right here to paint, although she did miss the beautiful view of the bay. But she could always go to the third floor of Building 50 and see it again, although from a further distance. She'd made some lovely sketches from there and painted a number of pretty pictures of the bay from that angle.

In a quandary now, she couldn't decide between marine blue and emerald green for the girl's dress, so she stroked a patch of each underneath the pig, which lay in the girl's arms.

"Oh, the blue looks wonderful!" She painted a few strokes and it looked perfect.

Another errant memory invaded her thoughts. Her little girl, Meg, had on a blue dress the last time Elizabeth ever saw her. And her little boy, Harry, had on a blue suit the last time she laid eyes on him.

"No," she said, squeezing more emerald green paint onto her palette. "Green will be better."

Working feverishly, she corrected the mistake.

She should have wanted to be a mother. The thought struck her as it always did: Unwanted and unwarranted, as far as she was concerned. Motherhood wasn't for everyone. Whoever decreed that it should be had apparently never been a mother. Some bastard of a man, obviously.

The asylum harbored a number of women who agreed with her. There were female residents who'd had nervous breakdowns after being overworked on their family farms with a bunch of children to rear. Others became afflicted by puerperal as a result of childbirth, fever and urinary infection. That sounded absolutely horrible to Elizabeth. And then there were those who suffered severe depression after childbirth. She certainly could understand that.

There were others, however, that she didn't understand. In her cottage especially, there were aging women who had not adjusted to the change of life, feeling as though they weren't real women if they could no longer reproduce. Poppycock! Elizabeth was too young for it now but looked forward to the day when she experienced the change and wouldn't have to deal with her monthly curse. It was nothing but a bother. She'd never felt as if she had to spit out babies in order to be a woman.

Men and women alike were here for a variety of other reasons, as well. Some were mentally retarded and some of the older ones had become feeble minded with age. There were those who had general poor health, intemperance, and business failures. Some drank too much. Others threatened suicide. She'd even heard of people being committed for religious excitement, nostalgia, and seduction. Some had physical disabilities like peg legs, hair lips, and epilepsy. There were the consumption patients scattered throughout the place, those who Dr. Munson was trying to collect next door in Cottage 25. And there were those who simply had no place else to go but the asylum. Not to mention the wives who'd been "put away" by their philandering husbands.

A hodgepodge group of outcasts to be sure. Elizabeth smiled. They were, after all, her people, as close to a family as she would ever get.

She stuck her paintbrushes into the jar of turpentine, wiped her hands on a rag, took off her apron and hung it on the peg on the wall, and patted her hair. It was time to go down to dinner with her family. This was pot roast night, one of her favorites.

8

"Excuse me, Miss." Meg looked up into the bespeckled sea blue eyes of a ruggedly handsome young man in a suit. Her heart did a little flip.

No, don't you dare! she warned herself. *Men are scum, remember? I'm off the bozos for at least the summer.*

Her heart flopped when the handsome man smiled.

"We were wondering if you know how to play euchre. We need a fourth." He jerked his thumb toward two older gentlemen sitting at a table across the aisle one row behind her in the first-class train car.

She blinked. "What?" *Well, that was stupid!* she reprimanded herself. She'd been half hypnotized by the clack-clack of the wheels on the rail and the endless miles of green trees flashing by the window. Coming back to the present felt like coming out of a fog.

"Euchre. Would you like to join us?" He raked a hand through his mass of sandy-colored hair, giving Meg an urge to run her fingers through it herself.

"Oh. Euchre. Yes. I used to play, but it's been years. I'm afraid I wouldn't be very good."

"That's okay, because I am very good. You can be my partner."

Damn! He smiled again and held out a hand.

Meg took his hand and let him gently help her to her feet. He led her to the gentlemen's table.

One man slipped out to let her scoot in by the window. She wore a Chanel sitabout dress of green satin, and the fabric of the flared skirt swooshed along the leather seat as she skimmed over it. Her long pearls clanked on the side of the table and she placed her hand over them to still them. Having taken off her cloche hat earlier, she touched her hair but then thought better of it, realizing it betrayed her nervousness. Daintily, she folded her hands on the table.

"Hello," the man next to her said. "I'm Walter. Glad you can join us." He sat back down now that she was settled in.

The man on the other side of the table had been pushed over when the handsome man sat beside him, so he didn't stand up. But he graciously reached across the table and said, "Just call me John."

Meg shook hands with him and with the man at her side, and said, "Hello. I'm Meg."

"Charmed, I'm sure," Walter said.

When she looked at the handsome man, his stare made her blush. "And you are?" she asked.

"Oh," he said, blinking as if coming out of a trance himself. "I'm Jed."

Meg reached across the narrow table to offer her hand once more, but instead of shaking it Jed took her fingers in his, lifted her hand, and gently kissed her knuckles. His lips were warm, with a slight touch of moisture that lingered sensuously on her skin.

Her heart flipped and flopped.

"Hello, Jed," she managed to say.

"Okay!" John announced as he dealt the cards. "First jack deals!"

John won the deal and the game ensued. Euchre had been around this area since French fur traders were the first Europeans to settle the Great Lakes region. Everybody in Michigan seemed to know how to play. Meg had learned from her nanny when she was ten, and played with her and the upstairs maids every Friday night when her father went to town council meetings. How she'd loved those nights! Her nanny and the maids were fun, not stuffy like most of the other adults she met, her father's friends and business associates. The upstairs card games lasted for two years until Meg left for boarding school when she was twelve, so it had been a long time since she'd played. But once the men reminded her of the unusual basics, like jacks being the high cards instead of aces, the knack of the game came back to her. Plus, her partner, the handsome man named Jed, hadn't lied about being very good. They soundly won the first game.

An hour and a half later, when night began to fall, they stopped play long enough to partake of beef sandwiches served by the porter, and then for her to enjoy an after-dinner cup of tea and the men to each savor a glass of scotch whiskey. Back to another hour of play once they finished their meal, Meg and Jed beat their opponents eight games to seven. Walter, an especially jolly fellow, had thrown up his hands and said, "I give! The match

SECRETS OF THE ASYLUM

is yours!" Amicable John had agreed and they'd asked the porter for more whiskey.

"Well, done!" Jed said, this time shaking her hand.

"It was all you," she insisted.

Before he could respond, the conductor came through the car, bellowing as he had all day, to announce the final stop. "Union Street station, Traverse City, next stop! Twenty minutes. If this is not your destination, you're out of luck because the run ends here!"

Walter stood to let Meg slide out of their seat. She'd been shocked at how much fun she'd had with these strangers, her mind diverted from her troubles. Table talk revolved mostly around the game but she did glean that they were all lawyers in her hometown. When she told them she was going home to visit family but said no more about that, all three of them were polite enough not to pry. After thank you's all the way around, she returned to her own seat to start gathering her things, pulling her satchel down from the net shelf above her seat.

Jed suddenly appeared at her side. "Excuse me," he said, not apologetic at all. "But I wanted you to know how much I enjoyed our game. Thanks again for joining us."

"My pleasure," she said, honestly.

The train jolted to slow down causing Meg to lurch forward, bumping into Jed's chest. "Oh! I'm so sorry," she said, automatically putting her hand on his chest to steady herself. As if having put her hand over fire, she jerked it back to slap it onto her own chest with a gasp.

Clearly not concerned with etiquette and the inappropriateness of her gesture, the handsome man reached out to take her shoul-

61

ders and help her catch her balance. A shockwave of lust trickled from her shoulders down to more sacred parts of her body, making her wonder if the sudden red blotchiness of her skin gave away her shame. She didn't recall ever feeling like this with Robert.

"That's okay," he said. "Listen, maybe we'll see each other again in town."

She hardly dared look him in the eyes, so urgent was her desire. When she forced herself to glance his way, she nearly melted away into his arms like one of those damsels in love in a tawdry romantic novel, many of which she'd secretly read with fervor. Oh, the ardor in Edith Wharton's *The Age of Innocence*, a serial in Pictorial Review magazine, which Meg had devoured last year the moment each installment came out. And then there was the story of passion in D. H. Lawrence's *Women in Love*. And…. She made herself stop. This was reality, not a racy story.

"Perhaps," she said answering Jed, half statement and half question.

The train stopped abruptly and, quick as lightening, passengers started jostling to disembark. Not knowing what else to say or do, Meg grabbed her satchel, threw her fox stole over her shoulder, and plopped her cloche onto her head. Without much choice in the throng, she followed the stream of people to the door, down the steps, and onto the platform.

Steam from underneath the train car swirled up and encircled her, leaving her feeling disoriented. Carefully, Meg stepped out of the mist and looked back at the door of the car, hoping to see Jed once more. One by one, a number of other people appeared and left the train, each seeming to take a lifetime to get out of the way so she could see the next in line.

But Jed did not appear.

Maybe he'd already disembarked, she decided, so she turned to look at the crowd of people greeting passengers on the platform. Walter was walking away with a man who looked like a driver. John's greeter was a nice-looking woman about his age, so she was probably his wife. Their attention remained riveted on each other and he didn't see Meg looking around.

Then she saw him, the handsome man, Jed, standing across the way with a beautiful woman. She had her arms around his waist and he, being considerably taller than she, wrapped his arms around her shoulders as they embraced warmly. Worse yet, there were two young boys, maybe three and five, grabbing Jed for their share of hugs. The man stooped down to embrace them tightly. It was clear they were all joyously happy to see each other.

So, Jed the handsome man was married with two children! He'd flirted with her, wanting to see her "again in town." How insulting. Did she really look like the kind of girl who would get involved with a married man? *What a bozo!*

Just then Jed's gaze lifted and landed on Meg. Their eyes met for the split second it took her to turn away.

"Margaret!" There was no mistaking her father's deep voice. Meg did an about face to see her father, dapper as ever in a gray wool coat and matching fedora, standing next to his driver, a string bean who she recognized as the former livery driver. Her father rushed toward her.

"Hello, Father," she said, dropping her satchel to the ground and accepting her father's quick, stiff embrace. The man stood over six feet tall and for the first time she noticed gray hair at his temples, which only added to his air of stateliness.

"It's so good to have you home!" Herbert Ambrose Sullivan declared, holding his daughter out at arm's length to look her over approvingly. "You look as pretty as can be! Here, let's find the rest of your bags," he said as the driver picked up her satchel, "and Sam here can take them to the motorcar. Wait until you see the new Ford Limousine we have! You'll love riding in it...."

Meg did her best to focus on her father's words, but couldn't resist a glance back. Jed, the handsome man, walked away with his family, his back to her. But then, like a magnet drawn to metal, he turned his head and met her gaze.

She turned her back on him, took her father's arm, and walked away.

Bozo! she thought.

9

By seven o'clock, a brilliant dawn of prismed light had awak-
ened the earth. Abby felt aglow with renewed vigor as she walked
through the forest from her cabin to the big house. The crisp
morning air, dewy moss, and cavorting squirrels all gave her a
sense of joy at being alive.

She reached the house, skipped up the steps of the back stoop
and entered the backdoor, going straight into the kitchen as she
did three or four times a week for a morning ritual of tea and
biscuits with Cook and the servants.

But today, unlike other days, as she reached for the handle of
the screen door a jolt of awareness struck her as strongly as a bolt
from the blue. She knew this was the day. She could feel it in her
bones.

The girl had come home.

"Abby!" Cook exclaimed, turning away from the big, black
wood cook stove just long enough to wave Abby in. "Come in,
dear. Sit! Today we have flapjacks." Cook's tall, fair, large countenance couldn't help but belie her Nordic heritage.

Abby placed the basket of flowers she always brought from her garden, yellow tulips today, on the center of the plank kitchen table and then dutifully plunked down, feeling at home. She loved this kitchen. For many years, Cook and the other old-timers here had brought her solace. Their friendliness plus the delicious smells of this room, not to mention the food that always followed, gave her a sense of belonging. That was something for a clairvoyant half-Indian half-white woman who so often felt accepted but not as though she truly belonged.

Even Lizzie, her one intimate close friend, who'd welcomed her with open arms at her cottage, still had always had an air about her that said, "This is my place and you are welcome to visit." The necessary secrecy of their acquaintance added another layer of feeling removed from feeling as one. In this kitchen, Abby felt as though she could curl up in the corner and announce she'd decided to stay forever and no one would object.

She looked in the corner. As usual, Kitty lay curled in a drowsy fluffy ball on her pillow. The stray gray cat had shown up ten years ago in the dead of winter, almost frozen to death, and when Cook brought her in out of the cold, the feline smartly decided never to leave. Winter or summer; snow, rain, or shine; the sweet girl seldom left this kitchen.

Abby peered around Cook's hefty frame to see that she poured glops of flapjack batter into three hot iron skillets on the stove. The sizzle of steam from each one revealed that butter greeted the batter in those pans.

Abby's mouth watered.

"Would you be a dear," Cook said without turning away from her work, "and pour the tea?"

Abby got up and grabbed the tea kettle, its whistle having just let loose, off the one burner not being used for skillets.

A fresh teabag sat in each of the eight teacups circling the tabletop. As she poured boiling water into each cup, Abby asked, "Are we having flapjacks today instead of biscuits because Miss Meg is home?"

Cook turned, a moment of surprise crossed her face, and she smiled. Looking back at her stove, she said, "Yes, that's it. Of course, you would already know she's here. Mr. Sullivan and Miss Hannah always just want biscuits and tea, but he ordered these today because they're Miss Meg's favorite." She took a spatula and edged one fluffy delight out of its skillet and plopped it onto one of the china plates stacked on the worktable beside her stove. Handing the plate to Abby, she said, "Here, dear. Let me know how they are today."

The aroma alone almost made Abby delirious with anticipation. "You know they'll be good!"

She sat back down and glopped fresh creamy butter and homemade maple syrup onto her flapjack. The butter came from Mr. Hollis' farm. The maple syrup was her own contribution, having learned from her father how to tap the maple trees for sap and make this sweet syrup, which she stored in large clay jugs. She'd bring a jug to Cook, who would dole it out into smaller amounts in glass jars like the one sitting on the table. Abby also knew how to cook up the syrup to solidify it into sugar, a staple in the Chippewa diet. Cook loved that, too, and Abby was more than happy each spring to share her goodies.

In the old days, when spring was at hand during the Moon of Snowblindness, the month of March, the Chippewa would use toboggans and their dogs to move out of their winter retreats deep in the forest to the maple groves for the tapping of the trees. Each family would work a stand of trees, using a handmade stone axe to make a cut into the bark of each maple tree and sticking a cedar spout into the cut. Then they'd put a makuk, a birchbark bucket, under the spout. Each day the syrup that had dripped into the makuks would be collected and cooked into sugar that would be used throughout the year. This was a staple in the Chippewa diet, so the collecting of the syrup was a very important ritual for families and tribes.

For this annual task, Abby still used the same tools her father had made and taught her to use. She tapped about twenty trees each spring and delighted in sharing her jugs of maple syrup with Mr. Hollis, the garage owner, the mayor, other longtime visitors to her cabin, and most of all, the crew of the Sullivan household.

Abby sure was happy to have that syrup right now as she ate Cook's fabulous flapjacks. She swallowed a big bite and turned in Cook's direction, saying, "Cook, I have only one question: What on earth are you wearing?"

"Hmph! Miss Hannah says we have to dress in these slave get-ups for a while until Miss Meg gets used to our new ways. These horrible things are like the ones we used to have to wear before Miss Hannah came." She pulled at the ridiculous white starched collar of her stiff blue uniform dress. "You'd think this was 1891 instead of 1921."

"I've never known Miss Hannah to make a bad decision," Abby noted, "but this one's a whopper. Those look just awful."

"Yeah, well, if I keel over with apoplexy because I can't breathe, tell her I'm sorry but I won't be able to make lunch."

Cook had doled out plates of flapjacks all around the table, and all the servants and Sam the driver magically appeared, like clockwork, greeting Abby as they came in.

Everyone got busy chowing down but it was the young Irish one, Peggy, who seemed to be bursting with news she couldn't suppress any longer. "Abby, did you know that Miss Meg came home last night? She's so sophisticated and beautiful you won't believe it!"

As more flapjacks got passed around, followed by butter and syrup, everyone chimed in with reviews of the young woman's attire, hairdo, makeup, voice, demeanor, and more. Peggy went into an animated description of her shoes. The few at the table who'd been employed by the Sullivans long enough to have known her mother agreed that Miss Meg was the spitting image of the woman from whence she had come.

An unbid thought hit Abby: The girl might look like her mother, but she hoped Meg turned out to be more emotionally stable. As much as Abby loved Lizzie, she clearly was not in the best of mental health. She did live, after all, in a mental institution.

Abby suspected the same ominous thought had occurred to others, but none were crude enough to mention it.

By the time Abby had heard every detail about the prodigal daughter's appearance, the head housekeeper, Miss Hannah, came in and said it was time to serve Mr. Sullivan his breakfast.

"Hello, Abby," she added kindly. "What a glorious day out there, isn't it?"

Abby readily agreed but almost broke into laughter. Miss Hannah also wore a stiff blue uniform dress. Without even realizing it, the woman stuck her finger in the collar and stretched her neck. Abby didn't have to be a fortune teller to see that these pretentious dresses wouldn't last long.

Everyone started leaving the table and hustling about, so Abby rose, too, to leave. Cook already busied herself making flapjacks for the family so Abby said thanks and bid them goodbye.

"Abby, dear!" Cook called. "Don't forget that." She pointed at a small burlap bag on a bench by the backdoor.

"Thank you!" Abby said as she left.

She felt grateful for the people she thought of as her "kitchen friends." Having come here for as long as she could remember, Cook had always given her food to take home. She peeked inside the burlap bag and today found five biscuits, a slab of cheese, a roll of butter, three sugar cookies, and beef jerky, each in its own roll of parchment paper.

Even though Cook's outstanding flapjacks had filled her up, she just might need to have an extra little snack once she got back to her cabin before her day of readings began.

She looked back at the big house. The girl was in there. Meg had come home.

The place would never be the same. Meg's mother, Elizabeth Sullivan, had been in the asylum for fifteen years. The Sullivan house needed more youth and laughter and love. She hoped Meg brought those things with her. If not, it would be hell to pay.

10

"Hello, Mrs. Sullivan," Dr. Whitmore said as she entered his outer office in the administration section of the main building of the asylum.

"Good morning, Dr. Whitmore," Elizabeth replied politely. Then nodding at his secretary, who sat behind her desk typing, she added, "Hello, Neddie. My, you look fetching today."

Harried and overworked, fifty-year-old Neddie looked up and grinned without breaking a stride in her typing.

The psychiatrist held his office door open, his patient entered, and he followed. Closing the door and locking it with a key he drew out of his pocket, he turned to Elizabeth and grabbed her upper arms, pulling her to him where he could plant a lush kiss on her lips.

"Oh, Lizzie, I've missed you so," he groaned when they finally parted. "Once a month isn't enough! Please let me schedule you more often."

Elizabeth smiled, drew herself away from him, and unwrapped the long scarf she'd thrown on around her neck. Taking one end of the scarf in each hand and flipping it behind her, she sashayed to the davenport, teasingly fluttering the soft fabric across her butt like a belly dancer at the county fair.

"Oh, Lizzie!" the doctor exclaimed, his eyes bugging out their sockets.

It had always amazed Elizabeth how easy he'd been to seduce. Well, how easy it was to seduce most men. She'd been coming to this office once a month for three years and he still slobbered all over her every time he turned the key in the door lock.

She sat on the davenport, held her arm out to make a show of carelessly dropping the scarf onto the floor, and unbuttoned the top three buttons of her cotton shift dress. Pulling her skirt up above her knees, she crossed her bare legs. Now she thought the prestigious doctor might faint.

"Come, Charlie," she said. "Sit here." She patted the spot beside her.

Dr. Charles Whitmore couldn't get there fast enough, dispensing of his suit jacket and suspenders in the few short steps it took him to reach her side. He loosened his tie and unbuttoned the top of his white shirt.

Grabbing her again, he pressed his body to hers but this time she turned her face away when he tried to kiss her. "Now, Charlie," she said. "Remember the rules."

He hung his head and said, "I know. I know. It's just so hard not to kiss you." He moved his hands to her chest, reaching inside the open neckline of her dress to fondle her ample breasts. She couldn't abide too much kissing but didn't mind having him play with her bosom. In fact, it humored her that such a simple thing aroused him so quickly and completely.

She moved her hand down to stoke the pathetic little hump in his trousers and leaned into him to whisper in his ear, "Yes, I would say it's hard all right."

That was it. After he frantically pulled down his trousers, it only took five minutes of fellatio, seventy-six strokes every time like clockwork, and the good doctor was spent.

Elizabeth rose, buttoned up her dress, fluffed her hair, picked up her scarf and wrapped it around her neck, and went to the cabinet beside his desk where she pulled out two glasses and their most recent bottle of moonshine whiskey. Pouring an inch of booze into each glass, she turned to hand one to him. He'd fallen asleep, sitting upright against the cushions, trousers crumpled around his ankles, snoring.

Elizabeth sat his drink on his desk, found one of the *Motion Picture* magazines he kept hidden in his desk drawer just for her, and sat in what was his chair when he did therapy with patients. She sipped her drink and looked at the photo of a pert actress on the cover. She didn't know who the actress was, not surprising seeing that she hadn't been to a picture show in fifteen years. They were still called flickers last time she'd seen one at a nickelodeon store. They had movie night here once a month, but she didn't much care for mingling with the whole crowd of residents and never went.

She flipped through the magazine, finding that for $1 down she could get a set of aluminum pots and pans on thirty-day free trial. Also for $1 down she could get a wolf lynx fur scarf or a richly embroidered wool serge dress. None of which she needed. She scanned more pages until coming to "The Answer Man." She adored the advice the "answer man" gave to people who sent forlorn letters, many about their love lives. Elizabeth figured the answer man had to be a woman, the advice generally being so witty and wise.

The doctor woke up with a jerk and a snort. "Oh my! Did I fall asleep again?" He fumbled to pull up his trousers.

"Yes, Charlie. But I don't mind." She put the magazine back in the drawer and stood. "Here's your drink." She took it to him.

"How wicked of us to drink so early in the day," he said as he stood and walked to his desk. He swallowed the contents of his glass in one swift gulp.

"Well, we have to pass the time somehow," she said, "seeing that we have—let's see," she looked at the clock on the wall, "twenty minutes left of our appointment time."

"Ah," Charles said, leering at her chest, "time for another go at it, if you know what I mean."

"Oh, Charlie, you never give up, do you? You know the rule. Once is all you get. That'll make you want me all the more next month."

Resigned, he nodded. Placing the empty glass on his desk, he pulled up his suspenders and put on his suit jacket. He pulled out the neatly folded white handkerchief in his jacket breast pocket and dabbed at beads of sweat on his face.

Sitting down at his desk, he shuffled papers while Elizabeth walked about the room, looking out one window and then another at the lush green yard. They chatted blandly until the official time for their appointment was up, and she stored the bottle and glasses back in the cabinet where she found them. He got up and unlocked his office door, opened it widely, and loudly declared, "That was a most productive therapy session, Mrs. Sullivan. We'll accomplish even more next month, I'm sure."

"See you then, Dr. Whitmore," she said. "'Bye, Neddie." This time the secretary didn't acknowledge her.

Elizabeth swayed her hips as she left the office, knowing the doctor's eyes would be glued to her rear end until she was out of sight.

Once outside, she felt free. Little did the psychiatrist know she needed that drink each time to erase the taste of him from her mouth. Still, as much as she abhorred doing that to him, it was better than being forced to sit there with him asking her questions about her sexual desires, and then listening to him explain her id and her ego.

Id and ego my ass! Who in the hell does that Sigmund Freud think he is, telling women about their sexual desires? He doesn't know squat about my sexual desires. Probably doesn't know anything about his wife's sexual desires, either. He is one serious nut case who belongs in this nut house more than any of us nutheads.

Until he'd shown up at the asylum a few years ago residents hadn't been insulted with any of that psychobabble mumbo-jumbo. They'd been free to be crazy in peace.

Oh well, she didn't have to worry about any of that again until next month. Walking out of the enormous, three-story building that sprawled out forever, the one they'd started calling Building 50, she wandered around the vast green yard with its patches of fragrant flower beds and majestic tall trees, taking in the scent of the lilacs bushes as she went. She didn't want to go back to her room yet; she didn't even want to paint right now. She liked having the first appointment with the doctor at 8:00 a.m. so she could get that over with and go on with her day. But today she felt restless. She knew, of course, what niggled at her. Her daughter Meg, now twenty-one years old, would soon be home, if she wasn't already.

On his last visit a week earlier, Herbert had told her all about it: Meg's break-up with her fiancé, the ensuing heartbreak, and her father's invitation to come home, at least for the summer.

Now that she was of age, would her daughter want to see her? Did she want to see her daughter?

Elizabeth knew that curiosity would get the best of her and that she would allow Meg to visit, if the girl wished. The real question was whether or not Herbert would allow it. Seeing that Elizabeth was considered by law to be incapacitated, Herbert was her guardian, regardless of new laws giving women more freedoms. Because she was deemed insane, he decided who did and who did not get in to see his wife, except for her friend Abby, who found her own way onto the property.

If a meeting with her daughter did happen, though, she hoped it held some hope of being fun. She welcomed a little excitement in her life.

11

"Good morning, Father," Meg greeted Herbert Sullivan as he read the paper and drank coffee while sitting at the head of the lengthy table in the formal dining room. "I'm surprised you're still here. I was so tired from my trip I'm afraid I overslept."

"Oh, hello, dear. Sit here beside me." He folded his newspaper and set it aside, and patted the empty spot at the table to his left. She sat as instructed. "No worries. I'm glad you got a good rest. I'm not going to the office today; I took the day off to help you get settled back in. I already ate and I must say that Cook's flapjacks today are excellent! Well, they're excellent every time she makes them. I hope you'll have some."

On cue, a servant came in with a glass of orange juice and a plate of said excellent fare. "Thank you!" Meg said. "They look delicious!" While she slathered the flapjacks with butter and flooded them with maple syrup, and dug in, her father looked at her thoughtfully.

"Meg, I must say, you're as beautiful as ever."

Her mouth full, she swallowed hard in order to respond.

"You're my father," she said. "It's your job to think your daughter is beautiful." With that she shoveled in another mouthful.

He chuckled. "Be that as it may, any person in their right mind could see that you are a beautiful young woman. I bring that up as a way of saying you're still the same person, Meg." Struck by the use of her nickname, twice now, rather than his usual use of her full first name, Margaret, she wondered what had caused the sudden change. She'd noticed an unfolded napkin to his right. Had someone else had breakfast with him? Did that person caution him to relax around his daughter? "I'm so sorry about what happened to you with that horrible lout in Chicago," her father continued, "but we'll just put that behind us and carry on.

"If there is anything you need, like time alone to think or to walk the gardens or to read, whatever you need, just let me know. On the other hand, I know of a number of young women's organizations in town, should you care to hear about them. Some do charitable work; some merely drink tea and gossip and call it something else; but they all seem to gather nice women together to socialize. Our parish has one such group," he added, alluding to the St. Francis of Assisi Catholic Church within which Meg had been raised.

The servant, a pleasant looking middle-aged woman in a stiffly starched blue uniform, brought in a plate of bacon. Meg thanked her again and stabbed a fat slab onto her plate.

"Father, I just don't know yet what I intend to do." She cut up the bacon and took a bite. "This is delicious, too!"

He smiled. "Comes from our own little farm here."

"Maybe I'll take up cooking." Meg polished off her flapjacks and proceeded to attack the rest of the bacon.

"And maybe I'll slop the pigs myself."

His sudden jovial, teasing manner shocked Meg. She'd never heard her father sound, well, fun before. What on earth had changed the man? She liked it.

The door to the kitchen swung open and the head housekeeper, Hannah, entered with a silver pot of steaming coffee. "Hello, Meg! We're all so glad you're home!" Hannah went to Meg's father and refilled his cup without asking, obviously knowing his preference. "Would you like some coffee, dear?" She held up the pot.

Meg. Dear. A warm welcome. Is this what changed my father? Meg wondered.

"Thank you, Hannah," she said instead of asking out loud the snoopy question that pressed on her mind. Hannah was a handsome middle-aged woman whose neat chignon of brown hair revealed streaks of blondish-gray. She wore one of the crisp, blue servant's uniforms. "I'm glad to be home," Meg told her, "embarrassing as it is that my fiancé dumped me."

"Oh, Margaret!" Meg's father said, forgetting her nickname in his haste. "Let's not think of it that way."

Hannah, on the other hand, set down the coffee pot on a hot pad, put her hands on her hips, and laughed. "I think that's rather healthy," she said. "Get it out. The man is a lousy cad. Good riddance, I say. You, young lady," she said, wagging a friendly finger at Meg, "have much better things in store for you. That's plain as the pretty nose on your face.

"Now, would you perhaps prefer a cup of tea?"

Meg had known this head housekeeper since her first became employed here seven years ago, having seen her when she came home on holidays. She'd never given the woman a second thought. Now she thought she liked her—a lot.

"No, thank you. I'll take tea this afternoon, please."

Hannah nodded and went back through the kitchen door, giving Meg a chance to take a long look at her father. Her statement about being dumped had unnerved him. He'd always been protective of her, yet this time seemed more obvious than usual. Still, as soon as Hannah spoke up he relaxed. In fact, everything about him seemed more relaxed. The whole house seemed more informal, some of the stiff upper crust principles of etiquette having fallen away, such as the head housekeeper speaking up without being spoken to. The only thing indicative of the formality of the past were the servants' starched blue uniforms.

Her father filled the silence. "Would you like to go riding today, my dear? The weather is grand. We could ride up the peninsula and take in the scenery. We'll take a picnic lunch."

"Oh, father, I'd love that!"

"Good! I'll go have the horses saddled. I'll meet you in the stables in, say, twenty minutes?"

"Perfect," she said as they both arose from the table. On a whim, Meg stood on her tippy-toes and kissed her father's cheek. The man actually blushed.

"Why, thank you, my dear. That was very sweet." Appearing not to know what to do next, he started for the vestibule. "See you soon!" he hollered as the front door shut behind him.

Meg went out of the dining room, walked into the grand vestibule, and looked around this mansion that had always been her home. The Victorian style of the house retained its beauty, even though the style had fallen out of favor for new homes. This, however, was a classic. The oak staircase with its intricately carved banister rose to a spacious landing with a glorious stained glass window then turned to reach the second story of the house.

In the window scene on the landing an angel in a flowing white robe held a fluffy white sheep as she walked barefoot in a green pasture. Her ethereal angel wings fanned out behind her against a vivid blue sky. When Meg was little she named the angel Angela and had always considered the holy apparition to be one of her best friends. It heartened her that the window drew the eye the moment one entered the front door, as if Angela the angel blessed everyone who entered here.

She'd imagined one like it in her own home one day, the home she thought she'd have after she got married. Well, that dream was dead, at least for now.

Meg walked up the stairs and stopped on the landing, taking a moment to sit down on the cushioned window seat below Angela. From here the view of the vestibule calmed her. She'd noticed when they came in from the train late last night that the Persian rugs were new, replacing darker ones of deep reds and navies. These in light shades of aqua, green, and beige added a sense of airiness to the space. Flipping off a shoe, she ran her bare toes over the sumptuous pile beneath her feet. The chubby cushions on the window seat were new, too, a light-colored fabric that complimented the carpets. She wondered if all of this was also the work of Hannah, the head housekeeper.

Even the immense gaslight chandelier that hung from the center of the second-floor ceiling to the top of the open first floor had been switched, too, with the new one being soft shades of stained glass rather than the old one of multifaceted crystals.

She'd become used to the brighter electric lights in the city, even in her own townhouse, but it didn't appear that electricity had yet found its way to Traverse City, Michigan. She liked the soft glow of the gaslight.

Yes, her home felt even more comfortable than ever before. It made her feel girlish and she got up to sprint the rest of the way up the stairs. Abruptly, however, Meg turned a corner and bumped into an upstairs maid, one she'd never met.

"Oh, I'm so sorry," Meg said, stooping down to help the girl pick up the clean towels that Meg had knocked out of the girl's hands.

"That's alright, Miss Sullivan. I didna hear ya comin'. 'Tis as much me fault as yers," she said in a cheerful Irish brogue.

They gathered all the towels off the floor and stood up, and the maid took towels out of Meg's hands to collect them all into her own arms. The freckle-faced, red-haired girl looked to be about twelve years old.

"Well," Meg said, smiling at her, "you know me, but I don't know your name."

"Why, I'm Peggy. Peggy McVeigh. Been workin' here fer a year, ever since me family came here from Ireland. We traveled all the way 'cross the ocean 'cuz my older brother got into trouble with the law when he came to work in the lumberyards. But me ma is soberin' him up. Yer pa gave me pa a job on his shipping docks. We're so grateful. Glad tah meetcha." She clumped the towels into the crook of one arm and held out a hand.

Surprised, Meg shook her hand. "Peggy, how old are you? If you don't mind my asking."

"Fifteen in a month, I swear!" She jostled the heap of towels back into both arms.

"Do you like it here?"

"Oh, yes, Miss Sullivan! I like it very much, even though Miss Hannah said we'd better wear these silly starched uniforms when ya come home." She looked down disgustedly at her prim blue get-up. "At least fer a little while, so things won't be too different fer ya at first. She says once ya get used to the changes around here we can be ourselves again."

"I see. I'm sorry you have to be uncomfortable for me. I'll try to get used to things as quickly as possible."

"Ah, I can't thank ya enough for that, Miss Sullivan. 'Cuz Cook's 'bout to die in this thing. Ya know, she's got a lot more skin to cover with this scratchy cloth than the rest of us." She raised her rust-colored eyebrows in earnest.

"I tell you what, Peggy, I've known Cook all my life. I'd planned on going down this afternoon to see her anyway. I'll tell her that tomorrow she can wear whatever she wants. She's such a fabulous cook she deserves to be comfortable. How's that?"

"Oh, that's wonderful! Then will ya tell Miss Hannah the rest of us are dyin', too?"

"That I will."

"Thank ya, Miss Sullivan. I gotta go now. These towels will be needin' washin' again seein' they've been on the floor. But we can chat more later." Peggy headed for the servants' stairs at the end of the wide hallway, the ones that led straight down to the kitchen.

So, things are different now. Interesting. I can't wait to get to the bottom of this.

Meg went to her room to change for riding with her father, all the while thinking of how she'd genuinely liked Peggy. However, she had an ulterior motive for befriending her. Clearly, Peggy liked to chit-chat. She had no boundaries for family secrets. Either being too young to know that wasn't customary for servants and their employers, or being a foreigner not knowing proper etiquette in this culture, or things having loosened up so much in this house it didn't matter to anyone anymore, there was some reason Peggy behaved as she did. Whatever the reason, if Meg wanted to find out what went on in this house, Peggy would be a good source of information.

She couldn't wait to have another little chat with the girl.

12

Abby felt antsy, finding it hard to concentrate on the reading she was doing for the mayor. Of course, that was because the girl was home.

Yet the messages coming through so strongly for the mayor of Traverse City couldn't be ignored. She closed her eyes, placed her hands on the crystal ball, forced herself to focus, and took in the missives from beyond. When she opened her eyes and told him that, yes, the "blessing of the blossoms" could be expanded to become a large event, the mayor was ecstatic over the support of his idea. Abby told him the religious ceremony conducted each year by a priest at the behest of local farmers to bless their cherry crops could attract visitors from far and wide. Local merchants could be involved; there could be a parade of floats made from motorcars and trucks; they could elect a queen; the high school band could march; war veterans could be honored; food could be sold; and there could even be a cherry pie contest.

The mayor left her cabin as giddy as a boy who just got his first feel of a loose girl. Abby felt happy for him. She'd been reading for him ever since he came home from college and went into business twenty years ago.

Most people would be surprised to discover how many businessmen came to her, most in secrecy at her cabin. For the two mornings a week she also did readings in the backroom of a garage in town, most of the folks weren't locals so they didn't care about privacy.

Abby and the garage owner, who'd once been a farrier full time and still shoed horses on the side, had enjoyed an amicable arrangement for years. He gave her a small space, a table, and two chairs in exchange for free weekly readings of his own. His business had prospered mightily over the years and he credited the fortune teller with guiding him, especially when prohibition struck and she reassured him that every law enforcement officer in town would look the other way when he sold moonshine under the counter, especially if they got a discount. She'd been right.

Abby watched the mayor drive away in his snazzy Model T Ford, took down her "All-Seeing Abby" sign, and closed the door. Quickly, she cleared the room with her sage and feather. Then, needing time to reflect about what to do with her discovery at Lizzie's cottage, she sat down in her rocker and summoned her ancestor spirit guides.

They remained silent. She'd tried many times to get them to tell her about Lizzie, but they'd always refused. Why, she didn't know.

"So, I'm on my own," she sighed. Finding what laid beneath Lizzie's cottage had been startling, totally shocking. She'd had no idea it had been there all these years, right there almost under her feet every time she visited.

The ladder under the trapdoor in the floor led down to a cave. Rather than a cellar being dug and a cottage being built on top of it, the cottage had been built, long ago by some unknown settler, on top of the entrance to a cave. It was very clever, actually. Abby could imagine the original dwellers, perhaps some of the first white people in the area, using the cave as a root cellar for storing food. She hadn't had enough light to venture too far but heard spring water trickling somewhere up ahead. That meant fresh water flowed right at hand. The cave could have served as shelter in a storm, too.

Limestone caves dotted these hills, carved out long ago when the Arctic glaciers slowly melted and crept down the landmass, cutting grooves and lakes and caverns into the bedrock as they went, like giant monsters clawing and digging their way south to reshape and mold everything in their path. Petoskey stones, pebble shaped rocks made of fossilized coral, were just one of the unusual materials left behind, still washing ashore on local beaches. Abby had buckets full of them she'd picked up from her very own beach.

She'd seen caves all over these hills but none deeper than about ten feet burrowed into the side of a hill. Just the short distance she'd seen in Lizzie's cave went about fifteen feet back and then turned a corner, so she was anxious to take a lantern to explore deeper into its mysteries.

But the biggest mystery broke her heart. Perhaps, she thought, she was being petty. However, she and Lizzie were so close, why did her friend keep the cave a secret? Was she hiding something?

There was no doubt Lizzie knew about the cave. Not only was the trapdoor obvious beneath the rug, a painting, too dull in candlelight to discern, sat against one of the stone walls down there. Everyone, she supposed, needed some secrets and privacy, but that seemed extreme. If a cave existed under her cabin, Lizzie would have been the first, and maybe only, person she'd take down there. Clearly, she and Elizabeth "Lizzie" Sullivan had not been as close as she thought.

She wondered if Lizzie was ever truly close to anyone. One part of her exuded warmth and charm and love. Another part of her remained closed to the world. Even to her best friend.

There was a lot Abby didn't know, but one thing was certain. No matter what secrets Lizzie held in her heart, with all her heart Abby would always love the Lizzie she knew.

13

"Excuse me, Lizzie," Jenny said apologetically. *"Do you think* you could spare a few moments to help me with something? I'm so excited I'm not thinking straight and I need your clear head to help me."

Elizabeth wiped her paintbrush with a rag as she listened to her neighbor's request. She'd been surprised when she heard a knock at her door as that so seldom happened. And shy, depressed Jenny, of all people, never bothered her. At the moment however, Jenny looked almost radiant. Maybe even happy. She actually had some color in her usually wan cheeks.

"Sure," Elizabeth said, curious. "What can I do for you?" She gestured for Jenny to come in, but the woman shook her head no.

"I need you to come meet with this lawyer who's in my room right now! My sister finally found someone to help me get a divorce!"

"Jenny! That's great! Let's go."

Without even bothering to change from her designer silk lounging robe, Elizabeth tossed her towel onto the floor and stuck her paintbrush in her pocket, and followed Jenny next door.

When they entered the room a handsome young man stood staring up at the painting of a barn that Elizabeth had given Jenny. He strode toward them, hand extended. "Hello, I'm Jed O'Neill," he offered, shaking Elizabeth's hand. "You must be Lizzie Sullivan."

"Glad to make your acquaintance," Elizabeth said.

"Mrs. Pennington has told me what a kind neighbor you are. She tells me she trusts your judgement, which is just fine. And she said you gave her that painting. It's exquisite! You have amazing talent."

"Why, thank you," Elizabeth said.

"Did you also do the one in the hallway of the three Labradors?"

"Yes, so many people here seem to miss their dogs, I thought they'd enjoy that one."

"Lizzie gives away her paintings all the time," Jenny interjected. "Half the rooms in our cottage have one and I think just about everybody who works here has one. She's so generous with her work. I love this one.

"I miss my farm. But not my husband."

"Why don't we sit down and talk about that?" the lawyer said, looking at Jenny Pennington for permission to sit at the one table in the room.

The living quarters in Cottage 23 were much more comfortable than those in the central building, the one known as Building 50. Each of the rooms in Cottage 23 was an adequately sized space with large rectangular windows reaching toward the high ceiling, allowing for lots of natural light. Supplied by the asylum were a table and two chairs, a small bed, white linens, a white blanket, a down pillow, a nightstand with a kerosene table lamp, and three candles in candlestick holders. Residents of 23, deemed more stable than many other patients, enjoyed the privilege of possessing matches for lighting the lamp and candles. Whatever type of valise and clothing they arrived with stayed with them, like the wicker case sitting on Jenny's floor under a window. A side table held a water pitcher and glass, filled twice each day by workers who came by with supplies and a fresh bucket of well water.

All-in-all, it was a better living situation than many residents had ever known in their private homes. But Elizabeth's room was, of course, much more opulent than Jenny's and the others, with Herbert having met his wife's many demands. Jenny's Cottage 23 room, on the other hand, was paid for by her sister, who'd been appalled upon discovering the conditions under which Jennie lived in the central building. Although clean and well-tended, she's had a nine-by-six-foot room, a cell really, with one small window. With Jennie's husband being a mere farmer, and a brute of one at that, he couldn't nor would have given her anything better. Her sister's wealth aside, Jenny had told Elizabeth she didn't want to ask anything more of her sister, she so appreciated this room, so she lived sparsely. Her room held just what it came with, except for the painting.

"Yes," Jenny responded to the young lawyer's request that they sit, her voice quavering in barely contained excitement. "We'll sit here." She motioned toward the table and then looked confused as there were only two chairs. "Here," she said, "I'll sit on the edge of the bed."

The lawyer and Elizabeth politely sat in the chairs and Jenny perched herself on the end of the bed, facing them.

"Mrs. Pennington, I'm sorry you didn't get the message that I would be coming here today. Permission from the administrative office came to us just this morning. It took some arm twisting by my uncle, the judge, but he got it done without your husband being contacted. Someone was supposed to tell you I'd be here at this time. I do apologize."

"Oh, I don't mind." Jenny beamed. "I'm just glad you're here."

"I do need to tell you up front that your sister expected another lawyer in my uncle's law office, but that man has a horrible cold and is recuperating. I just arrived in town two days ago. And I passed the bar last month. I hope that's not a problem."

"Why no, not at all."

"I promise to do my best for you. Seeing that this is my first case, you can imagine I want to start off my career with a bang, so you can count on me."

Elizabeth studied Jed O'Neill's sharp blue eyes, square jaw, and thick sandy-colored hair. He looked as Irish as they come. Behaving unlike herself, she preferred to remain silent to see what this greenhorn would come up with. She hoped not a bunch of blarney.

"Okay, I need to ask you some questions in order to get started. I understand from your sister that your husband had you placed here and that he refuses to get a divorce. Is that correct?"

Tears sprang to Jenny's eyes. "Yes, that's right."

"Why do you think he wants to stay married to you, if he doesn't want to live with you?"

"He wants to control me! He's an animal! He used to beat me. When I wouldn't stand for that anymore he decided to ruin my life by taking my children away from me."

Elizabeth had never seen the woman show so much emotion and reached out to pat her hand.

"This question is indelicate, but I must ask it: Do you think you are insane? In other words, is this where you need to be?"

"No!" Elizabeth exclaimed. "Mr. O'Neill, you have no idea how many women are here merely because their husbands wanted to get rid of them. It's a crime. It's immoral. It's ungodly. We keep hearing about suffragettes and women's rights and new laws for women, but believe you me we don't see any of that in here." Now her own emotion had got the best of her.

"Jenny?" the lawyer queried, looking for her answer to his question.

"No," she whispered. "I might be shy but I'm as sane as a saint. I'm certainly saner than that Satan of a man I married."

"How long have you been here?"

"Three years. My youngest was only three when they took me away. She's six years old now and probably doesn't even remember me." She started to sob.

Elizabeth looked around the room and found a linen handkerchief on the nightstand. She brought it to Jennie, who dried her eyes.

"Would you like a drink of water?" Elizabeth asked her.

"No, thank you. I'm fine."

"There are new laws, ladies," Jed said, "new laws that will help this case. And other cases like it." He looked pointedly at Elizabeth. "The biggest factor here is to get you declared sane by the officials here; that needs to come first. Then you'll be free to leave and get a divorce. If you are sane, your husband will no longer be considered your guardian by the state and he can't stop a divorce.

In order for you to get custody of your children in the divorce, we need proof that he's an unfit father and husband. My uncle is a judge; he says he's seen this a number of times. If we can prove that your husband has been leaving the children alone, for example, while he goes out to drink or cavort with other women, we can get it done."

Jenny gave up a small grin. "That should be easy enough. He can't spend half a day sober and he chases every skirt in town."

"Oddly enough, in this case, that's a good thing. It'll help immensely. Our goal is for you to have grounds for divorce, get back together with your children, and start a new life."

"Oh, that sounds wonderful! My sister wants me to bring the children and come live with her in Grand Rapids. Do you really think we can do it?"

"We'll certainly give it our best. If he's as bad as you say he is, he'll end up cutting his own throat. I think we have a good chance.

"Well, I'd better get to work! I'll be back in three days to give you an update." He stood, donned his hat, and nodded. "It's been a pleasure, ladies. I'll see you again soon." With that he left.

"Oh, Lizzie! What do you think? Is it really possible?"

"Yes, Jenny. I think it really is. There might be justice for women in this world after all. And you'll be one of the first in line to get it."

After a congratulatory hug, Elizabeth went back to her studio and continued to paint.

14

Meg entered Sleder's and looked around. Supposedly a restau-
rant, everyone in town, including her fourteen-year-old maid
Peggy, knew it was a speakeasy tavern. No wonder it was so
crowded.

Upon further inspection in the muted light, though, she
could see only men; professionals in suits, workmen in shirts and
trousers, and farmers in overalls; standing at the long ornate bar
with its brass rail, and sitting at oak tables and booths. It was a
beautiful room with mahogany and cherry as well as oak wood
abounding in the furnishings and accoutrements. She looked up
to see a tall ceiling of stamped tin. Stuffed animal heads lined the
walls, including a number of deer bucks and a buffalo. A sign on
the wall said: "Good will is good business—Case of Beer $1.50
w/ *free* double shot of whiskey and a beer." Dotting the floor were
numerous spittoons.

Dozens of masculine eyes turned in Meg's direction, taking
her in from head to toe. She straightened her spine and lifted her
chin, refusing to be intimidated.

Most surprisingly, all those fellows drank from teacups. Some of their large, work-worn fingers could barely hold the dainty handles. She knew that teetotalers they were not.

Two burly police officers sitting at a front table got up and walked out without paying, staring at her as they parted to pass her on each side. For a moment, she thought they would speak to her so she ignored their impolite inspection. They walked by, and she heard the door open and shut behind her. She took a deep breath.

"Hello, Miss Sullivan. Are you lookin' for the women's room?" A young lad she'd never seen before in her life had appeared at her side and asked the question.

Peggy had warned her about that, saying "everyone in town" knew that Herbert Sullivan's daughter had returned home from the big city because she'd been jilted by her hoity-toity fiancé. They would all know who she was. But this kid knowing her was really too much!

"The what?" she asked.

The answer didn't come from the boy, however, as her father's driver suddenly showed up at her elbow. Sam said, "Excuse me, Miss Sullivan. I saw you come in here and want to make sure you find the women's room. Hi, Louie."

"Don't worry, Sammy," the kid said. "I got 'er."

"Thank you, Sam," Meg said, struck by how her father always seemed to make sure someone kept an eye on her.

She'd told her father she was going to a restaurant to meet an old friend she'd known during summer visits home. When he'd asked the friend's name and she brilliantly came up with a bogus alias, he'd been confounded because, he noted, he knew just about everyone in town. Her then additional fabrication about the friend only visiting her grandmother during summers, too, until recently when she moved here permanently, seemed most clever. She even added the brilliant touch that the granddaughter and grandmother didn't have the same last name, but she didn't remember the grandmother's last name. Her father had looked at her for a moment with a furrowed brow, but then said he was pleased she was reconnecting with old friends.

No doubt the tale of this little debacle in the tavern would meet her sire's ears in the morning, if not sooner, thanks to Sam the driver.

"Okay then," Sam said, holding the door open to make sure she left.

"The women's room," the boy smiled up at her. "Com'on, I'll show you." He ushered her back out the front door.

Sam headed down Randolph Street toward the limousine, which was parked between a horse and buggy and a horse tethered to a hitching post. As they drove into town she'd been struck with how many people here still traveled by horse and carriage, or just horse. Obviously not nearly as large a percent of the population here owned a motorcar as what she'd become accustomed to in Chicago.

As the boy led her around the side of the building she looked back, wondering if Sam would sneak right back into the tavern as soon as she was out of sight.

They walked down a path at the side of the building. "Women aren't allowed in the tavern," he explained. "Boy! Did you see those men's eyes buggin' out at you? They don't get to see somebody pretty as you very often." He chortled.

"Thank you… Louie, it is?"

"Sure. Ever'body knows that. 'Cept you, I guess." He threw her a cockeyed grin. "Louie Sleder."

"Oh. I see. Well, now I know, too."

She carried on the conversation as amicably as possible, rattled as she was that women weren't allowed in the tavern. How parochial. She thought that went out in the last century. But it wasn't the boy's fault, so she chatted as best she could while they walked the length of the building.

"Aren't you a little young to be working in a tavern, Louie?"

"Oh, no, Miss Sullivan. I've been workin' here since I could walk and will pro'bly be here 'til I croak. My parents own the place and their parents owned it before them.

"Hey! Did you mean to go to the courtin' room? That's where men and women can be together. If you don't mind my sayin' so, I don't think you want to go in there."

"No. No, I'm not interested in a courting room. The women's room is perfect for me." *A 'courting room'? Really? Could this town possibly get any more backwards?* she thought.

"Here we are. This door right here." He opened the ordinary-looking door for her.

"Thank you, Louie. You're a very gallant young man."

The boy beamed. "No problem, Miss Sullivan. You come talk to me anytime you need somethin'. Thing is, though, you just gotta come in this door."

Meg stepped into the room and heard the door slap shut behind her.

She could see that she was overdressed. Her ermine wrap, something she'd wear to the grocer's in Chicago, proved to be an embarrassment here. Her elbow-length black gloves were really over the top. Her green silk sheath dress seemed more acceptable, as a number of women around the room wore similar, although not tailored or silk, sheaths. After all, the style was all the rage. A few even had long strings of pearls about their necks, albeit it fake, imitating the real ones Meg wore. It was clear there wasn't as much wealth around here as what she was accustomed to.

She tugged at one of her dangly diamond and pearl earrings, considering pulling off the pair and stowing them in her bag. Too obvious, she decided, seeing that women's bobbed-hair heads had already turned and wide kohl-lined eyes from all corners of the room stared at her.

She'd only come here because Peggy reassured her that here she would find nurses from the asylum. Peggy had left out, or didn't know, the part about the women's room being separate from the tavern. Peggy said her brother, the one arrested a number of times for drunk and disorderly, always bragged that he could bag a nurse at Sleder's any time, night or day. What the girl probably didn't know was that her brother must spend his time in the nefarious courting room. But then, Peggy insisted her brother was an "eejit."

An Irish lad's eejit status aside, this seemed to be the place to be to meet women in town. Meg had lost her taste for speakeasies but three days earlier when her father had refused her request to see her mother, she'd known she needed to take matters into her own hands. Her plan was to cavort with the locals, find a willing player for cash, and have an asylum nurse sneak her in to see her mother. According to Peggy it had been done before, especially for patients like Mrs. Sullivan in the houses called cottages.

"May I offer you a table, Miss Sullivan?" A pleasant woman, another stranger who knew her name, posed the question.

"Why, yes, thank you. For two, please. I'm… I'm waiting for an acquaintance." Of course, she had no clue yet who that companion might be.

The woman led her to a small table at the side of the room. "May I bring you one of our special root beers?" she asked.

Meg looked around. Almost every table held women drinking from tea cups. Most of them had stopped staring at her, although a few leers lingered.

"Is that what most of your patrons are having?"

"Oh, yes! Women love our root beer." The woman winked.

"Yes, that sounds good."

Meg took off her gloves, sluffed her fur stole off her shoulders to let it hang on the back of her chair, and took in the place. This room was much smaller than the men's, more like sitting in a parlor. Being nighttime, the lights were dim. It was a cozy room.

Still, she'd rather not have to be here. The chance she could pull this off, she now realized, was slim. Seeing that everyone in this small town knew everything about everybody else, the odds she'd get away with her plan didn't look so good anymore. It had sounded much more promising when she'd conjured it up with her fellow plotter, Peggy.

It all started when her father refused her request to visit her mother.

That evening Peggy had knocked on her bedroom door to thank her for talking to Miss Hannah. The starched blue uniforms gone, Peggy and the other servants wore plain white cotton blouses and straight mid-calf black skirts, with black hose and shoes, the outfits they'd been wearing for some time before Meg came home.

After a chat about style, Meg asked Peggy outright if there was any gossip about her father having a woman in his life.

"Oh, yes, Miss," Peggy said. "Everyone knows that! He and Miss Hannah are in love. They have been for a very long time, before I came here. She was head housekeeper at another business man's house, someone your da knew, so he met her there, and then she came to work here. But they can't wed, of course, seein' that yer father is married to, well, ya know, yer mother in the loon... um, asylum.

"Cook has worked here since yer father was a wee lad, and she says he used to be more like his mother, God rest her soul, and she was prim and proper as they come. But her husband, God rest his soul—ya know he started out as a shanty boy! A mere wood-cutter. Imagine that! And he built all of this." She spread her arms and looked around, agog. "Anyways, he's yer grandfather and he was a grand man. Everybody loved him. Yer father, Cook says, has become more and more like him over the years. Miss Hannah has helped him 'loosen up,' as Cook puts it.

"Isn't that grand?"

Meg had listened closely, her breath catching in her throat. So, her father was, after all, in love with his head housekeeper. He did not love her mother. Was that why he'd had her mother committed?

Meg's reverie of her conversation with Peggy evaporated when a Sleder's server placed a pretty china tea cup in a matching saucer in front of her. "Here you go, Miss Sullivan, your tea."

Yet another person who knew her name.

Meg lifted her cup to take a sip of "tea." Placing her cup back on the saucer, she chuckled. She'd like to see the bourbon and rye teabags that made up this brew. It was good, so she sipped away.

Looking around as she drank, she wondered if there was a "mark" in the room who could help her. She hadn't thought through how she'd approach someone who looked like they might be willing. If she revealed her plan to the wrong person, she could be had and get into trouble. Then she'd never be able to see her mother.

A few days earlier, the day after she first arrived home, she and her father had a beautiful afternoon together riding up Leelanau Peninsula. Their home sat up the peninsula five miles from town on the west side of Grand Traverse Bay, and they'd ridden seven miles further up, sometimes on the beach and sometimes on the dirt road that led to the Grand Traverse Lighthouse on the tip of the peninsula. They hadn't gone all the way, as the peninsula was a thirty-mile stretch, but it'd been an invigorating ride. She'd never seen her father so jovial and, again, the word that came to mind was fun. True to his word, he'd even brought a picnic lunch.

That evening she'd gone into his study and requested to see her mother. She hoped their new friendly father-daughter relationship had buttered him up enough to grant her request. But he'd turned her down, calmly saying he didn't think it was a good idea. He gave no further explanation. Seeing that he was her mother's guardian, Meg needed his permission to enter the asylum. So here she was, eyeing up a roomful of women wondering if a potential co-conspirator sat within sight.

She didn't have to wonder for long.

The young woman had a round face, innocent looking as all

get out. She'd attempted to put a wave into her limp blond hair but it had spurned the style. Still, with her soft eyes and gentle manner, she was attractive. She wore a pink shift and little jewelry, adding to her natural, innocent femininity. Uninvited, she sat down at Meg's table.

"Hello, Miss Sullivan. Would you like to see your mother?"

That's all it took. Within minutes Meg and the asylum nurse named Petunia had planned a clandestine nighttime visit a few days hence, when Cottage 23's supervisor would be on holiday.

Their plot complete, nurse Petunia went back to her table of friends. Meg paid her bill and left Sleder's women's room walking on air.

"Meg!"

Startled at a man's voice, as little light found its way to the side of the building, she turned but hastened her pace toward the front of the tavern. When the man stepped out from under a tree where she could see his face, she kept going.

"You! What do you want? Why are you skulking there in the dark?"

He caught up with her and matched her stride.

"I'm not skulking. I'm waiting for you."

"How did you know I was here?"

They'd reached the front of Sleder's and Meg was relieved to be under a gas streetlight. Men inside the tavern could see her through the front windows. Surely some gentleman in there would be chivalrous enough to save her should this thug attack.

The man grinned and took off his fedora. Thick, sandy-colored hair spilled out around his face. He wasn't wearing his spectacles, making his eyes more vibrant than ever. "Oh, everybody in there," he said, jerking a thumb at the tavern, "knows you're here. I was at the far end of the bar with my uncle and saw you come in."

"Do you know what time it is? My father's driver will be back any moment. That's our car down there." She pointed at the limousine, although she could see that Sam was nowhere in sight. Still, she wanted this Jed bozo to know she wouldn't be alone for long and dawdled over putting on her gloves to avoid looking at him.

"There's a bench over there. We could talk until he gets here."

"Why on earth would I want to talk to you? Mind your own beeswax, please, and leave me alone!"

"Meg... Miss Sullivan," he corrected himself given her hostility. "We're old friends. Weren't we great euchre partners on the train?"

"Yes, and then we got off the train, where your wife and children met you! You slob. Don't talk to me anymore."

"My... wife?" Jed O'Neill slapped his forehead. "You mean my... *sister and nephews.*"

Meg turned to face him. "What? Your sister?"

"Yes, Miss Sullivan, my *sister.* And *her kids.* Not mine. My brother-in-law didn't come because he was sick in bed with a bad cold, although he's feeling better today, thank you very much."

"Oh, well, then, I'm sorry. I misread the situation." She gnawed at her lower lip.

"I can promise you I'm not married. Haven't had time. Went to college out of high school, went to war in France, came home, got my law degree, and moved here to set up practice. See? No time for a wife and kids."

"You... you...." She felt like a fool. "You fought in the war?"

"I did. Spent far too much time huddled down in cold, muddy trenches. Glad it's over. Glad I survived to be here, in fact. Will being a war veteran entice you to talk to me? Because if it will, I'll tell you all about it."

"I'm sorry," she relented. "I thought, well, I thought you were a married man trying to flirt with me. It insulted me to think you thought I was that kind of girl."

"Oh, no, Miss Sullivan. May I call you Meg again?" She nodded. "Meg, you don't look anything like that kind of girl."

"Did you know my last name on the train or did you hear it for the first time in there?" She tilted her head toward the tavern.

"In there. Everybody in there seems to know you're the daughter of Herbert Sullivan, one of the most prominent businessmen in town. On the train, you were just Meg."

The door to the tavern opened and Sam came out. "I'll pull up the car, Miss Sullivan," he said, hustling down the sidewalk.

Jed smiled at Meg and she felt her whole body relax. It was a beautiful smile. She smiled back. "I have to get used to being back home in a town of only six thousand people after being in the biggest city in the country for so long. Chicago has over two and a half million people. And I must say that relatively few of them know who I am. But everybody here does. So, you probably already know that my fiancé in Chicago left me and I've come home a brokenhearted woman."

"Yes, but they didn't use words that were quite so kind about your fiancé. Don't worry. Everybody thinks the man must be a bozo and it's his loss."

"Bozo. That's the very word I used at the time." She felt it prudent not to reveal that's precisely how she'd thought of him, as well.

The black limousine pulled up in front of them.

"Well, I have to go," Meg said, as Sam hopped out and came around to open her door.

"Wait! Can I see you again?" Jed asked. "I could get together an entire team of people to play cards if you don't want to be alone with me." Meg couldn't help but notice that he nervously circled the rim of his hat in his hands.

Sam's eyebrows lifted as he continued to hold the door. He looked at Meg, then at Jed, then back at Meg expectantly.

"Do you ride horses?" she asked Jed.

"Sure do. My uncle still owns some nice ones."

"Can you get to the beach on the west side of the bay in front of our house at two o'clock tomorrow afternoon?"

"Sure."

"I'll be riding there. Why don't you join me if you can?"

"Yessirree. I'll be there." He settled his hat back onto his head and smiled again, looking as dapper as one of those Hollywood actors.

Just as it had when she'd first met the handsome man on the train, Meg's heart flip-flopped. That, she knew from experience, probably meant trouble. But her heart insisted she find out for sure.

Meg got into the car and threw Jed a little wave.

Sam closed the door and tipped his driver's cap at Jed. "Well done," he said.

15

Abby wasn't expecting anyone on a Saturday morning, so the knock on her cabin door came as a surprise. She put down the herbs she'd just picked out of her garden and had started to bundle for hanging from the rafters to dry. Wiping her hands on a towel, she quickly threw the purple and yellow primrose flowers she'd cut into a vase of water, not wanting to leave them dry for too long.

She finally reached the door and opened it.

"Hello. Abby? I hope you don't mind my dropping by, but I've been told you might be able to help me."

Abby froze. Why in tarnation hadn't her ancestor spirit guides warned her of this? Sometimes she thought they entertained themselves by leaving her high and dry. They'd undoubtedly be laughing their heads off, if they still had heads.

She smiled. "Hello, Meg. Please come in."

The young woman entered her cabin and looked around. "So, you know who I am," she said.

"Of course. Everyone in Traverse City knows who you are.

But in all fairness, anyone who's lived here for more than twenty minutes is known by everyone else in town.

"Please, come, sit." Abby led Meg to the table. ""Did you ride over?" she asked, noting her riding attire.

"No, but I'll be riding this afternoon, so I went ahead and got ready."

"Ah, that's nice."

"May I get you some herb tea? I just brewed some fresh ginger-mint, from my own garden."

"Oh, that would be lovely."

Actually, Abby didn't care about tea as much as she needed a moment to absorb what was happening here. Lizzie's daughter sat right here in her cabin, looking every bit like Lizzie had looked when Abby first met her. Except for the modern clothes and haircut, it could be the same woman. She busied herself getting her tea kettle off the coals in the fireplace and pouring the aromatic liquid into the two best cups she could find, the only two she owned that weren't chipped.

Meg, in the meantime, occupied herself by swiping imaginary lint off her riding breeches and straightening the collar on her checkered blouse, while surreptitiously examining the contents of the cabin. Giving up the pretense, she said, "Abby, your cabin is lovely! So… charming." She turned all the way around in her chair to take in the entire space. "Your kitchen area is so sweet with those striped curtains."

Abby brought the tea and joined her guest. "Why, thank you, Meg. I love it here. I've lived here all my life."

"And your bed is beautiful." Meg pointed to Abby's four-poster bed in the corner, the posts draped with fabric which Abby pulled down when she knew people were coming. Not expecting anyone today, the bed sat in full view. But normally, she didn't think people needed to be looking at something as private as her bed. "Did you make that quilt and those ruffled pillows yourself?" Meg asked.

Abby chuckled. "Yes. It usually surprises people to find out I love to sew. They tend to think Indians only fish and hunt. My mother was a good seamstress. She taught me."

Meg continued to look around and Abby knew she might be sizing up the place as many people often did, their false assumptions about the Chippewa shattered by this pleasingly clean and domestic home. Abby didn't spend money on furnishings or clothes, but she did keep her home and her person spotlessly clean, as had been Chippewa tradition since time immemorial.

"You have a lot of books. You like to read?" Meg asked.

"Oh, yes, I love to read."

Then Meg saw it, the one thing that Abby knew could open the gate to the girl's past.

"That painting above the fireplace! It's beautiful!" Meg got up and stood in front of the painting of the forest, having no idea she stood so close to her own mother's work. "Look at that fawn peeking out from behind the tree. It's so well done it looks like I could reach out and touch the sweet thing. Is this painted by a local artist?"

"Um, yes. A client. Gave it to me… as payment." Abby impulsively decided to keep that gate closed, at least for now.

Meg returned to her chair, looked back at the painting, and then looked at Abby. "I'm sorry if I'm too nosy. I'm a bit nervous. I've never done this kind of thing before."

"That's okay, dear. Lots of people feel that way the first time. And I'm proud of my little home here. Did you know your grandfather gave this plot of land and the cabin to my parents? Herbert Ambrose Sullivan, Sr." She said the name with near reverence. "He was a generous, kind man. Because my father's family had lived in this area for generations, when your grandfather bought the land he let my parents stay right where they were. They so appreciated that, and so do I, of course."

"I've always heard that my grandfather was a kind man. And I've heard the shanty boy story a hundred times." Meg sipped her tea and smiled across the table.

Abby smiled back. "Yes, a self-made man."

"Meg, do you remember being here once when you were a little girl?" Abby pointed in the direction of her bow and quiver of arrows standing in a corner.

Meg looked at the weapon and squinted in contemplation. "Yes, I believe I do. I figured that must have been you, must have been this cabin I was in, although it was dark at night and stormy so I didn't really look around much, except for seeing that." She nodded at the corner. Meg looked at her intently, causing Abby's chest to ache, so mindful was she of her mother. "I snuck away from my nanny because I was sure my little brother must be in the woods and the big people hadn't looked in the right places. I wanted to find him. But all of a sudden I realized I was lost. All the trees looked alike and it was getting dark. I didn't know which way to go to find our house. I was terrified! And an Indian woman — you — came along just as it started to rain cats and dogs. We were near your cabin so you brought me in here first. You wrapped me up in a blanket and started for my house in that storm. My dad was in the woods, soaking wet, hollering my name and half crazy. He was so happy to see us! He carried me home and I never saw you again. I never thanked you. Did my father ever thank you?"

"Oh yes, your father came here the next day to offer his personal thanks. That was very nice of him. In fact, the men in your family have always been kind to me. Your grandfather, Herbert senior, even insisted that I come and live in the big house when my parents died. But I knew your grandmother didn't like the idea and, besides, I couldn't imagine living with her, so I begged to stay here. That's when your grandfather insisted I come to the big house for breakfast at least a few times a week. If I didn't show up for a few days he'd send someone over to check on me. You come from a family of good men, Meg."

"I didn't know that about my grandfather and you. The old shanty boy had a heart. That warms my heart. And I'm glad my father came to thank you for taking care of me."

"Oh, no thanks were needed. I knew everybody at the big house would be frantic to find you so we couldn't wait for the storm to end. When we came in here for the blanket, you saw my bow and arrows, and asked me if I would use it to shoot the man who took your brother. Believe me, I would have if I'd known who to aim at."

"I don't remember that but it sounds like me. I missed my brother so much. I still do. I think all the time about how old he'd be now and what his life would be like. I think he'd be my best friend."

Abby reached across the table and took Meg's hand. The young woman used the other hand to dab at the moisture at her eyes. Abby let silence soothe their memories as they sipped their hot tea for a couple of minutes. Then she decided it was time to move on and ask the necessary question.

"What brought you here today, Meg?"

"Well," Meg said, fingering the edge of her tea cup, "I've decided on something and one of the servants at the house said you're good at helping people decide if they've made the right decision. She said you are friends with the servants there and come over in the morning a lot. It's the Irish girl, Peggy, the most recent upstairs maid."

"Yes, the servants at the house have always been very kind to me. I consider them to be good friends."

She didn't want to reveal that she and Meg's mother had been close for years. That they had always kept secret, knowing that a wealthy white woman and poor Indian woman being friends would never be acceptable in their town. They both would have been run out on a rail. Even the servants in the house didn't know. Elizabeth knew that Abby had been visiting that kitchen since she was a child, but back when she was still at home, Elizabeth never came down. For one thing, she wasn't up yet that early in the morning. But, more importantly, they wanted to keep their relationship private. They both enjoyed it too much to lose it.

Meg said, "I can't believe I never saw you in the kitchen when I was a kid. I wasn't allowed to go in there much. I think my nanny thought I'd be in Cook's way. But when Nanny took her afternoon tea in her room Cook always snuck me into the kitchen for my own little 'teatime.' How I loved that."

"That sounds like Cook. Such a generous, loving woman. Your nanny used to come down to have tea and biscuits with us early in the morning sometimes, before you were even out of bed. She was a nice woman. I'm glad that after you went to boarding school she married that widower with small children. Last I knew she's been very happy."

"Yes, Cook got a letter from her last year. Those kids are grown up now and the oldest is married and has a child. She's a grandmother."

"But! You didn't come to talk about any of this, did you?" Abby patted Meg's hand. "This decision that you've made: What is it?"

"I know you ask... spirit guides..." she faltered, "for information. I've always known you were here but never had the nerve to come before, so this is hard for me. But this is the problem: I've made arrangements to sneak into the asylum to see my mother. I haven't seen her since they took her away when I was six years old. I want to see for myself if she's really insane. My father says she is but he won't tell me what makes him think so or why he had her committed. If she's in there because he wanted to get rid of her—some men do that, you know—then I want to help her get out.

"I know that my father is in love with our head housekeeper, Hannah."

Ah, Abby thought. The girl has either heard house gossip or is very perceptive. Of course they were in love; everyone at the house and most people in town knew that. But Abby didn't feel it was her place to reveal that to this young woman. She needed to be strong enough to confront her father for answers to some questions.

"And you think your father had your mother committed so he could be with Hannah?"

"Maybe. I don't know. She's only worked there for seven years but they've known each other, from what I hear, much longer."

So, it was household gossip she'd been hearing.

"Why don't you ask your father?"

"You mean, just march in and ask him?" Meg sounded incredulous.

"You don't have to march. You could simply walk up to him and ask. Find a good time, like when he's reading his paper in his study."

Meg gnawed at her lower lip. "I, I never considered that."

"Didn't you just turn twenty-one years old?"

"Yes."

"You're a grown-up now, Meg." Abby reveled in giving advice to this girl. It made her feel motherly. Lizzie's daughter had been in her humble cabin for less than twenty minutes and already Abby loved the girl.

She hadn't even asked her ancestor spirit guides to come through yet, but it was time. "So, your question is whether or not you're making a mistake by planning to see your mother. Is that what you want me to ask the spirit guides?"

"Yes," Meg offered in a mere whisper.

"Are you afraid you'll find out she truly is insane? What do you fear should you find that out?"

Abby almost expected Meg to cry but instead the young woman showed enormous strength. She was more of a grown-up than Abby had suspected. Meg sat up straight and spoke clearly. "I don't know if I can handle knowing for sure. I know that's what everyone already thinks. But if I know for sure I can never again pretend that it might not be true."

"I see. Let's ask the spirit guides what they think of all of this." Abby placed her palms on the crystal ball out of habit, even though she didn't need it to communicate with her ancestors. She closed her eyes, slowed her breathing, and let the trance come over her. "Dear ancestor spirit guides," she rasped, "please help this young woman with her dilemma. Should she visit her mother in the asylum or should she leave well enough alone?"

The message came through so strongly it felt to Abby as if the spirit sat beside her and shouted in her ear.

"Yes," Abby said to Meg. "Go." The fortune teller paused, listening. Stunned at what she heard, she knew she couldn't tell Meg the spirit guide said she must go because it would be the only chance she would have to see her mother. "Go," Abby repeated and opened her eyes.

Meg sat transfixed.

Abby felt conflicted. She didn't want Meg to see her mother. She, too, feared what she might find out for the same reasons Meg feared going. Yet, as usual, the spirit guides had spoken through Abby and she had no control over what they said. She felt exhausted.

"That's all they can say about it at this time," she said.

"That's all I need. Thank you so much, Abby. I hope you won't mind if I come to see you again sometime."

"No, I don't mind at all. That would be nice."

Meg drank the last few sips of her tea, pulled four dollars out of her pocket, and laid the folded bills on the table.

Abby patted her hand. "You don't have to do that, dear. I'm glad to do this for you. You feel like family to me."

Meg smiled, Lizzie's smile. "Please take it. I wouldn't feel right otherwise. At least this time." She started to rise from her chair and then halted, plopping back down. "Um, this is rather silly, but I do have one more question about something else."

"Yes?"

"I'm going riding with a young man this afternoon. A very handsome, nice young man, I think. I want to tell him about my mother. My fiancé in Chicago broke up with me when he found out about her.... Oh, you know about that, don't you?"

Abby shrugged.

"I still forget sometimes; everybody knows everything in this town. Okay, so he dumped me because of my mother. I want to tell this new man right away, so if he can't handle it I won't waste my time. What do you think?"

Abby cocked her head and looked at Meg thoughtfully. "I think he already knows," she said.

"Oh. Of course. Everyone knows." Meg laughed. "I should have known. It's going to take me a while to get used to living in a small town again." She stood up, but Abby stayed in her chair.

"Meg, dear, the spirit guides tell me this is a very good man. You will have a wonderful ride this afternoon."

At that, Meg Sullivan beamed. "Thank you, Abby! I hope to see you again soon." She shot a long glance at the painting above the mantle before leaving the cabin.

Once Lizzie's daughter left, Abby took the folded dollar bills, went to the fireplace, pulled out a stone near the edge on the side, and pulled out a small burlap sack. She pulled on the strings that opened the sack and placed the money inside, along with hundreds of other one-dollar bills. She closed the sack, carefully secured it back in its hole, and replaced the stone. The sack was almost full, which meant she'd soon need to put its contents in the most recent metal box buried in the yard along with all the other metal boxes full of cash.

Abby was a good Chippewa. She knew how to prepare for the future.

She poured herself another cup of tea, sat in her rocker, and pondered what to do. It confounded her that the spirits had said this secret visit would be Meg's only chance to visit her mother. What did that mean? Meg would see her mother but then be caught and never allowed in again? That seemed the most logical explanation. And then Meg might be even more intent about getting to know more about her mother by going through her cottage.

Abby had wanted to visit Lizzie's cottage one more time to explore that mysterious cave but had been afraid to go lest Meg be walking around and see her going through her mother's things. Abby wanted to see if she needed to get rid of anything in the cottage — she had no clear idea of what it might be — that would cause the young woman distress. Perhaps there were indiscreet paintings, lurid books, or unsavory magazines. She'd never seen those things herself when she visited there, but she hadn't ever gone through the place and Lizzie did have a decidedly wild side. Now, though, how could Abby possibly examine the cottage with Meg about?

Her ancestors were mum, so Abby decided to finish bundling and hanging her herbs. That she could handle.

16

"Hello, Herbert. Come in."

"Elizabeth." Herbert Sullivan, hat in hand, stepped into her room and she closed the door. Without another word, as was the routine that had developed over the years, he sat at the table, keeping his hat in his lap. As usual, he was fastidiously attired in a suit, dress shirt, and tie. A natty silk handkerchief peeked out from his pocket. He sat up so straight Elizabeth imagined the starch from his shirt had infiltrated his body. He never completely settled into the chair. It always seemed to Elizabeth as if her husband was reluctant to touch anything in her room. Let alone her.

She joined him and picked up the silver teapot off its silver tray, and poured hot water on top of a teabag that sat in a Blue Willow cup. All of this, of course, like everything else in her room, had been provided by her dutiful husband. Like all her clothes, he'd also paid for her latest outfit, which she wore today, a delightful lavender morning frock. Its delicate fabric graced her gentle curves deliciously, with a low neckline framing her décolletage and the mid-calf length showcasing her shapely gams. Turning sideways in her chair, she crossed her legs toward him to emphasize her milky silk stockings and cream-colored heels with pearls on the buckles. She knew she looked stunning.

Not that Herbert would notice. He hadn't seen her as a real woman in years, possibly the only man on the planet who didn't find her alluring. Her little game of dressing to try to sway him had been going on for as long as she could remember. She hadn't won yet, but refused to give up. Not that she wanted him to touch her; the game alone amused her.

Her husband poured himself a cup of steaming coffee from the metal urn always provided for him by a nurse. He took a hasty sip as she dipped her teabag a few times, and drew it out to place it on the saucer.

He finally looked at her face. "Meg is home," he said without preamble. "She arrived by train a few days ago."

Elizabeth did her best to look surprised, even though she already knew the girl would be coming. Abby had told her that.

"Well," she said, "it was a month ago you told me her fiancé broke their engagement, so I guess this is no surprise."

"I'm glad she's home. Right now she needs to be around fam... people who care about her. She seems to be handling it well." He gulped at the rest of his coffee.

Elizabeth slowly sipped her tea, enjoying his discomfort and doing her best to drag out their conversation to force him, in his politeness, to stay as long as possible.

"Herbert," she said, "why do you still come here? Hannah brings me everything I ask for. I'm curious about your visits." She sipped slowly on her tea.

Her husband looked stricken. "Why, it's my responsibility. You are, after all, my wife."

"Ah, I see," she said, setting down her teacup. "I did my duty to you as a wife by providing children, one of which you still love today, so my reward is your monthly presence in my asylum room, where you had me committed. Is that it?"

He reddened. "Elizabeth, we both know this is the best place for you. I thought you were happy here."

"Oh, I am. Happier than having to share a bed with you. But I just wonder if you ever feel even a twinge of guilt that you've had your wife put away."

He stood abruptly and secured his hat on his head. "As usual, Elizabeth, our conversation is going nowhere."

Herbert walked to the door, reached for the handle, and turned back to her. She didn't get up, continuing to calmly sip her tea.

"Is there anything you need this month?" he asked.

"Let's see…. Besides one of those fabulous Rolls-Royce Silver Ghosts I've seen in magazines, with my own driver to take me wherever I want, there's a list there on the stand by the door of the paint I need."

He picked up the piece of paper, stuck it in his pocket, and left.

Elizabeth stared at the closed door and laughed.

17

Meg could see him from half a mile away. *She'd been watching* anxiously, thinking she saw a man on a horse about a mile up but losing sight of the image where the shoreline meandered in and out of knolls and sand dunes that barred a straight view to Traverse City from the beach. But when he rounded the final curve there remained no doubt: Jed the handsome man kept his promise. He rode along the beach from town, coming to see her.

She clicked her tongue and lightly pulled the reins to coax Millie to head in that direction. The mare clopped along nonchalantly in the sand, headed for the man and his horse.

Waving vigorously when he first saw her, he tapped his dark brown horse to gallop toward her. She waved in return but didn't press Millie, old as she was and not inclined to be in a hurry anymore. Her father only had two good riding horses left because he had a motor vehicle. Seeing that he owned a large chunk of Ford Motor Company stock he felt it his duty to set an example for the town and felt certain it wouldn't be long before more and more cars were seen on the roads. In the meantime, it turned out it was customary to let the two head groundskeepers borrow the two remaining horses on Sundays. But he offered to get Meg a nice riding horse if she pleased. Half of the stables had been turned into a garage but the other half could still hold four of the animals. She'd told him she'd like very much to have a good horse to ride, but for now was stuck with sweet, docile, graying, old Millie.

As Jed neared, Meg could see that his horse was a spry, young quarter horse. And that Jed appeared to be much the same.

Their horses finally came head to head. The riders smiled at each other.

"Hello, Meg," Jed said as he dismounted.

"Hi, Jed." She got down and patted Millie's neck. "Beautiful day for a ride. Glad you came."

"Oh, I wouldn't have missed this for the world. My only concern was that you wouldn't show up." He smiled again, flashing broad, white teeth. He took off his hat, tussling his sandy hair and, once again, just like on the train, Meg had an urge to run her fingers through it. Rather than a proper riding outfit like hers, he wore Levi blue jeans, a blue-and-white ticking shirt open at the collar, and well-worn but polished boots. No spectacles today. Incongruous with the rest of his attire, his felt fedora hat completed his look. She found his potpourri of clothing style to be utterly charming.

"Of course I came. I keep my word," she said.

"Oh, I'm not implying you wouldn't. It's just that my pursuing you must have come out of left field, so I was afraid you might feel like you don't know me well enough for us to ride out here alone. I realized I never even told you my last name."

They'd led their horses to the shoreline where the beasts walked into the fresh, cool water, lowered their heads, and lapped up their fill. Meg and Jed stood side-by-side, just outside the reach of the benign waves. The sky above reigned blue with sunshine peeking through scattered, puffy, white clouds. A slight breeze made the warm spring air comfortable. It couldn't be a more perfect day, Meg thought. Yet Jed had been right; she'd considered not coming. Not because he didn't seem trustworthy but because meeting him would break her promise to herself to stay away from men for at least the next few months, seeing that they were all bozos.

Bozo this man was not, even though she'd thought so for a while. At least, right now it didn't seem as if he was an idiot like so many men.

She said, "You are Jed O'Neill, nephew of Judge Daniel O'Neill. Originally from Detroit, you and your sister used to come here every summer to stay with your uncle. Your sister fell in love with a young lawyer here and stayed. Now you've come to join your brother-in-law in keeping up the judge's old law practice, which he can't do anymore, being an officer of the court and all. You plan to stay, too."

He let out a low whistle. "You must have been talking to your father. He and my uncle are good friends, from what I understand, and are even euchre partners on occasion."

"Oh, no, not my father. That all came from my maid Peggy. That girl is a wealth of information. But when I told my father I was going riding on the beach with Jed O'Neill he knew exactly who I was talking about. He seemed pleased."

He threw that dazzling smile of his at her again. It became harder and harder for her to keep her "avoid all bozos" vow to herself.

The horses backed away from the water, looking at each other. His horse huffed. Millie turned away from him, no longer having any patience for young male displays of superiority.

"You rode a long way," Meg said to Jed. "I only had to come from the house." She pointed up the hilly dune, where spires from the big house were visible. "Do you feel like riding some more?"

"I'd love to," he said. Thrusting his foot into the stirrup of his saddle, he mounted. Meg did the same and they were off, trotting north up the beach.

They rode beside each other for another mile, not pressing the horses into a gallop. It went without saying that Millie wasn't into running full steam anymore but they had a pleasant ride anyway. The exercise warmed Meg; she opened a couple more buttons of her blouse and rolled up her sleeves. She looked at Jed to see that he'd undone another button and rolled up his sleeves, too. It seemed they felt comfortable with each other, any sign of formality already having fallen away.

When they reached a dune that stretched into the water, eating up the flat beach and making anymore riding that way impossible, they stopped and got down. While the horses drank, they each splashed water onto their faces.

"That feels good!" Jed offered.

"Let's sit over here for a while." Meg pointed toward the rising side of the dune. "We can tie the horses here." They tethered their horses to a large bush and walked a few yards away to plop down in the cushy seat of sand, looking out over the west arm of Grand Traverse Bay. On the other side of the water sat the long peninsula that jutted into the bay across from them, Old Mission Peninsula. From this side of the bay they could see tiny images that told them that peninsula was dotted with small farms, a large cherry tree orchard, and a cow pasture. It presented a pleasing, restful scene. They couldn't see it but knew the east arm of Grand Traverse Bay stretched out on the other side of that narrow landmass and beyond that arm of water the western shore of Michigan headed north to the tip of this part of the state.

Long ago, somebody had nicknamed the lower peninsula of Michigan the Mitten State because on a map it looked like a hand held up with the thumb on the right. This bay lay between the ring and pinky finger.

"It's beautiful here, isn't it?" Jed said. "When I was a kid, my uncle and sister and I used to ride our horses up there." He pointed straight across the water at Old Mission Peninsula. "I love it out there at the old mission church and lighthouse."

"Yes," Meg agreed. "It is beautiful here. I thought I'd miss Chicago more than I do. I'd almost forgotten how pretty it is here. That is, until the snow hits in December."

They both laughed. "Even that is pretty, so crystal clean and sparkling white. For about a month. Then I'm always ready for it to go away."

"Yeah, but you have at least two more months to wait. But when it breaks and spring comes, there's nothing better."

He nodded his concurrence, looking out at the water. When he turned his head and his blue eyes rested on her face, Meg fairly melted. They sat so close to each other their shoulders touched, giving her an urge to grab him and ravish him with kisses, her whole body tingling at the very thought. Inching her shoulder away from him and looking at the bay, she said, "Jed, before we get to know each other any better, I want to talk to you about something."

"Okay," he said.

"It's about my mother." She pulled her knees up and wrapped her arms around them, finally looking at him again.

"Yes. She's in the asylum," he stated matter-of-factly.

"You know about that?"

"Sure. I remember my uncle talking about it a long time ago, and when I told him I'd met you he told me all about it. It's a sad situation, Meg. I'm sorry."

"You understand that most people think she's quite mad?"

"Yes. That's what Uncle Sean said, anyway."

"And you still want to be my friend?"

His face softened and he put a hand on the back of hers, stroking her smooth skin. "Yes, I want to be your friend. I don't care if your mother is in an asylum or in Timbuktu or in prison. You aren't her. It's you I'm interested in, not your mother."

Meg turned her hand over and let their palms meet. "It's just that, well, my fiancé..." she faltered, unable to finish the sentence.

"He left you because of your mother. Hasn't anyone told you he's an absolute ass?"

That broke the morbid spell that had started to consume her and Meg broke into a smile. "No, no one has put it quite that way. Although father said he's a moronic idiot."

"That, too. I don't know the bore and hope I never do, but anybody who would do that isn't worth a plug nickel. Are you still pining for him, Meg?"

"Strangely, no. You'd think I'd miss a man I intended to marry. But now, here, it seems like that was all a childish game. I think...

It's hard to admit, but I think I let myself get engaged to him because I just didn't know what else to do with my life. That's not a good reason to marry someone. I'm glad it didn't work out."

Jed let go of her hand and put his arm around her shoulders, slowly pulling her to him as they looked at each other. She didn't resist. With the gentle caress of a Valentino, he wrapped his other arm around her waist and kissed her lips in a long melding of desire.

Holy moly, it was never anything like this with Robert! Meg thought. This was an entirely new terrain of emotion for her, so desirable it was frightening. When their lips parted, she drew back and looked away.

"I'm sorry," he whispered. "Too much, too soon. I just couldn't resist."

Looking at him again, she said, "It's okay. It's just, well, it is a bit soon after promising myself that men are trouble and I wouldn't have anything to do with one."

Jed removed his arms from around her and laughed heartily. "I'll have to work to prove to you that's not me."

"You are making me consider changing my mind. That's a big step."

"Thank the stars for that.

"But, listen, Meg, there's something I need to tell you now."

"Oh, oh. Is your mother in an asylum, too?" She lifted her eyebrows and tottled her head.

"Nah," he said, shaking his head. "But I did meet your mother, just the other day, next door to her rooms. I've been hired by a woman in Grand Rapids to try to get her sister a divorce so she can get out of the asylum and go back to her children. The woman

I'm representing, her name is Jenny, asked your mother to join us for our first meeting. I hadn't expected to meet Elizabeth Sullivan and was surprised. I know you haven't seen her in a long time, so I wanted you to know."

Meg's eyes flared in disbelief. Here she'd conjured up a secret, complicated plot to sneak in to see her mother in the middle of the night and this man had walked right in during the middle of the day and talked to her!

"What's she like?" she asked, almost breathless.

"Well first of all, there's no doubt you're her daughter. You two look just alike, except you're the younger version. Both astoundingly beautiful. Oh, you're blushing. Somehow, I can't picture her blushing, even though she didn't say much, seeing that we only talked about Jenny's situation. Jenny's husband basically had her committed to get her out of the way so he could do whatever he wants, including drinking and holing up with other women."

"What did my mother wear?" Such a girl question, she realized after asking it.

"I didn't pay much attention to that—some kind of long, flowy thing. Pretty colors, I do remember that. I wasn't there very long. I did see a couple of pretty pictures she painted, one she gave to Jenny. Apparently she's quite generous in giving them away. I'll be going back next week. My uncle says he doesn't have a problem granting the divorce, so we'll be able to get this done."

This was it. Meg knew that if she was going to tell Jed about her plan to see her mother it had to be now. Wild thoughts skittered through her brain. Maybe she didn't need to sneak into the asylum; maybe he would take her when he went. No, he was probably too ethical for that. His law practice was too new; he couldn't chance it. She didn't really know him yet, luscious kissing aside, and he might report her plan to his uncle who would tell her father who would be mightily dismayed with her. Jed might see her plot as unscrupulous behavior and would never want to see her again. He might never kiss her again!

She said, "I hope things work out for Jenny. I know there are other women there in the same situation. It's an awful thing. It's good Jenny has a sister who cares about her enough to find you to help her.

"But, Jed, you know all about my family. You've even met my mother. Tell me a little about your family. I know you're from Detroit and you have an uncle, a sister, brother-in-law, and two nephews here. What about your parents?"

"Oh, my parents are great. My grandparents, on both sides, came over from Ireland when they were young and first married. Things were bad in Ireland and they were destitute, with barely enough money for passage but big dreams for a better life. My mom's parents eked out a living farming outside of Detroit. I loved going to the farm and helping them out when I was a kid. They were happy here. They've both passed on. My dad's parents worked right in the city and finally got a haberdashery shop there. They both still work in the shop, although they've passed it on to my parents. Everybody works there every day, although gram and gramps mostly just visit with people now. They're a lot of fun, still talk with thick Irish brogues. I loved growing up with them; we had apartments next door to each other. I worked in the shop up until college, and at first I think they all were disappointed that I don't want to take over the shop one day. But I was always fascinated with Uncle Sean's talk about the law. I think

I knew by age twelve that would be for me. Now I they all say they're proud of my choice.

"But, as you can see, hats are still a big deal to me." He pointed to the fedora he wore. "This, in fact, is my lucky hat. They make sure I have others, but this is the one I trust to make things go well for me."

Meg realized she got lost in his eyes as he talked, drawn to him in ways no young woman should be drawn to a man she hardly knew. "Your family sounds wonderful. And I like your lucky hat," she said, wrestling with herself to take her mind off of Jed's eyes, Jed's lips…

Pushing her way out of the side of the dune, she stood up, swiped sand off her behind, wiped her hands together to get any tiny grains off her palms, and said, "Well, we'd better head back."

Jed didn't get up for a moment, the pause obvious. "Sure," he said, pushing up and matching her stride as they went to the bush and untied their horses. Hopping on, they rode back the way they'd come.

Once they reached the spot where they'd met, they pulled up and stopped.

"My father asked that I invite you in for refreshments. Would you like lemonade, or perhaps something a little stronger? Father doesn't mind and imbibes himself. Brandy is his favorite."

"Would *you* like me to come in?"

"Oh, yes," she said honestly, her conflicted emotions at least allowing her that. "Come on, there's a good path that leads to the gazebo, then up to the house."

Halfway up the hill, Jed hollered over at her. "What's that? It's such an intriguing place." He pointed to her mother's cottage.

"It's where my mother used to go to paint. No one's been in there in years. I've been thinking of breaking in to look it over."

"Really?" Jed craned his neck to look back as they rode by. "If you want help, I'll be glad to do it."

"You're on!"

The house was all activity when they arrived, with field workers scurrying up to take the horses. When they went inside, her father took long strides out of his study to meet them in the vestibule and shake Jed's hand. The servants scampered about busily fluffing parlor room cushions and bringing lemonade, and then the illegal whiskey. Cook came in herself with a plate of freshly baked sugar cookies. Peggy, although being the upstairs maid, appeared to ask if they needed anything else. Meg wasn't fooled; they all wanted to see the man she'd brought home.

After an hour of congenial conversation, with all three of them appraising the many positive aspects of living in the beauteous and busy small town of Traverse City, Jed excused himself. He'd been invited to his nephew's fourth birthday supper that evening. Her father asked if he and his uncle might be able to join them later in the week for dinner. Jed said he'd be pleased to come and would have his uncle call to set a day, as his schedule was busier than his nephew's. The gentlemen said their goodbyes in the parlor, shaking hands one more time.

As she walked Jed O'Neill to the door, Meg became struck with the absence of all the voyeurs. She and Jed stepped outside the front door and he took her hand.

"I had a lovely afternoon, Meg. Can I see you again, before dinner later in the week?"

"How about tomorrow," she suggested, "to see if anything was left behind in my mother's cottage?"

"Yes, I'll be here! What time?"

"Well, we go to mass then have Sunday dinner. How about 3:00?"

"Okay. I'll drive over this time. See you then." He leaned closer to her, their faces just inches apart as she lightly laid her hands on his chest and he held her elbows. But knowing there were undoubtedly prying eyes coming at them from all directions, they simply smiled at one another and backed away.

One of the outdoor workers appeared with his horse and Jed road off.

Meg stepped out to the flagstone walk in front of the long front porch to watch until he disappeared from sight. As she turned to reenter, she looked up to see Peggy's cherub face pressed to the glass above.

18

"Hello, my friends!" Abby announced her arrival as she entered the backdoor of the big house and went into the kitchen. "What a beautiful Sunday morning. And look at what I brought for you today! Fresh out of the woods yesterday." She plopped a big basket of morel mushrooms on the kitchen table, with her usual flowers in a separate basket beside it. Today the flowers were dainty white trillium and bluebells.

"My-oh-my! Look at those fat babies!" Cook clapped her hands together when eyeing the morels. "You found so many! Thank you, thank you." She used her apron to wipe flour off her hands and grabbed Abby for a hug that buried the much smaller woman in pillows of chest and arms. When Cook let go, Abby took a deep breath. "I'll tell you what," Cook said, "we'll fry up a big mess of them right now for breakfast. We'll have scrambled eggs, too. Later I can fry the rest to go with the family's dinner. They'll be delighted!

"Peggy, dear, check the bread, would you please? Sarah's out right now collecting the eggs. This will be a grand breakfast!"

Cook got busy preparing the iron skillet for their feast, stoking the wood fire in the stove's belly to increase the heat and using a wooden spoon to drop a large glob of lard from its jar by the stove into the skillet. The lard sizzled loudly, announcing the coming of good eats.

"Abby, don't ya know we have a lot to tell ya?" Peggy interjected in her Irish way of turning a phrase. She opened the oven door to reveal three golden mounds of bread. Using the edges of her apron to cover her hands, she pulled them out one by one and set them on a towel on the table. "Meg brought a young man home yesterday! And what a looker he was. Could put that John Gilbert to shame, to be sure. Maybe even Rudolph hisself."

"I want to hear all about it," Abby reassured her, pouring herself a cup of tea and sitting down at the table. Kitty jumped up on her lap, rubbing her head on Abby's chest. Abby stroked the cat's back and received an appreciative purr in return. Then, as quickly as she'd come, Kitty jumped down as if she had an appointment somewhere else, and scampered out of the room.

Abby grabbed a paring knife that lay on the table and pulled over the basket of mushrooms, slicing each one once lengthwise for better frying.

Seeing that it was ten o'clock in the morning, Abby's usual time for dropping by on a Sunday as the family would be at mass, she knew that Cook and the other servants had already come back from early service in order to prepare Sunday dinner to be served early in the afternoon. It was the most elaborate meal of the week, pot roast, baked chicken, rack of lamb, venison chops, or steaks with all the trimmings plus dessert. But Cook always had the preparations well in hand so the mood in the kitchen was relaxed and jovial. On other days, when Abby came shortly after dawn, they had a short visit over tea and biscuits until the family arose, but on Sundays they all could afford to take their time and enjoy a big breakfast together.

Monday was the only day they never met, as it was the servants' day off. Cook, having no family, simply slept in on Monday mornings. Most of the others went home late Sunday afternoon to spend the night and next day with family, returning to the big house either Monday night or early Tuesday morning.

Abby had anticipated that this day promised to be especially gossip-worthy. She felt certain her friends would be all abuzz with news of the young man Meg brought home the day before. And seeing that it was Sunday they'd feel at leisure to talk longer than usual. Peggy's comment confirmed that a good gossip session boiled over for the telling.

She'd decided not to tell them she already knew a bit about the young couple. She saw them on the beach while she'd been in the woods near the water. Talking about him would seem like a betrayal seeing that Meg had asked her about him during her reading. The spirits had said he was a good man. The girl needed a good man after that scoundrel she'd had in the big city. Abby hoped this young man was it. When she saw them they seemed happy. He was certainly good looking enough.

Cook's assistant Sarah returned with a basket full of brown eggs. She greeted Abby warmly, and went about cracking and stirring eggs in a big porcelain bowl.

Peggy filled Abby in on Jed O'Neill's visit while Cook scrambled the eggs and mushrooms, and fried thick slabs of Canadian bacon. Sarah got a block of butter out of the icebox and put it in the center of the table, and then sliced the steaming bread, the smell wafting through the room. Peggy set the table and Abby got up to retrieve a jar of Cook's homemade apple butter from the pantry. There was no way she'd have fresh bread without that scrumptious apple butter that Cook made each fall, using fresh Spy apples. Then Abby poured tea for everyone.

Peggy opened the swinging kitchen door and hollered, "Come and get it!"

Within moments the other three servants in the house showed up, licking their lips, swiping their hands together, and saying, "Oh, yum!" "This smells fantastic!" "Morels! The first of the year!" Sam appeared out of nowhere. Everyone clamored to sit around the table.

"My mouth is watering!" Cook declared. "Eat up!" She passed the morels, eggs, and bacon. Bread went around next, and everyone dug in with more moans of approval than conversation at the beginning of the meal. Eventually, though, talk wandered back to Meg and the man they called her "beau," and they all agreed it looked like a good match.

After an hour of good food and good company, and after helping clean up, Abby left. Walking through the woods to her cabin on this pleasant day, she made a spur-of-the-moment decision. She never went into town on Sundays to see Lizzie, as her friend spent the morning at mandatory services in the resplendent asylum chapel and the afternoon enjoying a scrumptious dinner in her cottage dining hall. Lizzie had often told Abby how much the asylum's careful attention to making Sunday holy meant to her. She described in detail how the guest ministers gave rousing sermons while sunlight streamed into the cavernous, Victorian-styled room through the tall, rounded windows with stained glass at the top. The organist was excellent and residents let loose singing rousing hymns. And the holy day dinner always outdid even the best of the excellent weekday meals.

Of course, Abby had never seen the chapel or the inside of any of the asylum buildings. She would never have been allowed inside, but that was okay because of the secret nature of their friendship, anyway.

Most of all, Lizzie spoke of the images conjured up during Sundays for her paintings: light shining through stained glass, faces exuberant with venerated joy, heads bowed in reverent prayer.

Everything, it seemed, generated pictures in Lizzie's mind for painting. It had long been clear to Abby that her friend was abnormally obsessed with her art. She'd read that many proliferate artistic geniuses throughout history had been quite mad in one way or another. Vincent VanGogh, Bugatti Rembrandt, and Alexander Henry, just to name a few, died grotesquely at their own hands. Abby speculated that allowing oneself to become obsessed with a solitary talent provided an escape from facing real life.

In spite of her friend's shortcomings, Abby found it difficult, if not impossible, to fault her. Lizzie's art was, after all, brilliant. In another day and age when women could be more accepted on an equal footing with men, Elizabeth Sullivan would be an independently wealthy and famous woman, Abby had no doubt.

But today she was labeled as insane.

The notion that kept drilling its way to the surface of Abby's consciousness, a notion she continuously struggled to suppress, was that perhaps Lizzie was truly insane. Perhaps her art was not a manifestation of the suppression of women in society but a sign of individual innate lunacy.

It was that thought that propelled Abby to turn off the path to her cabin and walk through the woods to the beach, where she could go to search Lizzie's cottage and its secret cave one more time. She'd been struggling with this idea since discovering the cave, knowing she'd been avoiding reality herself. There was something down there. Maybe just a hiding place for special paintings, maybe just a cool storage space for bottles of wine, or maybe something more sinister. Abby genuinely didn't know what she expected to find. But she had known she'd need to go during the day in order to get as much light as possible from above. Plus, she admitted to herself, the cave scared her. It was downright spooky and, she feared, haunted. The very thought of nighttime down there gave her the heebie-jeebies.

Casting that silly thought from her mind, because if anybody alive shouldn't be afraid of ghosts it should be her, seeing that she talked to them all the time, she hurried down the beach, climbed up the path, and went inside Lizzie's cottage. Now was the perfect time. It was daylight and Meg would be at the reception after mass for another hour, with more time added on to drive home from town.

Standing stone still in the middle of the space, Abby looked around. The room felt warm and inviting. The paintings emanated a soothing aura. Mottled light filtered in through the windows. The cottage seemed to beckon her to stay.

Glad she'd come, she allowed herself the luxury of sitting on the chaise lounge. First, she took the faded afghan and covered the chaise so that she could rest her body on the clean underside of the throw, the side that had been hidden from dust all these years. With a long satisfying sigh, she settled herself onto the chaise and looked out at the sparkling bay. How many hours, days, months, had she spent right here while Lizzie painted? She couldn't even venture a guess, they'd spent so much time here during the years they knew each other before Lizzie was taken away.

Abby closed her eyes and remembered the good times. Finally, she arose and went to the side of the fireplace where she moved the painting of the cemetery scene, flipped back the rug, and opened the trapdoor. Lighting two lanterns, she took one down and placed it on the floor a few feet into the cave, then went back for the second one to carry with her.

This time the rock cavern didn't seem so mysterious or frightening. Instead, she saw walls and floor and ceiling constructed of layers of innocent enough limestone. The ceiling rose far enough to allow her to stand up straight as she walked inward to reach the large painting that sat on the floor at the end of this corridor. It turned out to be yet another cemetery scene, a tranquil single cross in springtime with colorful wild flowers sprouting up at its base.

Turning right at the painting, now she could see that the cave took a bend to continue for about thirty feet, the ceiling opening up to allow for more headroom and the floor slowly tilting down. A gentle spring trickled out of a crevice in the wall to slide down to a natural three-by-three-foot cistern carved into the rock, and then out again in a stream that disappeared into cracks along the side of the floor. The cistern held a fresh pool of water that would be perfect for personal use. Abby walked down the slanted floor, following the stream. She continued far enough down the second corridor to see that it culminated in — yes — she could see it clearly enough now to decipher none other than a mass of enormous budding hanging vines.

"Vines! They could never survive inside a cave without light," she informed herself needlessly. So, the cave had a second outlet into the side of the hill, probably not far above shore level. The greenery hid that entrance from view on the outside and prevented exit from inside at the same time. However, at one time the vines would have been much smaller and that opening must have been accessible. "This is one fascinating cave!"

She thought back to her walks on the shore. A number of spots had wild vines with giant leaves that grew on grassy knolls to hang down over the dunes. In the winter when the leaves fell, the mangle of barren brown veins still prohibited a view of what laid beneath.

Turning back the way she'd come, she lifted the lantern to examine the painting. Why was this one down here, but no others? She looked behind it. Nothing but a pile of stones that looked like they'd been picked up from the floor to clear the path, and stashed there rather than hauled up and outside. The painting would have been no more than Lizzie's way of hiding the unattractive pile of rock.

Abby took the lanterns up, one by one, and closed the trapdoor. There was nothing down there to worry about. She carefully replaced the rug and the painting that sat at its edge, blew out the flames of the lanterns, put them back where they'd been to cover their same clean circles surrounded by dust, and surveyed the room one last time. Paintings and more paintings. There was absolutely nothing here that would cause distress for Meg.

Relieved, Abby left Lizzie's cottage and hurried home to enjoy a quiet Sunday afternoon.

19

Elizabeth stuffed the sandwich she'd made herself into a little paper sack and put it in her pocket. Taking the scarf that hung loosely over her chest, she threw each end over a shoulder to wrap it around her neck. Then she retrieved her sketch pad and pencil from their hiding place behind the open dining hall door and snuck out the front door into the balmy spring air. Compelled by the urge to draw the asylum's prize cow, Traverse Colantha Walker, she scurried away and fled behind a couple of buildings until out of sight of any administrators who might happen upon her playing hooky. She had more freedom than a lot of residents, but all of them were expected to keep Sunday sacred.

Running into half a dozen miscreant elder resident men behind a barn smoking pipes and roll-your-own cigarettes, and chewing tobacco, she smiled and waved as she went by. Today wasn't one of the smoking days when tobacco and "plug" were given to any residents who wanted to partake. She watched one of the men ignite his pipe with a small match and knew they were supposed to have a ward employee light up for them in a designated smoking room, as they weren't allowed matches like the people in some of the cottages, like her cottage. She recognized them as former shanty boys, lumberjacks, who in their younger years had been strong and independent, moving from one stand of forest to another as they worked. Like others here, they'd grown too old to wield large tools. It wouldn't matter anymore if they could as the lumber business had died in the area. These boys had helped deplete the timberland. Seeing that shanty boys had lived such a gypsy lifestyle, in their old age many of them had no roots and no place else to go but the state asylum. She felt sorry for them.

They waved their approval of her escape from indoors.

Elizabeth fleetingly considered asking if she could have a cigarette, as she'd been contemplating trying it out, but decided against joining that pack of grizzled ruffians, and went on her merry way.

Finally, she reached Traverse Colantha Walker, the prize cow.

"Hello, my love," she cooed. "You just stand nice and still like that, chewing your cud so I can sketch you. Okay? You look a great deal like some men I just saw, chomping on their plug. Did you know that?"

Traverse didn't respond but did do as she was told.

Elizabeth sat down on the warm grass and drew.

She'd completed a sketch that she found to be particularly delightful and started to eat her sandwich when her peace and quiet were interrupted.

"L-li-lizzieee!" Dr. Charles Whitmore staggered down the path from which she'd come, drunk as a skunk. Quite an image for a supposedly esteemed psychiatrist. "Liz-liz! I needa talk to you!" His feet became tangled on each other and he tripped, almost falling over. He wore a suit but his shirt hung out in front and his tie sat askew. He carried a brown glass whiskey bottle that sparkled in the sunlight as he flailed his arms about like a madman.

Elizabeth looked at Traverse. "What an idiot. He doesn't know enough to piss downwind."

The bovine mooed agreement.

"Liz-she my love," he said, stumbling his way to her side.

Elizabeth methodically rewrapped what was left on her sandwich, put the little package into her pocket, stood up, put her hands on her hips, and faced him down, although his breath almost knocked her over.

"What the hell are you doing here?" she demanded to know.

"I… I need you. Once a month ish… isn't enough, Izzie, I need you now."

"What about your wife? Why don't you go back to your house in town and bother her? And leave me alone."

"Sh-she's not like yo-o-ou…." He lunged at her, grabbing at her shoulders as if to take her down, and Elizabeth whacked him up the side of the head. The doctor swayed, looked skyward, and fell flat as an ironing board onto the ground.

Elizabeth doubled over and shook her hand to try to eradicate the sting. When she looked up, three of the old shanty boys stood glaring down at the unconscious psychiatrist. Elizabeth froze, sizing up the situation.

"Mrs. Sullivan, we saw the drunk doctor here coming in your direction so we followed him to make sure you were okay," one of them said. They all broke out into grins and one scratched his head. "But we see you can take care of yourself."

Elizabeth straightened her spine, patted dust off her skirt, and offered a big smile. "Thank you, gentlemen. But he was pretty easy to handle, seeing that he could hardly stand up in the first place."

The men guffawed and one asked, "What should we do with him?" They all looked at her.

Elizabeth looked around and honed in on the pasture full of cows and cow patties. "How about in there? You can just toss him over the fence."

With little effort, the old boys picked up the much younger man and gently dropped, rather than tossed, him over the fence.

"We'll walk you back," one said.

She picked up her sketch pad and pencil, took hold of an end of her scarf that had come loose and cast it over her shoulder, and they all looked back at the hump of human form on the ground. Dr. Whitmore slept soundly, mouth agape, and curled into a fetal ball in the cow pasture, a glop of cow dung two feet from his head.

Elizabeth walked back to Cottage 23 under the protection of the shanty boys.

20

Jed O'Neill arrived ten minutes early, pulling his uncle's black Model T Ford Coupe into the Sullivan driveway. Meg already sat in a rocking chair on the front porch in anticipation of his arrival. It was a gloomy, gray day, causing her to wrap herself in a warm sweater and making her wonder if the foreboding weather meant this adventure they were about to embark upon might be folly. But the moment that Tin Lizzie chugged up the road, her spirits lifted.

He wore brown trousers with a light wool plaid shirt, in acquiescence to the promise of cool rain. His spectacles peeked out from the breast pocket of the shirt. And his fedora sat proudly as ever on top of his head.

Meg thought he looked swell.

Jed approached the porch, took off his hat and held it over his chest, and smiled up at her. Meg came bounding down the steps and threw her arms around his neck, planting a warm kiss right on his lips. *The servants be damned!*

He grabbed her around the waist and twirled her around as

they laughed. Finally finding her feet, Meg said, "I'm so happy to see you."

"I couldn't be happier." Holding her at arm's length, the twinkle in his eye said he told the truth.

"Come!" She took his hand in both of hers and pulled him toward the house. "Father wants you to come in and say 'hello' before we go down to the cottage."

"He's okay with what we want to do?"

"Well, I don't think he's thrilled. But he knows it's inevitable. He's okay."

They went into the house and Herbert Sullivan met them in the vestibule as he came out of his study. After a sturdy handshake and an offer of a "pick-me-up," which Jed deferred to after their return from the cottage, the young couple headed out.

"I'm so glad you agreed to do this with me. I keep thinking it needs to be done but then I lose my nerve," Meg said as they crossed the gazebo and went down onto the sand dune.

"Why do you lose your nerve?"

"I don't know. Just afraid of what might be there, I guess. I don't really know my mother at all." The thought of sharing her plan to secretly see her mother crossed her mind, but she tossed it away. It was too risky.

Only twenty feet from the cottage it started to sprinkle, so they grabbed hands and ran. Jed pushed the heavy door open and without fanfare they walked into her mother's cottage.

"Oh, my lord! Look at all those beautiful paintings!" Jed was agog.

"I knew she painted but had no idea it was like this!" Meg marveled as she touched one after another of the canvasses.

Jed craned his neck to look in every direction. "The place is run-down but nothing that couldn't be fixed with some elbow grease and paint."

Meg stayed glued to the artwork of her mother. "Look at this one! It's fabulous!" She pointed to a partially finished portrayal of a lady in a yellow dress lounging on a hammock in the gazebo with the bay behind her.

Jed came over and looked over Meg's shoulder, wrapping his arms around her waist from behind. "It's exquisite," he agreed.

Rain suddenly beat a steady rum-a-tum-tum on the roof, solidifying their solitude in this shelter.

Meg turned within his arms, melting into his embrace as they kissed once more, this time deep and lingering. When their lips parted, they looked into each other's eyes, startled at the intensity of their desire for one another. They kissed again, their mouths unable to remain apart. Jed's hands roamed down Meg's back to knead her derriere and she found herself matching his caresses with her own, feeling the breadth of his shoulders then running her hands down the muscles of his back to land on his slim waist. Her breasts afire, she was shocked to find them rubbing against his chest, as if of their own will.

As deftly as if she were a feather, Jed picked Meg up and laid her on the faded chaise lounge, stretching himself out beside her. Their hands groped and fondled while their lips parted only long enough for them to breathe.

The rhythm of the rain served as a metronome as their bodies undulated to the beat on the rooftop.

"Jed... Oh, Jed...." Meg moaned repeatedly with no pretense of being capable of finishing a sentence.

A bolt of lightning pierced the sky beyond the murky windows, for a split second illuminating their glistening faces, highlighting their ravenous intent.

When his hand went to the buttons at the top of her blouse and fumbled in their urgency, a woman unknown to Meg helped him unbutton her blouse. The foreign hand attached to her arm guided his hand inside her silk chemise to her bare breast.

A clap of thunder drowned out her scream of delight.

Meg's stray hand slid down Jed's torso until she grasped the waistband of his trousers. Now it was Jed's turn to moan like a tormented creature. Meg tugged on the band and it was then she thought he just might die.

With one arm around her back, his other hand left her breast and grappling with the hem of her skirt to gather it up.

That alien woman who had possessed her body aside, Meg somehow managed to recall her vow to herself to stay chaste until marriage.

"Jed," she whispered. "Jed, dear…."

Eyes glazed, he looked at her. "What?"

"I've… well, I've promised myself I would stay a virgin until my wedding night."

He lifted his head and looked at her quite stupidly. His hands stopped moving. "You mean you've never…? Not even with your fiancé?"

"No. Never." She didn't add that with Robert she'd never felt a wanton need like this.

Jed sat up, smoothed down her skirt, and said, "Oh. Well, then, I need you to take your hand away." He looked down to where she still held onto his waistband.

"Oh! Yes, of course." She let go and lifted her hand to let it dangle in the air, not knowing what else to do with it. He took it in his hand and kissed it, then took her arm and helped her sit up beside him, and they swung their legs to the floor. She looked at him sideways while buttoning her blouse, wondering if he'd be mad at her. Robert always got mad when he tried to do anything, not that they'd ever done anything like this, and she stopped him.

"Meg, I'm so sorry," Jed said gently, placing a hand on her knee. "I can't seem to keep my hands off you. I think you like me, too." He grinned.

Teasingly, she looked up at him. "What gave me away?"

He lifted his eyebrows and pointed to where she'd held his trousers in a vice grip.

"Oh, yes, I guess that was a dead give-away."

"There's only one thing for us to do to remedy this situation."

"What's that?"

"We need to get married. Meg Sullivan, will you marry me?"

Meg had read of women swooning in romantic novels and always thought that was mere fiction. Yet she swooned.

"Yes, Jed," the foreign woman inside of her said. "I'll marry you."

Slowly, Jed O'Neill wrapped his arms around his intended and held her tight. "I love you, Meg."

As if speaking an unknown tongue, Meg found herself saying, "I love you, too."

She'd never said that to Robert.

To veer away from her desire, Meg asked the question that probably pressed on every young woman's mind upon first making love with a man. "Jed... Um, well..."

"What is it, Meg? Oh, you want to know if I've made love to lots of other women."

"Well, I was wondering…"

His snicker came as a relief. He pulled her close, kissing her forehead. "To tell the truth, I was wet behind the ears all through high school. Not that I didn't want to be with girls; they didn't want to be with me. I was skinny as a rail. Wasn't an athlete except for loving to swim in the Detroit River in summer and ice skate in winter. And I loved swimming and riding horses when we came up here in summer. But in school I wasn't a football player or anything like that. Nothing that would attract girls. Started wearing spectacles for reading when I was twelve. Not a muscle on my body until I was eighteen. I didn't start looking like a man until college.

"I finally got a girlfriend in college and we dated until graduation, but when it became obvious she expected a marriage proposal, I couldn't do it. I couldn't picture a whole life with her. She was furious and dropped me like a hot potato. So, I know what that feels like. After that I was in the war in France."

"Did you have any… girlfriends… in France?"

Sheepishly, he looked at her sideways. "Well, I was in *France*."

She squinted at him. "I might want to hear about that someday, but not yet."

"Good. Let's change the subject and look through the cottage, like we said we'd do."

They got up from the chaise lounge and went back to surveying the place. She commented on a pretty cemetery scene by the fireplace. Jed joined her to look at it but that just led to more kissing so they went to opposite sides of the room. Meg had anticipated that exploring her mother's cottage would be a momentous event in her life yet it couldn't compete with her need to be with this man. Lust and love, she realized, outbid her desire to learn more about her mother.

But the paintings were wondrous, and she and Jed agreed they needed to be sold, with the money donated to charity. Meg felt certain her father would agree to that.

They also decided not to share their marriage plans just yet, believing that everyone they knew would think they had lost their minds seeing that they'd only known each other for a week. For another few weeks, they would let it be their secret and then they would shout it from the rooftops.

In their love-lust delirium, neither of them noticed the smudged dust spots around the lanterns, the faded and fresh portions of the chaise lounge, or the trapdoor under the rug. If they'd been able to think clearly, they might have known someone else had recently been there.

By the time the rain stopped and they went back to the house to visit with her father, they were able to do their best to act like normal human beings. There was tea for her and illegal Walker's Old Highland whiskey for the men. Meg watched them drink their liquor and became thunderstruck with the notion that she wanted to marry this Jed O'Neill.

When Jed drove the Tin Lizzie away from the house at dusk after telling her he had to leave early in the morning to take the train to Detroit to get a deposition for a case and wouldn't be back until Tuesday, she realized she hadn't given another thought to whether or not she should tell him she was going to secretly see her mother tomorrow night, Monday.

It hadn't even crossed her mind.

21

"Hello, Hannah. Come in." Abby opened the door so that her monthly guest could enter her cabin.

"Hello, Abby. Happy Monday morning. How are you today?" the head housekeeper of the Sullivan house, and mistress of Mr. Sullivan himself, asked.

"Oh, I'm fine! I see that Sam drove you, seeing that it's a bit chilly and cloudy today." Abby poked her head out and waved at the driver waiting in the Sullivan limousine. He waved back.

"I'll be right out!" Abby hollered and turned back into her cabin. Hannah had gone to the fire to warm her hands.

"Yes," Hannah replied, "once he takes Herbert to work in town for the day, Sam is always so willing to take me wherever I want to go. I don't know what I'd do without him."

"He's a gem, for sure." Abby poured a cup of coffee from a steaming pot sitting on the hearth and said, "I'll be right back."

She left the cabin and took the cup to Sam, handing it to him through the open window.

He threw out the cigarette he'd been smoking and readily

took the cup, saying, "How is it an Indian makes the best coffee in the country?" He winked at her and blew on the steamy brew.

Abby guffawed. "Oh, you old charmer, you. Listen, my friend, why don't you come in for a reading some day? I'd love to know what the spirits have to say about an old scallywag like you. Aren't you curious?"

The wiry, weathered guy laughed. "Abby, you know me better than that. I just want to handle today. Tell me where to drive today. That's all I need. The future is too much for me. If I make it through today, each day, tomorrow will always take care of itself. See what I mean?" He took a long draw from the cup.

Abby pondered his words for a moment. "Sam, that just might be the most profound philosophy of life I've ever heard. I think you've got something there." She smiled at him and turned to go back into her cabin.

Inside, Hannah had already poured them each a cup of coffee and sat down at the table, so Abby sat across from her.

"Here we go," Hannah said as she pulled a small box out of her handbag and set it on the table. The shared box of Hershey's Kisses was a tradition between the two women. The box may be unopened now but by the end of the hour, every little piece of bite-sized, conical-shaped chocolate would be gone and the box would be full of nothing but wadded up aluminum wrappings. For all the time it took a Hershey's factory worker to hand-wrap each piece of chocolate, it only took one second to rip off the tin foil to get to the treat.

Abby waited for her guest to imbibe first and Hannah obliged right away. As Hannah chewed, Abby said, "How are things going up at the big house now that Miss Meg is home?" She opened her own kiss and popped it into her mouth.

Hannah swallowed and took a sip of coffee before answering. "Oh, Abby, she's such a lovely young woman." She pulled her shawl off her shoulders and folded it on her lap. The ruffled pink blouse she wore favored her rosy complexion. "I'd give anything to be like a real mother to her, but we want to give her time to adjust to our... situation."

"Wouldn't you think she's already guessed? Or been told? You do have Peggy living in that house."

They each ate another chocolate kiss and sipped at their coffee.

Hannah smiled and for the hundredth time, Abby thought about how this middle-aged woman might not be traditionally pretty, with a face a bit too long and hair a dull brown except for the few touches of gray, but somehow her demeanor, expressions, voice, and eyes rendered her comely and appealing. Also, her heart. Abby could see why Mr. Sullivan fell in love with her.

"I suppose," Hannah said. "Sometimes Herbert and I worry that we're treating her too much like a child. She is a grown woman now. But, on the other hand, she'll always be his little girl. He adores her. I think he wanted to go to Chicago and wring that Robert's neck for breaking her heart. But she seems to have recovered well, so it's all probably for the best. She wouldn't get over Robert so easily if she'd been madly in love. She even has a new friend, the judge's nephew. He seems like a very nice young man."

"Ah, yes, the new lawyer in town, setting up practice in his uncle's old firm. And his sister's husband already works there. I think they'll be very successful."

"Do the spirits say that?"

Abby smirked. "No, it just seems that way to me.

"Okay, let's look at what the spirits have to say today. What would you like me to ask them?" Abby ate another chocolate, foregoing the crystal ball with Hannah, who'd been coming here long enough to know better than to believe in a mystical glass orb.

Hannah ate another piece of chocolate and looked at the ceiling in contemplation. When her gaze came back down to Abby she said, "I've been dreaming lately about Harry. Even though that happened before my time, I feel as if I know him and should be able to find him."

Startled, Abby didn't know how to respond. Lately, thoughts about little Harry had been invading her mind, too, fifteen years after his disappearance.

Hannah asked, "What do the spirits think that means?"

Abby's spirit guides had always remained silent on the topic of Harry, her questions as to his whereabouts always lamentably unanswered. But for Hannah's sake, she wanted to try one more time.

She closed her eyes, folded her hands in prayer on the table, and said, "Dear ancestors, we thank you for your presence and guidance on this day. My friend Hannah and I are grateful for any answers you may be able to provide. Please hear our plea about Harry Sullivan. It's a heartbreaking mystery to us as to how he disappeared. Now we want to know why he has been on Hannah's mind. Is there something we need to know? If we search again will we find him? Does he need us? We will honor your guidance in this matter."

The fortune teller sat still, lost in her netherworld. Her mind roamed, searching, searching, and landed nowhere. After a few of minutes of silence from her ancestors, she opened her eyes.

"I'm sorry, Hannah. The ancestors have never had anything to say about Harry and they won't reverse their silence today. They have nothing to say. I'm sorry."

Hannah ate a kiss and nodded her head. "That's okay, Abby. It can't work all the time. Besides, I can't help but wonder if their silence isn't a message in and of itself."

"I've wondered that myself." Defeated, Abby ate another kiss and drank her coffee.

"Well, then, I have one more question: Do the spirit guides think that this friendship between Meg and Jed O'Neill could develop into something serious?"

"Oh, yes, definitely!"

"The spirits think so?"

"No, just this woman's intuition."

Hannah said, "That works for me. I'd love to see that work out. Of course, if he's as good a guy as he seems to be.

"That makes me think of one more question. I know, I thought I was done. But talking about Meg and Jed makes me long to know something I've always been afraid to ask: Will Herbert and I ever be able to marry?"

"Yes!" The answer came through so loudly it relieved Abby to know her guides had not abandoned her altogether. "In fact, I see a tombstone that says Hannah Sullivan, 1877-1971. Is that the year you were born?"

"Yes!"

"It's saying you'll die when you are… What is that? Ninety-four. And you die as a Sullivan. Hannah, you are going to be one wrinkled up old lady," Abby teased.

Hannah beamed. "To hell with the wrinkles, I'm just so happy

I can be Herbert's wife. I only hope it happens before all those wrinkles start setting in."

"I hope so, too."

They chatted amicably for a while, eating the last of the Hershey's kisses and finishing their coffee. When she left, Hannah put two silver dollars on the table, even though Abby had often asked her not to pay, because everyone in the Sullivan house was so kind to her. But Hannah always insisted this was different and if she ever came to be head housekeeper in Abby's cabin she'd charge for her work, too.

Abby walked out to the car with her and commented on the gloomy sky. Sam hopped out to go around and open the front passenger door for Hannah, as she refused to sit in the back all by herself. Giving the empty coffee cup back to Abby, he bid her farewell and they drove off.

Abby watched them bounce down her dirt road, wondering why the ancestors refused to reveal anything about Harry when they were so willing to share so much else with her. It was a mystery for which she had no answer and they certainly were not willing to give her one.

22

Elizabeth scrutinized the canvas before her. Traverse Colantha Walker stared back at her with brooding eyes.

"Am I beautiful or what?" the woman imagined the cow mooed at her.

"You are gorgeous!" Elizabeth cooed.

Satisfied with her work, she cleaned her brushes, took off her apron, and went into the next room to check the clock. Two hours until Meg would be here.

Her daughter. She found it hard to think of it that way, it had been so long since she'd seen her. Meg had been six years old the last time she'd laid eyes on the child. Elizabeth had been a mere twenty-three. Now she was thirty-eight. Where had the time gone? It flew by. Especially being holed up here in an asylum.

Sometimes she fancied demanding her release. But then she'd try to picture where she'd go or what she would do. No images ever came to mind.

Elizabeth admitted to herself she felt excited about the possibilities of the visit with Meg. It would undoubtedly bring some excitement into her life. Her daughter had lived near or in Chicago for almost ten years. She'd been engaged to one of the most prominent young men in the city. Certainly Meg would display some of the pizazz that kind of relationship would require, even if it hadn't worked out in the long run. Hopefully she'd be a flapper with a lot of flare and they could talk about fashion.

After a run down the hall to the water closet, Elizabeth came back to her room and opened the wardrobe. What should she wear to meet the girl? Shoving aside the skirts and blouses she thought of as her "asylum rags," she culled through her designer clothes. Mostly lounging robes she enjoyed wearing while she painted and morning dresses for Herbert's visits, she went through the robes first. A colorful, gaily patterned, silk duster by a designer named Beer spoke to her. She pulled it out and held it in front of her, turning to the full-length mirror.

"Yes. This is it."

Throwing the gown down on the bed, she looked back into the mirror, turning her head from side to side, trying to decide what to do with her hair for this occasion. Usually loose or in a rushed topknot, tonight would have to be something fancy.

"Up," she decided. "I must put it up, like that movie star I saw in *Photoplay Magazine*." Sometimes she confiscated the magazines Dr. Charles Whitmore bought for her to read in his office and snuck them home with her. Unfortunately, she'd used up all the ones she'd had to use as blotting pads for her paint brushes, so she didn't have any left. She wished she'd kept some. But she felt certain she her artist's memory had imprinted the photograph of the actress into her mind well enough that she could replicate the hairdo herself.

Working on it for twenty minutes, she finally got her way-ward black locks pulled back into a silver hair clasp at the back of her head, with wisps of curls left loose to frame her face.

Tackling her face next, she pulled her makeup box out of the drawer in her nightstand and laid it on the table. She never wore makeup during a routine day. She didn't think she needed it. But she liked to use it to heighten her tease of Herbert when he came, and now for this. Carefully she powdered her face with the new pink powder puff Hannah had brought during her last visit, and then she lined her eyes with black kohl. Rummaging through a dozen tubes of lipstick, she came upon the brightest red she owned and lavished it on. Smacking her lips together, she stood back from the mirror and evaluated the look.

"Perfect!"

Slinking out of her asylum rags, she slithered into the duster, gathering it at her feet, stepping into it, and pulling it up so it wouldn't muss her hair. With the duster being floor-length, she didn't need stockings so she would forego those and went straight to her red heels.

Topping it all off with her diamond and pearl jewelry, she looked in the mirror one more time.

"I do believe that at a speakeasy they would say I'm the cat's meow or the cat's pajamas. Prettier than the *Queen of Sheba*. Only this isn't as risqué as those costumes worn by Betty Blythe in the movie. At least, *Photoplay Magazine* said they were indecently risqué. That Betty must be quite the dame!"

After packing up her makeup box and stowing it away, she picked up the No. 5 Chanel bottle from her nightstand and spritzed twice, once on each side of her neck. The new perfume with its fresh hints of jasmine, rose, sandalwood, and vanilla sent her reeling. The scent's creator, Coco Chanel, had created a masterpiece, as far as she was concerned.

"Well, that's it," she said with one last glance in the mirror. "I hope that girl appreciates my efforts."

23

Meg could hardly breathe she was so filled with anticipation.
The other night with Jed she'd forgotten all about this but now,
without the distraction of the smell and feel of him beside her,
this became all consuming.

She'd once again told her father she'd be out for the evening,
this time meeting an old friend at the Dreamland movie theatre
in town to see a nine o'clock showing of *The Kid* with Charlie
Chaplin. How she hated lying to her father, but she couldn't imagine what he'd do if he discovered the truth.

Peggy had helped her hatch a plan to get out of the house:
Sam would drop her off at the theatre on Front Street and she'd
tell him to pick her back up at eleven-thirty. She'd buy a ticket at
the booth out front where Sam could see her go into the theatre.
She would wait ten minutes, by which time Sam would most
likely be on his way to Sleder's tavern. Then she would leave the
theatre to meet Peggy's "eejit" brother Patrick on the corner for
a ride in their family's horse and buggy. He'd give her a ride to
the corner of Elmwood and Green Drive in front of the asylum,

where Petunia the nurse would be waiting to take her to see her mother.

The night in the women's room at Sleder's when Petunia had approached her, they'd made plans for the clandestine rendezvous but she hadn't considered how difficult it would be to figure out how to get from her house to that corner. Peggy's devious little mind had no problem with that conundrum.

Between the nurse and eejit brother, Meg was shelling out twenty dollars, a lot of moola to be sure, but worth it as far as she was concerned. She was finally going to get to see her mother after fifteen years.

The plan came off without a hitch. Her father had a business dinner that evening so wouldn't be home anyway. That morning when she'd told him she'd be going to a movie he'd barely commented, buried as he was in the newspaper. Sam fell for it hook, line, and sinker, dropping her off and driving away toward the tavern. Peggy's brother Patrick showed up right on cue, stone sober, ruggedly handsome, and spectacularly charming.

"And ya must be the Miss Meg me sister talks about nonstop without taking a breath, like a seanchi. That's an Irish orator who never runs out of stories. Ya have quite an admirer there and I must say I can see why!" He offered her a hand to help her into the carriage.

"Thank you. And you are, no doubt, her brother Patrick." She settled into the small, open, two-seater beside him.

Patrick McVeigh clicked his old dray to a start, headed through the residential area between downtown Traverse City and the asylum. The way was dully lit by gas lamps on the streets. Gas, oil, and candlelight flickered in the windows of the well-kept Victorian houses in pretty neighborhoods, homes that had stood since the boom of the lumber era that first hit this area more than fifty years earlier.

"Miss Meg, I must say ya look fetchin' this evenin'. To be sure it'll be a nice visit with yer ma and she'll be pleased with the beauty of her daughter." Meg could see that this eejit Irishman wasted no time turning to lady-killer yammer.

"Thank you," she said, hating to admit to herself she'd needed the compliment as she'd spent an insecure hour trying to decide what to wear to see her mother. She and Peggy had finally picked a rather simple black dress accessorized with no more than her pearls. She left her diamond and pearl earrings, and any other jewelry, off and left her hair in its natural state of curls. She'd started with a bit of kohl around her eyes and a touch of pink lipstick, but wiped them off. After trying on and casting aside half a dozen dresses, their thinking had finally reached the conclusion that women in the asylum must not have much to wear or any makeup whatsoever and Meg didn't want to get so dressed up as to make her mother uncomfortable in her own undoubtedly drab attire. Peggy had pulled out a nice gray cashmere shawl to keep out the evening chill, one that could be left with her mother if the woman needed it. All-in-all, it was a plain outfit and anything other than what Meg would consider to be "fetching," but just right for this arcane occasion.

After a few blocks of listening to Patrick's chatter about how much he loved working the docks, Meg said, "Patrick, we don't have much time. I don't want to insult you but I have to ask you something. Do I have your promise you'll be back here in exactly an hour and a half to pick me up? You won't forget, or anything, will you?"

"Ah, to be sure, Miss Meg. I'll be right here. You've been listenin' to me sister Peggy, eh? That one's a talker, no?"

That's the pot calling the kettle black, Meg thought.

He continued, "You're afraid I'll get muddled and forget ya. Don't ya worry yer pretty little head about that. Our ma has kept me sober fer two months now and me brannigan, drinkin', days are over. That I swear. Don't ya know, yer da has even given me a good job on the docks with me da, so now why would I want to go ruin the best chance I've ever been given? You can count on me. To keep me mouth shut, too." He pressed his lips together in exaggeration.

Meg said, "Okay. I'm just so nervous, I had to ask."

"That I understand. Don't ya fret. It'll be grand, I'm sure."

They made it to the designated corner right on time. Petunia, dressed in her stark white nursing uniform and stand-up cap, with a blue wool cape draped over her shoulders, stepped out from the shadows when the buggy stopped. Patrick again offered a hand and Meg got down.

"Petunia," Patrick said. "I dinna know it was you we were meetin'. My, ya look stunnin' in yer uniform." He grinned down at the nurse.

"Hello, Patrick. I haven't seen you in a while. Where've you been keeping yourself?" Petunia batted her eyelashes.

"Here and there. Maybe we could get together for afternoon tea one day soon?"

"I'd like that. Come on, Miss Sullivan, we need to get going so I can be on the floor at the start of my shift. 'Bye, Patrick. Stop by my house. You know where I live."

Great, I'm paying people to flirt with each other, Meg thought.

She felt pretty certain, however, that this Irishman flirted with every living being on the planet that wasn't male.

"Come on, Miss Sullivan, we'll walk around the back of the buildings here where it's dark and nobody will see us coming." Petunia explained that they'd be entering the nurse's backdoor of Cottage 21, as that was where she worked. Then, however, they'd take a tunnel to Cottage 23, where Meg's mother lived.

"You did tell her I'm coming," Meg inquired.

"Oh, yes, Miss Sullivan. She thought it over for a minute and said okay."

"Do you know my mother well?"

"Oh, no. I work in the cottage next door. But from what I hear she has two rooms, one for living and one for painting. That's very rare around here. In fact, she's the only one and most people don't even know about the arrangement. I don't know how it happened other than your father has donated large sums of money to the hospital. Everybody knows he's a generous benefactor."

"I see. So, my mother still paints?"

"My goodness, yes. Beautiful paintings. There are patients—Dr. Munson wants us to call them "residents"—who have one of her paintings in their rooms and I know a number of nurses in her cottage have some, too. She'd very generous with her work."

They'd walked down a service road and reached what must be Cottage 21, as they entered a backdoor into a hallway with electrical lights illuminating the place with lightbulbs hanging from the ceiling every ten feet. Meg's body felt energized; stepping into the building made it feel real. She was actually within walking distance of her mother!

"You have electricity here," Meg commented. "I haven't seen any in town yet."

"Yes, we're ahead of the rest of the town. Dr. Munson made sure the hospital had its own power plant, built right into the original plans thirty-five years ago when the place first opened. He's always been ahead of his time. He also had the railroad bring tracks up to the plant so that coal and other supplies can be brought right to us. Sometimes the coal piles are three stories high, we use so much! Tons a day in the winter for steam heat. All the rooms have radiators in the walls. Our residents aren't denied common creature comforts. And we have hot and cold running water, piped right to the kitchens in each building, and water closets on each floor."

They'd reached the end of the hallway that seemed to be a work area and Petunia put her finger to her lips to signal silence. She opened a heavy door and peered around the other side.

"Okay," she said. "Nobody here. I didn't think so but we had to be sure. Come on." She waved Meg through the door into a small space that led to the top of a dark brick staircase. Opening a box on the wall, she pulled out a flashlight and turned it on.

"I don't see many of those, either," Meg commented.

"We need them to walk these tunnels. No electricity down here.

"This, by the way," she noted, pointing at a contraption on the wall with keyholes in it, "is the key switch to turn on the electricity. The building supervisor has the key and turns it on and off as needed. There's only electricity in the nurse's work areas, kitchens, and dining halls, but not the resident rooms. They still have oil lamps and candles in these cottages, but many residents in the main building can't be trusted to be around matches, so they don't have any light once it gets dark. They just have to go to bed."

They'd reached the bottom of the narrow stairs and now Meg felt completely spooked. This was one scary place, with two brick tunnels with rounded ceilings. They veered off in different directions and met where they were standing. Petunia flashed light into one, revealing stealthy pipes and wires.

"This one is mechanical. Only maintenance men are allowed in there. It brings the steam and water and electricity to these buildings. We go this way." She turned the light into the other tunnel and took off.

Petunia hoofed along with no trouble, the stubby beam of her flashlight bouncing off the brick walls ahead of her. For her own safety, Meg had to scramble to stay close behind. If any place on earth was haunted by vengeful ghosts, surely it would be a brick tunnel under an asylum in the dark of night.

"You're quiet back there. You all right?" Petunia asked without breaking her stride.

"Yes," Meg said weakly. "I'm fine."

Suddenly Petunia ducked. "Watch out for the cobweb!" she warned, too late.

Assaulted by a tangle of spider silk, Meg screamed and waved her arms wildly to get it off her.

Petunia turned around and laughed. "Oh my, aren't you a mess. Here, let's get this little fellow off you." She pointed the light at Meg's arm and calmly removed a white spider and gently placed it on the wall, where it jauntily walked away.

"It's white!" Meg exclaimed, swiping the last remnants of spider web off her.

"Yes," Petunia said, turning to keep going, "they're born down here and never see the light of day, so they're albino spiders.

"Here we are now." Another narrow staircase took them up to a door that opened into a hallway much like the one they'd first entered in the other building, again with electrical lights hanging from the ceiling. Petunia turned off her flashlight. "This is Cottage 23. Come, I'll take you to your mother's room."

In silence now they went through another door and entered a nice main entrance area with a checkered tile floor, a Persian carpet, and an ornate wood staircase. They went up to the second floor and after walking down a long, wide hallway decorated much like a parlor, they came to a door.

"This is it," Petunia said. "I'll be back in an hour."

With that she disappeared back down the hall.

Meg stared at the door. Reaching out to knock, she withdrew her hand and put it on her chest to quell her racing heartbeat.

To her surprise, the door opened, as if she'd knocked after all. There, silhouetted in the light of a gilded glass oil lamp and candles, stood Elizabeth Sullivan, her mother, dressed in a glorious duster robe of patterned silk, her luxurious black hair piled behind her head, kohl highlighting her vibrant eyes, bright red lipstick enhancing her full lips, and with dangly diamond and pearl earrings glinting in her dainty ears.

Meg stepped inside and her mother closed the door.

24

Suddenly the spirit guides wouldn't shut up.

"Really? Now?" Abby asked, hauling herself out of bed. It was late, after nine o'clock, and she'd been having a pleasant dream of riding in the Sullivan limousine.

Even though the day had cleared to be warm and sunny, and she could see stars through the window over her kitchen sink, telling her the sky had stayed cloud free, the chill in the air caused her to pull on her shawl and go over to stoke what was left of the day's fire. Taking two thin logs out of the wood box, she crisscrossed them on top of the ambers and sat in her rocker, watching the dry maple take the flame. The heat it put off felt good.

She settled back into her chair, folded her hands on her belly, and said, "Okay. What is it?"

The message that came through at first surprised her but she quickly realized it made perfect sense. Of course, Herbert Sullivan wouldn't want his daughter to see her mother, and of course Meg would then plot a way to see her.

Tonight, they were saying. Meg would see her mother tonight.

"What am I supposed to do with this information? Why tell me?" They never talked to her about Elizabeth Sullivan, her Lizzie. Was this message about Meg?

She concentrated, listening for revelations.

Yes, it was about Meg Sullivan.

"Will she be hurt by Lizzie? Or disappointed? Or will their meeting go well?" Abby knew that last option was hope beyond hope because Lizzie didn't exactly have maternal instincts. But she could always wish.

"What?" She listened some more. "You're saying it doesn't matter how the meeting goes, good or bad, Meg will need a friend?"

Abby cocked her head in concentration, waiting for more. Nothing more came.

"That's it? You got me out of bed for that? Of course, I'll be her friend! For three reasons that you know good and well. Her mother is my best friend. The Sullivans have done so much for me, I'd do anything to repay them. And Meg is such a delightful woman, I like her anyway.

"Is that it? May I go back to bed now?"

Then the words came into her head, clear as day. "Meg needs a real mother."

"Ah, I see. Hannah? Of course. I'll do whatever I can to help that along. I'll encourage Hannah to give up the pretense and let herself love the girl."

The spirits became silent, satisfied they'd been heard and with what they heard in return.

Abby didn't actually see her spirit guides; rather, their voices came into her head. Three of them from the distant past of her heritage made themselves available to her. More than that, since the age of four she'd known they were there to protect and guide her. Not every moment of every day but when she was in need and when she called upon them to help others. Out of the thousands of ancestors she must have, these three were the ones who wanted to give useful information to the living.

They refused, however, to become involved with unscrupulous people or nefarious plots. Abby feared that was why they refused to communicate with her about Lizzie and Harry.

They also refused self-centered, insufferably boring people, like that Nola from a few days earlier. Oh, they would answer stupid questions, alright, but with glib and stupid answers that she didn't dare repeat. Like the time the unattractive teenager wanted to know if she should go to Hollywood to become a movie star. The ancestor said of course, the girl had the same chance of being a star as the ancestor had of making it to the silver screen. Abby could swear those ancestor spirits entertained themselves with some of the people who came her way.

Stoking the fire one last time for the night to invite a little heat into the room, she put up the poker, laid her shawl on the rocker, and yawned broadly.

"Dang it, did they really have to get me out of bed for that? As if I didn't already know…"

Abby went back to bed. Cuddled under the cozy pile of quilts she'd hand stitched herself, she closed her eyes and fell fast asleep.

Her dreams consisted of a wedding someday for Hannah and Herbert, a new friend in Meg, and chocolate kisses.

25

Elizabeth opened her door to a mirror image of herself seventeen years earlier. Except she would never have allowed herself to look so drab.

"Hello, mother," the young woman said.

"Hello, Meg. Do come in." She swept her arm in an invitation to enter her room.

Her daughter walked to the center of the room and turned a full circle. "My," she said, "you have a beautiful place here. It's so lovely." She touched the back of the chaise lounge, but quickly withdrew her hand.

Elizabeth could see that Meg felt uncomfortable, not knowing what to expect or what was expected of her. To keep the conversation innocuous and hopefully put the girl at ease, Elizabeth looked around herself. "Yes, it surprises most people. They think that everyone in an asylum lives like an animal."

"Did you paint this picture?" Meg asked about a whimsical rendering of the asylum sheep on the wall above her bed. Meg stepped closer to look at it. "It's wonderful!"

"Thank you. I love painting farm animals. Actually, I love painting anything. I always say this one helps me count sheep at night.

"Here, let's sit at the table." Elizabeth pulled out two of the carved wood Victorian chairs with purple velvet padded seats and motioned to one. After Meg was seated, she sat down, too. "I've had them bring tea. May I pour you a cup?"

"Yes, that would be lovely."

Two Blue Willow tea cups with matching saucers sat on the table, with a Ceylon tea bag in each one. Elizabeth proceeded to pour steaming hot water into the cups from her sterling silver teapot, the one with an accompanying silver tray.

"Herbert makes sure I have all of the comforts I want, like this tea set. The nurse on this floor brings me hot water whenever I want. Isn't that nice of her? Of course, I know it's because Herbert pays an arm and a leg for them to take good care of me.

"Do you take sugar or cream?" She motioned toward a crystal cream and sugar set next to the tray.

"No, thank you," her daughter said.

"It's been a long time, hasn't it, Meg?" Elizabeth hated trifling repartee but knew it was expected in situations like this. She'd once been a master of "boring banter," as she'd thought of it, during dinner parties as a married woman. Make a benign statement, take a sip of your drink, pretend to listen, make another benign statement, and repeat the process ad nauseum.

"You look well," she said, and took a sip of her tea. Of course, she didn't think the girl looked well at all. But what else could she say?

"Thank you. It's good to be home."

"Of course, I heard about your breakup in Chicago. That man sounds like a perfect jackass." Although, she could see that if a man wanted a little excitement in his life, this girl wouldn't be it. She realized she'd hoped for just that with this visit: a young woman with city flare, flamboyant clothes, good jewelry, and fancy makeup. Maybe even smoking a cigarette in one of those long black cigarette holders she'd seen in magazines. Well, none of that fantasy had come true. Her daughter wore a plain black dress and hideous gray shawl, and no makeup or jewelry. She looked atrocious.

"Yes, the breakup was difficult. But I'm doing okay now," Meg said.

"Um," Meg hemmed, "I'm sure father told you your parents left me their townhouse in Chicago. I've lived there for the last three years. I'm so grateful for their generosity."

Elizabeth couldn't suppress an indignant huff. "Thank your father. He bought it for them under the condition they make our children their beneficiaries. They were in such dire straits at the time I met your father he bought them that place." The wry smirk felt just right on her face. "Without him, they would have ended up in the poorhouse. Or maybe in a place like this." She fluttered her hand around to indicate the asylum.

"Oh, I didn't know that," Meg murmured.

The younger version of Elizabeth looked out the window into the dark of night, causing Elizabeth to think, *She's contemplating telling me something else, something revealing, but doesn't know me well enough. However, I am her mother, after all. She's in a quandary. She wonders if telling me will bring us closer together, as if that would ever happen.*

"I… I'm glad to see that you're comfortable," Meg said, veering away from anything too personal. "I didn't know father had arranged all of this. I had all sorts of pictures in my head."

Elizabeth pulled the tea bag out of her cup and placed it on the saucer, and her daughter followed suit. Looking over the rim of her cup as she sipped, the mother took a long, measured look at this person who was her very own child.

She set her cup down. "I see that you're confused. Relax, Meg. You're sitting on the edge of your seat. You expected me to be miserable. Is that why you wanted to see me?"

Tension visibly dissipated from Meg's body as she sat back in her chair. Still, she took a long drink before answering. "Yes, I suppose that was part of it. I…. I wanted to know that and I also wondered…" She trailed off, obviously afraid to say what she wanted to say.

Not only did she look dull, she was afraid to speak up. *How tedious*, Elizabeth mused. She drank more tea to keep herself from filling in the tiresome gaps in the conversation.

"I've always wondered why father had you brought to this place." Meg finally spit it out.

"Ah, I see. You're wondering if I'm truly insane. The doctors say I am." Elizabeth took another sip.

"But, mother… May I call you mother?"

Elizabeth fought to keep from cringing. "If you wish," she said, knowing that was the least of what would be expected of her. She didn't want to cause a rift with this young woman. She didn't want her to feel as though they had problems to "resolve" together. There couldn't possibly be anything more tedious than that.

"Tell me more about what it's like to be here," Meg said. "Obviously, it's not what I expected."

Elizabeth enjoyed talking about the farm and the good food provided from their own bounty. She also described the excitement of chapel on Sundays. She told Meg that Herbert came once a month and Hannah brought her anything she'd told Herbert she wanted. She confessed that she liked Hannah. Her funny stories about some of the other residents got Meg laughing and the mood lightened considerably, thank goodness.

She ended with, "And there really isn't much more to tell about living here. I'm happy here."

Meg said, "I'm so glad."

"But, mother, there's one more thing I need to ask."

Elizabeth could see that her daughter had loosened up enough to get to the crux of what was on her mind. This was getting a bit interesting. The girl might not be so insipid after all.

Meg said, "I guess it's partly because I just turned twenty-one and feel more grown-up now, but I've been thinking about this for some time. I wonder if father had you put in here and declared insane just to do what a lot of men do: to get a wife out of the way."

Ah, so Meg was starting to think things through and speculate. Well, Elizabeth was determined to make her think it all the way through.

"'Get a wife out of the way' for what?" Elizabeth asked mischievously.

"I don't know. Maybe I didn't put it very well. But sometimes men want to be single or to even have a... another woman."

"You mean a mistress? I'm sure there are men who do have

their wives committed for that reason. In fact, my neighbor here has an unscrupulous husband. But your father isn't one of them. We may have been unhappily married, if that's what you've heard—and, yes, I was miserable—but one thing I can say about your father is that he's an honorable man. He had me brought here because he genuinely thought I was out of my mind after the loss of your little brother. I don't fault him for that.

"Do I think I'm crazy? Ha! No more so than any other living soul out there walking the streets. The difference is once I was put in here I started to like it. Oh, I screamed bloody murder at first but when I realized being in here gave me more freedom than living with a man I don't love, I settled in. Now it's my home. Best of all, I have all the time I want to paint.

"Would you like to see some more of my paintings?"

"Oh. Um, sure."

Elizabeth gulped down the last of her tea before it got cold and, again, her daughter copied her. She got up, took a lantern, and led Meg into her studio.

"Oh, my! Mother! There are so many. They're so beautiful. Look at this one!" She pointed to Elizabeth's most recent completed piece of Traverse the cow. "And this one!" Meg pointed to lilacs in bloom, and then roamed from canvas to canvas, marveling at the breadth of work. "You must have fifty paintings in this room alone."

The room exploded with Elizabeth's artwork, every inch of wall space covered. Even more sat stacked on the floor, leaning against the walls.

Elizabeth nonchalantly fingered a few of her precious creations and said, "I don't know. I just know I like to paint them."

After another fifteen minutes of fawning over her mother's work, Meg announced that she'd better keep track of the time, as Petunia would probably be here soon to pick her up. A knock on the door proved her right.

At the door, Elizabeth realized that Meg expected some sign of affection. It wouldn't hurt her to offer a hug, she supposed, but her daughter didn't make a move so neither did she. Meg merely wrapped her ugly shawl tightly around her shoulders and said, "Goodbye."

Once her daughter was gone, Elizabeth wondered why on earth she'd been so curious to see the girl. There wasn't much there of interest.

She hoped the boring young woman never wanted to come back

26

Meg opened the front door and turned back to Sam, who stood behind her on the porch, hat in hand, having insisted on walking her up. "Thank you, Sam," she said. "Good night."

"Good night, Miss Sullivan," the driver said, half bowing. "Sleep tight."

She tiptoed into the house and quietly closed the door. The stained-glass chandelier offered dim light in the vestibule as the vast house sat steeped in silence. And then she heard it, the ever so soft click of her father's bedroom door upstairs at the top of the open staircase. He'd been waiting up for her.

Gathering her courage, Meg made a split decision and marched up the stairs. On the landing, she looked up at Angela the angel in the stained-glass window and said, "Say a prayer for me, okay?" As always, Angela looked down on her with endearing calm. Meg went up the rest of the stairs, stepped up to her father's bedroom door, and knocked.

He opened up immediately, as if he'd been standing there with his hand on the doorknob.

"Oh, Meg. I'm so glad you're home. How was the movie?" he asked.

"Father, I think you know I didn't go to a movie. May I come in?"

Wide-eyed, he opened the door wider, throwing the light of a gas lamp into the hall. She stepped inside.

Her father had on navy blue cotton pajamas under a navy blue silk robe, with leather sheering-lined slippers on his feet. She'd seldom seen him look so comfortable. It helped put her at ease.

A quick scan of the room suddenly made her aware that it had a woman's touch. Her father stood staring at her while she glanced around, noticing the bed had barely been touched and a book sat on a table beside a wingback chair. When her eyes landed on a vanity with a woman's ornate silver-handled hairbrush, she made another instantaneous decision.

"Would you mind meeting me in your study? Don't get dressed or anything, just come down. And, father, may I invite Hannah?"

He stood mute for a moment and then said, "Why, yes, that's fine."

Meg went out of his room and down to Hannah's room at the end of the hall. A sliver of light peeked out from underneath the door. She rapped softly.

After a few moments, Hannah's door opened. "Hello, Meg," she said. She was dressed in a lovely silk robe and heeled slippers with a spray of feathers on the tops. Meg had so seldom seen anyone in this house in sleeping attire she found her father's and Hannah's casualness to be a relief.

"Father and I are meeting in his study. Would you join us? Please, come as you are."

"Of course."

Hannah and Meg walked down the stairs together. Herbert Sullivan already stood in the center of his study, looking flummoxed.

Everyone sat down, with Meg and her father on the divan and Hannah in a leather chair facing them. The older adults looked at her expectantly and Meg cleared her throat.

"Tonight, I went to see my mother...."

First, she begged that no one who helped her would get into trouble.

Her father looked from her to Hannah and back to her, and said, "Meg, I have a confession, too. We found out about your visit beforehand. We decided... Hannah and I decided that we should let you go. In fact, I should have given you permission in the first place so it wouldn't be so difficult for you. When your plan came to light, I talked to Patrick McVeigh to get reassurance that he'd keep an eye on you. He never drove his carriage out of sight of your mother's cottage. If I didn't think I could trust him, I would have stopped you and helped you make other arrangements. But you seemed intent upon this and seeing that you're twenty-one years old now, we thought you should have it."

Meg was stunned. "You mean Peggy told you?"

Hannah chuckled. "Oh my, no. But she told Sarah who told Cook who told me. I told your father."

"At about that same time," her father added, "Patrick called to tell me and ask what I wanted him to do. Peggy, of course, has no idea he did that."

"Patrick?" Meg queried, mulling over this revelation. "That traitor," she said, not unkindly.

"No, more like loyal to me," her father said. "He's grateful I gave him a job on the docks with his father."

"But Peggy spilled the beans, too," Meg said. That confused her. She'd thought of Peggy as her secret confidant.

"Meg," Hannah said, "don't be mad at her. She's just a child. She doesn't ever have to know about any of this."

"And Patrick is a good fellow," her father added. "He was more concerned about your safety than about making money."

Meg snickered. "Maybe so, but he let me pay him anyway."

They all laughed at that.

"Patrick doesn't intend to tell his sister that her brilliant plot was foiled. I hope you won't say anything, either," Hannah said to Meg.

"Oh, I won't. She means well. And she is a sweet thing. I enjoy her company.

"Well, then, would you like to hear how it went?"

"Yes, dear, I would like that very much," her father replied as Hannah nodded ascent.

She described her entire visit, ending with the fact that her mother seemed friendly enough, but somehow distant. Tears came to Meg's eyes. "I guess I've always had a fantasy that we'd meet and she'd be thrilled to see me. But she wasn't. Not really. She didn't even ask me anything about myself. She talked mostly about her paintings and how happy she is at the asylum."

Hannah got up from her chair and sat on the arm of Meg's side of the divan, and wrapped her arms around the young woman's shoulders. She drew Meg close, resting her chin on top of Meg's head. "I think that's one reason your father didn't want you to see her. She's like that with everyone, Meg, not just you. Even you."

Meg clasped onto Hannah's arms and let her head rest into Hannah's chest. It was the closest thing to having a mother she'd known since she'd been twelve years old and separated from her nanny. Hannah seemed like more of a mother than her own mother. She could see why her father loved his housekeeper. Affection for the woman warmed Meg's heart, replacing the forlorn sense of emptiness she'd felt all the way home from the asylum.

"She's right, Meg. The truth is your mother isn't always a very nice person. I tried to spare you that. But I see now I was wrong. You're old enough to know the truth." Her father reached out to hug her, too, and Hannah went back to her chair to give them their space together.

"Father," Meg said when they parted, "you're getting better at hugging. You're not so stiff anymore." Herbert Sullivan laughed so unexpectedly and so joyfully it made Meg laugh, too. Hannah's face harbored a huge grin.

When they quieted down, Meg said, "But I have one more thing to ask. I might as well spill all my suspicions. This one just came to me tonight on the way home. Maybe I'm slow, but it simply wasn't possible for me to consider such a horrible thing before." Her voice cracked as she continued. "Do you think mother had something to do with Harry's disappearance?"

Her father's face became struck with sadness. He took a deep breath and got up to go over to his whiskey decanter to pour a drink. "Would either of you ladies like a small glass?" he asked politely. They both shook their heads no. He returned to the divan and took one gulp, as if for courage.

"I've never wanted to believe it, Meg. I have absolutely no proof to say that she did. Nothing other than she wasn't happy being married or being a mother and suddenly he was gone. There was never a ransom demand. No sign of anyone having invaded our house. No one, not the police or the private detectives I hired, not even Abby, could ever find a single clue to what happened to him.

"My heart was torn in two. I thought I might die. I wanted so badly to comfort you but I couldn't even figure out how to comfort myself, let alone do that for someone else. Your nanny was a godsend during that time. She took such good care of you. She loved you like her own, Meg, and you deserve that kind of love.

"When you were twelve and she'd fallen in love and needed to move away to marry, I thought it might destroy you. But, of course, I couldn't let her feel guilty about that. She deserved happiness. So, I watched her go and did what I thought best for you. I've questioned the decision to take you to Chicago every day of my life since."

He took another drink of his soothing whiskey. "Eventually you seemed happy and that assuaged my guilt. Now, there's nothing more in the world I want than for you to be happy again.

"But to get back to your original question: I don't know if your mother hurt Harry. I don't know what happened to him. But I do know she's not well and that she needs to be where she is." He tipped his head back as he drained his glass.

For a long, measured moment, Meg looked at her father. His eyes pleaded with her to forgive him any wrong he might have done her. She said, "Thank you, father. That helps me a great deal. I saw tonight that you're right. She's where she needs to be, and even where she wants to be. My mind is at rest about that."

"I'm glad." Obviously relieved, he inhaled a deep breath.

"I think I'd like that drink now," Hannah said as she stood and went to the decanter. "Meg?"

"No, thank you. I'm tired." She got up and went to the study door. "Why don't you two enjoy yourselves while I drag myself to bed?

"And, by the way, I know you're in love. Everybody knows you're in love, so you may as well continue to live together like you were before I came home." She winked at them and turned to go upstairs.

27

At dawn, Abby hopped onto Mr. Hollis' milk cart as he drove down the main road and came by the trail that led to her cabin. Their first stop after that was the Sullivan house, where Abby jumped down and left their usual Tuesday morning order of four bottles of milk, one crock of butter, and one brick of cheese. As they drove away she waved at Cook, who came out to gather the goods from the backdoor stoop.

As was the routine two days a week, she rode with the milkman and they chatted amicably, today with the weathered little man explaining that his best milk cow, Betsy, was getting on in age and her udders had started to chap badly. He had three other Holsteins that had never been nearly as giving as she and feared he'd have to buy two new cows to replace that old gal when the time came.

Abby suggested bag balm to soothe the poor girl's mammary glands while being pulled and squeezed during milking. She knew where to get a jar from the local veterinarian and promised to have some by the time they rode home this afternoon. Mr. Hollis thanked her mightily.

As they stopped at farmhouses and country cottages outside of town, Abby would hop out of the cart and leave the orders on the doorsteps or porch stoops. After so many years, she knew the route as well as Mr. Hollis. Doing this chore had long ago become her way of paying him back for the rides to and from town.

By the time they arrived in Traverse City, he took her straight to the garage where she did morning readings two days a week. Usually the sun came up by now but it was such a gloomy, overcast day, the sun remained allusive. She waved as the horse cart pulled away, knowing she was lucky to have so many good friends that could help her and who she could help in return.

Going to her table in the back room of the garage, she found a dowdy, dour woman already waiting. It seemed the woman suspected her husband was cheating on her and wanted the spirits to tell her if the "scumbag" needed to be "stripped naked, horse-whipped, castrated, chained to a motorcar, and dragged naked down the street." Always finding it difficult to convince her ancestor spirit guides to cooperate when this level of hostility became involved, the fortune teller did her best, to no avail. All the spirits would tell her was to get this wrothy viper away from her.

Abby fibbed her way through, eventually telling the woman the truth: Her husband aside, she needed to deal with her deep-seeded anger. Until she did, nothing else would fall into place in her life. The woman stomped out of the garage, furious. She didn't pay.

The next three visitors weren't much more amenable and Abby counted it as an odd morning. One simply wanted to find a lost ring. It could be found, the spirits said, in the pocket of her apron. But the woman insisted she'd already looked there. Abby asked if she had a second apron. Embarrassed, the woman quickly threw down two one-dollar bills and left.

Another wanted to know which of two suitors she should marry. Neither, as it turned out. She said that was no help at all. After all, she insisted, she had to marry *somebody*. She tossed a silver dollar onto the table, half the normal fee, before storming out.

And the last visitor, a businessman in town, wanted to know if he should invest in a motorcar or if they were going to turn out to be folly. He reasoned that the roads couldn't accommodate them and places to get gasoline were scarce. Abby told him the spirit guides liked cars. He rejected their advice, mulling it over and coming to his own conclusion that those motorcars, even though popular at the moment in cities, would never catch on because they weren't practical.

"They don't make any sense," he said.

Abby repeated what her spirit guides said word for word. "Human beings often do things that don't make any sense."

He scoffed, paid with two silver dollars, and left. Abby didn't know why he'd come, being so intent on making up his own mind. Of course, however, she knew he was wrong. The spirits were seldom wrong, and if it seemed they were that was only because she'd misinterpreted what they said.

Abby bid goodbye to the garage owner and headed toward the veterinarian's barn to pick up the bag balm for Mr. Hollis' milk cow. Pulling her shawl over her hair as it looked like it might rain any minute, she walked through town seeking out interesting motorcars. There were none today, however. All she saw were standard Model T's, Tin Lizzies, scattered in-between horses and carriages. She'd hoped for a few classy Model T Runabouts, maybe even a burgundy one. Or a Touring Car with a cloth top. At least a snazzy jalopy. A police car, a lumber mill truck, and an ice truck went by, but nothing out of the ordinary. A few kids rode down the street on bicycles. That was it.

Then she went by the Union Street train station and saw something interesting. There stood Meg talking to her "beau," Jed O'Neill. He looked debonair in a professional black suit, white shirt, and tie. His hat sat on his head. Obviously having just come off the train, which at this time of day would have been the one from Detroit, he carried a leather valise. Meg looked jaunty in a flowered pink dress and pink sweater. They each carried a black umbrella.

Abby slipped behind a tree and watched. She wasn't close enough to hear but could see them clearly. Meg talked for a few minutes, gesturing animatedly. Jed listened intently and put a hand on her shoulder. Then Meg talked a bit more and shrugged, her hands spread wide. He nodded and took Meg into his arms. They kissed, right there in front of the train station, so smitten with each other they were oblivious to the rest of the world.

They are in love. Already, Abby thought. *That didn't take long.*

Abby walked away, wondering what they'd been talking about.

It started to rain as she entered the veterinarian's barn but by the time she left the shower stopped and the sun peeked out from between intermittent clouds. She decided to take a chance on the possibility of seeing Lizzie in the woods by the asylum.

The lengthy walk to their spot, however, didn't invigorate her as it had so often in the past. It used to be that the thought of seeing her friend built up her excitement to a fever pitch. But today, when she came through the trees and saw Lizzy already sitting on a blanket in their shed with a picnic basket beside her, rather than leaping with joy, her heart lagged.

Any mere pleasantness or pretense waned even more and more the longer and longer her companion talked. Lizzie's unemotional story of Meg's visit rattled Abby. The mother's unkind description of her daughter in no way matched Abby's impression of the young woman.

Dark clouds rolled in overhead, adding to the gloom.

When Lizzie said she hoped her daughter never came back, a wall crumbled within Abby's heart. Almost unable to breathe, she unexpectedly envisioned how carefully she'd built that barrier over the years in order to rationalize her affection for her friend.

Her appetite lost, Abby didn't finish eating the egg sandwich and apple Lizzie brought for her. Lizzie, on the other hand, had no problem downing all her lunch.

Excusing herself earlier than usual, saying she wanted to make sure to catch Mr. Hollis for a ride home as it might rain again, Abby left the woods a broken woman.

Her life, she knew, would never be the same.

The visit to Lizzie the night before must have been what Meg was telling Jed about. The girl had experienced, perhaps, the same kind of realization that had just hit Abby over the head like a blow from a sledgehammer. No genuine comfort or unselfish love would ever be found in the person of Elizabeth "Lizzie" Sullivan.

Abby knew now this was why her ancestor spirits never communicated with her about Lizzie. They despised her.

The Chippewa fortune teller trudged toward her meeting spot with the milkman, all the while contemplating what had made her bond so quickly and deeply with that woman almost twenty years ago.

Of course, she knew the answer all too well, one that wasn't new to her, although this was the first time she'd allowed it to reach fruition in her mind. There had been so many signs over the years, so many subconscious warnings, and, yes, even so much blatant proof. Their bond was unhealthy and unnatural, but not for the obvious reasons.

Oh yes, most people would think them evil for the kind of love they shared, "the love that dare not speak its name," as Lord Alfred Douglas wrote in his poem *Two Loves*. Oscar Wilde's 1895 "indecency trial," where the prosecution used that phrase as damning evidence, resulted in Wilde being convicted of "committing acts of gross indecency with other male persons" and going to jail.

The revelation that some people of the same sex were intimately attracted to each other had become common knowledge today. That didn't mean that most people accepted it. Even women's rights had come a long way in the last twenty years, but not that far. And regardless of new laws, new beliefs certainly had not reached a small town in a remote area of a Midwestern state. Some people might accept her, but others would have her committed to the asylum, right along with anyone else who didn't meet society's expectations of what they should be.

For the first time in her life, Abequa "Abby" Crane admitted to herself that she'd fallen for Elizabeth Sullivan for one reason and one reason alone: By the time they met when they were both eighteen years old, Abby had become desperately lonely. Her parents died four years earlier. With no immediate family; living alone since age fourteen; being an Indian outcast no matter how friendly others might be; not totally Chippewa and not totally white; never having had a physical relationship; and coming upon a beautiful, wild creature who had no qualms about initiating their affections... Abby admitted to herself that she'd been a total pushover for falling in love—with a woman or a man.

Blinded by a need for attention, derailed by sexual desire, and thwarted by her own obstinate denial, for twenty years she'd ignored the stone-cold fact that Lizzie was a damned shrew.

Suddenly it struck her that the things she'd loved about Lizzie, those things she thought she'd always love, were qualities she admired because she sought them in herself. The carefree spirit, attention to nature, and acknowledgement of being different could be respected. But there were too many other qualities within that woman's dark soul that Abby could no longer abide.

It was the mother's attitude toward her own daughter that had done it, once and for all. Abby felt maternal toward Meg the moment she met her. Lizzy's icy disregard for such a warm, loving young woman, her own daughter, had chilled Abby to the bone.

For some years now, Abby had been shoving away notions that she needed to break off their relationship. But every time the warning cropped up in her mind, her loneliness prevailed and within a week she'd be tromping through the woods outside the asylum to liaison with her lover. Now, however, she knew that she would never go back.

It must be much like, she surmised, a woman being married for twenty years and slowly over time coming to acknowledge that her husband is a brute, and getting a divorce.

She'd rather be alone for the rest of her life than be with Elizabeth Antoinette Wolcott Sullivan for one more moment.

Only the bag balm in her pocket gave her a slight sense of having done something a bit useful on this morbid, gray day. At least Betsy the cow might find some relief in what she had to offer.

28

With a steady hand, Elizabeth reached up to add a touch of deeper red to the rose.

"Damn it all to hell!" she groused. "This red paint is all over my hands."

Grabbing a rag, she swatted at her hands, to no avail. They refused to come clean. Looking down at her clothes, she realized that in her haste she'd forgotten to put on her apron and her white blouse was virtually ruined. Red paint stripes swathed across her chest.

"Hell, it's all over me!"

She swiped at her blouse with the rag but only seemed to transfer what was on the rag onto her clothes. There was no getting rid of this damnable color. Next time she'd have to paint a white rose.

It was bad enough trying to paint by lamplight, but the urge had struck her so violently she simply had to come into her studio to paint. Usually by this time of evening, right after supper as the sun set, she was lolling in her comfy bed in the other room, marveling at the spectacle she could see out her big windows. Being on the second floor of Cottage 23 and on a corner with two full walls of long windows, on clear nights she could see the moon rise in the east and a sky full of stars in the dark of night. In the morning when the wake-up whistle blew at seven o'clock, she'd open her eyes to the dawn, the level of the sun depending on the time of year. The scene looked different every day. She'd had them place her bed right in the center of the room to take full advantage of the view.

She could also see the tops of trees, which offered up all kinds of entertainment, including birds building their nests, spring-born hatchlings chirping away, and squirrels chasing each other in circles. Every now and then there was a bird ruckus where mother and father bird would have to holler and peck at predator birds who tried to get to their young. The noisy parents usually attracted help from other birds of their kind and the combined army usually won. Once in a while, though, a baby bird would disappear long before it could fly on its own.

If she walked right up to a window, she could look down at bushes and flowers planted alongside the cottage, like the lilacs and irises in bloom this time of year. When she opened the windows, like now, different smells filtered into her room, depending on the season and what was in bloom. It was one of the things Elizabeth loved most about her rooms here.

She'd painted many a scene, birds, squirrels, trees, flowers, clouds, sunrise, sunset, and the night sky, right from these windows.

But tonight was troublesome. Her painting had gone awry. She was filthy dirty with red paint all over her. She couldn't seem to do anything right.

Sweeping a loose lock of hair out of her eyes, she realized she'd just wiped paint onto her face.

"Good God! Will there be no end to this?"

She tried a clean rag. This time red paint came off on the cloth and she felt like she was finally getting somewhere.

Out of nowhere, a sound echoed from the other room. She stopped wiping herself down and stepped into her main room to listen. It came again. A knock at the door.

"Who in hell would be here at this time of night?" She tossed the rag aside and headed for the door.

"Oh, Jesus Jenny!" she swore when she tripped. "That damned lump is still there. Somebody needs to come and take that away."

Stepping gingerly over the large heap in the middle of the floor, she straightened her back and opened the door.

A deputy sheriff, young and good looking, and the sheriff, old and ugly as sin, stood there in spiffy uniforms.

"Hello, gentlemen. What can I do for you?" She patted the side of her head to fluff her hair.

She'd only opened the door halfway and stood in the way so they couldn't see into her room. Upon further inspection, she could see her cottage supervisor standing behind them, a normally ebullient woman now solemn-faced as a cadaver. And the night nurse in her white uniform who did final rounds after supper, and who had in fact been here not long before, stood by the supervisor, crying with a white handkerchief to her mouth.

What a crazy gang of people, Elizabeth thought. *Somebody needs to commit them to this place.*

"Mrs. Sullivan," the sheriff said, "we need to come in."

She opened the door wide and heard the nurse cry out.

"You stay here," Elizabeth heard the supervisor say to the nurse, which only intensified the yawping in the hall.

Elizabeth stepped back so the men and supervisor could enter. The young deputy went straight to the hump on the floor; the sheriff took Elizabeth by the elbow and guided her around it to the table, where he told her to sit. He sat down beside her and then looked over at the situation on the floor. The supervisor, having turned white as a ghost, looked down at the floor, nodded to the young officer, and left. The bawling in the hallway ceased as she presumably went away with the nurse.

"Mrs. Sullivan, I need you to tell me what happened here tonight." The sheriff seated beside her took off his hat and looked her straight in the eyes.

Elizabeth looked over at the clumped up mess on the floor. The young deputy had stood up and stared at her, as well.

A furrow formed between her eyes as she pondered the request. "What happened here tonight?" she repeated, confused by the question. "Well, I was trying to paint a rose…"

29

Meg caught herself staring at Jed, awe-struck. Her respect for the one she'd originally thought of as nothing more than "the handsome man" had just shot to the stars, knowing no bounds. His passion for the case he'd been working had earned her highest admiration.

"So, Jenny Pennington was released from the asylum today," he explained to everyone seated at her father's dinner table.

There was her father at the head of the table with Hannah on his right, looking stunning in a blue dinner dress. Next to Hannah sat Jed's uncle, Judge Sean O'Neill, known for years simply as "Judge." Meg sat at her father's left with Jed beside her.

Cook's dinner meal of roast beef, mashed potatoes, beef gravy, green beans, creamed corn, and buttermilk rolls had been spectacular. Now, even though they'd all agreed they were filled to the gills, none of them could resist Cook's German chocolate cake.

Jed finished telling his tale as they finished dessert. "It was easy to get her declared sane once I got a deposition from a woman in Detroit who'd moved to get away from Jenny's husband.

Turns out she'd been his mistress and he'd told her all about his plan to 'get rid of' his wife by having her put in the asylum. But the mistress got mad when he cheated on *her*." He shook his head.

"So, Jenny was released today and her sister from Grand Rapids came to get her and her children," he said. "A sheriff's deputy went with them to pick up the kids from the farm. I met them all at the train station this afternoon to say goodbye. They're all so happy! They'll be in Grand Rapids within the hour."

Judge interjected, "Yes, and now that she's declared sane, she can get a divorce, which I have no problem granting as expediently as possible."

Jed added, "That's my first case as a lawyer and it felt so good! I'm just afraid there are other women in the asylum in the same situation. Although, I know there are also those there of their own accord to get away from their husbands."

Meg liked how Jed talked so easily and openly at this table in her father's house, in her house. Her father had already reassured Jed that he could feel free to talk about working on an asylum case, as no one at this table was a stranger to the place. That made Meg love her father all the more. The new openness in their father-daughter relationship made her feel like a grown woman at last.

When every crumb of cake had vanished and coffee was served, Judge asked Meg if she intended to stay in Traverse City or return to Chicago.

"I'm staying here. Just today, Father called the butler on the phone to tell him. I've always thought of him as Frederick the Fossil, he's so old. But then I found out he was a retired police officer Father hired to keep an eye on me. I always wondered why his butlering skills weren't so great." Everyone tittered and looked at her father.

"In my defense," her father said, nodding acquiescence to her version of the facts, "I wasn't about to let my daughter live in the city without protection. Call me old fashioned, but I didn't care how much of an adult or flapper she fancied herself to be, I'm still her father."

"Well done!" claimed Judge.

"I'm just glad she's here to stay," Jed said.

"At first I felt badly about the house staff there," Meg said, "but Frederick wants to retire once and for all, Father has already found another position for the cook, and he's promised to find positions for the two maids. That makes me feel much better."

"Yes," Hannah interjected, "once they're all established elsewhere, Meg's townhouse will be put up for sale and then Herbert will let go with a sigh of relief." Hannah smiled at Herbert and Meg saw pure devotion there.

Judge looked intently at Meg. "Will you miss the excitement of the city?"

Meg cocked her head, thinking. Would she miss it? "No," she finally said. "It's a beautiful city, and I have my favorite walks and parks and restaurants and shops. I love the Field Museum of Natural History. I went to its new location at Grant Park just before I came home. I can spend hours in there. That's all to say I hope to visit from time to time but I have no desire to move back there. Traverse City is my home now."

She looked at Jed to see his reaction to this proclamation. She hadn't known such happiness could be seen in one's eyes.

"Oh, I tried to fit in there," she said as she noodled it out for herself. "I tried the exciting flapper life; I had high-class friends; and, yes, I even had a rich fiancé. But none of it ever fit right. It was like wearing a tight, corseted, ill-fitting dress. Being back here fits like a glove. No effort. No expectations. No judgements.

"I will admit, though, I miss the music in the clubs."

Everyone seemed amused by that.

"Thank goodness we have an excellent Victrola in the parlor," her father said. "I must confess, I've even come to like some of that jazz she plays."

"Speaking of jazz," Judge said. "Herbert and I have a little business to discuss about the Ford motor car store we're opening in town next week. The rest of you can go into the parlor, perhaps, and listen to some of that music. It'll only be a few minutes, then how about a rousing game of euchre?"

"Sure," Meg said, standing. "Hannah and I can take turns at a spot with Jed to beat the pants off you old rapscallions."

"You're on!" Judge said. "In the meantime, you young rapscallions go entertain yourselves."

Meg, Jed, and Hannah went into the parlor. This was a relaxing room, much more informal than it used to be before Hannah remodeled the house. In the same light tones as the vestibule, there were comfortable chairs and a davenport. A new Victrola stood on one wall. The only old piece of furniture was an upright oak piano.

"Do you play?" Jed asked Meg, pointing at the piano.

"Not a lick, no matter how hard I tried. But Hannah plays beautifully."

"Do you want to play for us?" Jed now asked Hannah.

"No, no," she said. "Not tonight. Meg wants some jazz!"

Hannah sat down on the davenport and Meg when to the Victrola.

"I have Eubie Blake's 'Shuffle along Broadway.'" She held it up so Jed could see the Victor Record and then placed it on the turntable of the Victrola. She wound up the phonograph player with the handle on the side and delicately placed the needle on the phonograph record. Jazzy music filled the room.

Meg challenged Jed. "Can you one-step?" she asked, holding her arms out and dancing solo.

"Are you kidding? Detroit does have its share of speakeasies." Jed grabbed her and twirled her around as they fell into a breezy one-step, covering the room with their moves.

Hannah smiled from the sidelines and clapped approvingly.

"How about the shimmy?" Meg wanted to know. She broke away from Jed's hold and wiggled her body in the dance that had taken the country by storm, causing her filmy green shift dress with its satin hip band to swish around her body while her long pearl necklace jiggled back and forth. With that, Jed stepped back, his finger thoughtfully to his cheek, teasingly studying Meg's performance.

"Whoo!" Hannah exclaimed. "That's a hard one to match!"

"Oh yeah?" Jed pointed at Hannah and said, "Watch this!" He stood next to Meg as she danced, and broke into a lively shimmy that managed to look both silly and swanky at the same time.

Now everyone laughed and clapped as the song ended.

"Here's one of my favorites," Meg said, switching records on the turntable. "The bells are ringing, for me and my gal…" trilled from the Victrola.

Meg said, "Here's a new dance that everybody does but doesn't seem to have a name yet." She started knocking her knees in and out, and kicking up her heels.

"Oh, yeah, I've seen that," Jed said, doing his best to imitate the moves.

Hannah fell back onto the cushions of the davenport, thoroughly enjoying watching this young couple.

That's when the knock came at the front door out in the vestibule.

They all stopped and listened. Meg took the needle off the record. The knock came again.

Hannah rose and said, "I'll get it."

For a reason Meg couldn't name, she felt an abrupt compression in her body, knowing this could be none else than bad news. She and Jed went to the parlor door, and on the other side of the vestibule saw her father and Judge come to the study door. They all watched as Hannah opened the front door to see a sheriff's deputy standing there.

He removed his hat and said, "Hello, Miss Hannah. I need to see Mr. Sullivan, please."

Her father took giant steps to get to the door, going outside alone onto the porch with the deputy, closing the door behind him.

Everyone else gathered in the center of the vestibule and stared at each other in silent wonderment until the door opened again. Her father stepped back inside.

"There has been an incident at the asylum," he said. "I don't know any details yet. Just that the staff wants me to come and talk to Elizabeth. I've been told that she's alright. There's just something we need to talk to her about. Judge, the deputy suggests you come with me."

Judge grabbed his hat off the hall tree and handed her father's hat to him. Both men nodded reassuringly to the others as they donned their head coverings.

Her father said, "We shouldn't be long."

Judge didn't say anything because, Meg suspected, he knew better.

The men went out the front door, leaving it open for Meg, Jed, and Hannah, and out of nowhere Peggy in the caboose, to trail out to the porch behind them. The deputy drove away in his car and her father went with Judge in his Model T, not having had time to rouse Sam for his own transportation.

No one on the porch said a word.

Meg noticed the moonlit sky had clouded over, making the night as dark as Hades. A chill had invaded the air. When she wrapped her arms around herself to fend off a burst of cutting wind, Jed put his arm around her and pulled her close.

30

Abby always feared that evil spirits would invade her nether-
world where she talked to her dead ancestor spirits. It had never
happened before, yet tonight morbid thoughts pillaged her mind
and plundered away any ability to feel a sense of faith in human-
kind. Had *they* finally come?

She sat in her rocking chair beside the fireplace, staring into the
flames, picturing the "fire and brimstone" of Hell. Of course, however, that was the belief of her mother's Christian Methodist reli-
gion. In her father's Chippewa beliefs, fire represented life, a good
thing. They believed that if a person was bad while living on earth,
they were tortured forever after when their earth bodies died.

The seer closed her eyes, her hands clasped in prayer, allowing
the essence of her safe place, her cabin, to sooth her. The warmth
of the fire in front of her allayed her fears. The knowledge of
candles and lanterns offering soft light throughout the space
gave her peace. The wind suddenly howling above her rafters did
naught but signal the reliable movement of the earth in the dark
of night outside. She need not be afraid.

The presence of her ancestor spirit guides was so palpable Abby felt her breathing relax, her chest rising and falling smoothly beneath her clothes. They had settled her nerves because they wanted her to know something.

She listened intently. This message had been a long time coming, they said. She hadn't been ready to hear it and they didn't know if she was ready now, but there could be no more coddling and waiting. She had to face a life-shattering truth. She had to face it at this very moment. Until she did, she could not move on with her life.

The flames of the fire shot up into the chimney with the revelation, sucking Abby's heart into the night sky with it, leaving her morosely empty inside.

She had known this for a very long time. Yet she hadn't let herself know.

Stunned, she sat still for a few moments. There was no question about what she needed to do next, it was just a matter of willing herself to do it.

The spirits bid her rise up out of her chair and get on with it. They would be at her side, they reassured her. They would never let the evil spirits of others invade her soul.

A sob grabbed her throat, one of gratitude and of utter gloom at the same time.

With the weight of the world on her shoulders, she rose to wrap a shawl around her shoulders. Taking a bright lantern from the table she went out the door, too possessed to think to close it behind her. Hearing it flap in the wind and not caring, she tread toward the beach.

A violent gust of wind caught her shawl and cast it away into the night. Abby carried on without pause. Gaining momentum now, her denial and fear stripping away layer by layer with each footfall in the sand, the sudden burst of blustery rainfall did nothing to stop her. The pitch black of the night scared her not. She sallied forth until reaching her destination.

Abby shoved open the cottage door and entered. Soaking wet now from the storm and dripping onto the floor, she stood for a moment as a fierce bolt of lightning flashed outside the grubby window, alighting on the bay as nature reminded all living creatures that it reigned supreme. She took methodical deep breaths as she went to the corner by the fireplace, shoved the painting aside to free the edge of the rug, pulled the rug back, and opened the wooden trapdoor.

Descending the ladder, she lifted the lantern high and burrowed into the belly of the cave. At the site of Lizzie's painting in front of the pile of rocky rubble, she slid the canvas to the side, set the lantern on the ground, and began digging with her hands.

When she came to what she sought, even though expected, her tears would not be denied. Abby fell to her knees, head in her grimy hands, and wept.

After a long while, her crying spent, she raised her arms in supplication to God and lifted her bloodshot eyes to the heavens. "Holy Spirit, Gichi-manidoo, God Almighty, our Lord Jesus Christ, and Mary Mother of our Lord, bless this place of final repose...." Her verdant voice lifted in an earnest plea to sanctify this place where such a heinous act had taken place.

What she must do next would be the most heartbreaking thing she would ever have to do. But do it she must. She rose up and went to do its bidding. This, too, could wait no longer.

31

"Herbert, what are you doing here this time of night?" Elizabeth asked as her husband entered her room. "You're all wet from
the storm."

Never before had she been glad to see him here, but tonight
with the hubbub from these annoying people perhaps he could
be helpful in getting them to skedaddle. She even forgave him
dripping rainwater on her floor. The sheriff wouldn't let her go
back to her studio and insisted she remain seated at the table. A
deputy held vigil at the door and a doctor of some kind had come
in to look things over. Her cottage supervisor came and went,
alternately whispering to the deputy and the sheriff. Some asylum bigwigs in suits appeared and left, looking ill. A few nurses
and residents had congregated outside the door trying to peak in
whenever it was opened, but the supervisor shooed them away.

"Good lord, Herbert," Elizabeth said to her husband, "will
you please make them all go away?"

Herbert looked at her, pulling his shocked gaze away from
the mess on the floor. He held his hat in his hand and she saw

the man who'd come in with him remove his hat, as he stared at the floor.

The sheriff got up from his seat at the table beside her, and said something to Herbert and his friend in a low voice. Herbert nodded and whispered something in return.

The sheriff and other man stepped away, and Herbert sat down beside her at the table, for the first time placing his hat on the other side of the table rather than holding it in his lap. Leaning toward her with his elbows on his knees and his hands outstretched he said, "Elizabeth, what happened here tonight?"

"What happened? Here? Well, let me see.... I was painting a rose and got red paint all over me. Then these people came to interrupt me. Now they won't let me go back to my painting." She pouted like a child.

Herbert looked at her in silence, his eyes glazed in what she interrupted as sadness. "No, Elizabeth," he said, "what happened with Dr. Whitmore over there?" He motioned toward the bloody lump on the floor.

"Oh." Her voice lowered in disgust. "Him. He came here, drunk as a skunk. He's not supposed to come to our rooms. He's never come before. But he came tonight insisting on having his way with me," she whispered, her eyes widening, "When I said no he got mad so I stabbed him with my palette knife. Good riddance, I say.

"Now may I get back to my painting? Please, Herbert."

Elizabeth watched her husband fail to breathe as his face drained of what little color was left in it. Eventually, he took a long breath. "Elizabeth, I need you to listen carefully." She stuck out her neck and leaned in, focusing on his eyes. "You've killed a man. That's against the law. They have to take you to another room, at least for the time being, one where you can't hurt anyone else. Hopefully, when everything gets sorted out, you can come back here."

"Oh, no, Herbert. Tell them I'm staying here. This is my home; this is where I live. I don't want to go anywhere else. Tell them to go away and leave me alone." She flipped her hand at the others in a gesture of good riddance.

Her husband cajoled for a long while, to no avail. Elizabeth would not move. When he suggested that she at least let the supervisor help her wash her face and hands, and find clean clothes to change into, she looked down at herself.

"Oh, this isn't paint, is it? It's blood. That horrible man's blood. Okay, she can help me. I want him off me."

The white-faced supervisor came in with a basin of warm water, a washrag, and a towel. With shaky hands the distraught woman washed her resident's face and hands. Setting the basin aside, she went to the wardrobe and selected a plain blouse and skirt.

Elizabeth stood up and started unbuttoning her blouse.

"Why don't we step in here to change your clothes," the supervisor said, motioning toward the studio.

Elizabeth frowned, finding that unnecessary. But if that would help make everybody go away, so be it. She went into the studio where the supervisor helped her into fresh clothes.

Elizabeth came back into her main room, grinning. Herbert stood talking to the sheriff and other man who'd come with Herbert. She heard the sheriff call the other man Judge. Walking up to the three men, she spread her arms and said, "See? Just like new. Now, will you make them all go away?"

Two men were putting Dr. Charles Whitmore's lifeless body onto a stretcher. They pulled a white sheet up his torso and over his face, only to watch the sheet turn red from blood that had congealed around the dead man's head. When the men scuttled the stretcher out of the room, the pool of blood left behind on the floor looked like a luminous red pond.

"Somebody needs to clean that up," Elizabeth demanded, pointing at the liquid life that had drained like a waterfall from the psychiatrist's neck.

Everyone in the room gawked at her in disbelief.

"Sheriff," Herbert said in a deep, dull drone she'd never heard before from her husband, "may I have a moment alone with my wife." Phrased like a question, it had been a demand.

The sheriff nodded at the others and everyone left the room. The sheriff closed the door behind him.

Elizabeth and Herbert stood face-to-face next to the table. Hands loose at his side, back straight, and head high, in that sinister voice he said, "Elizabeth, did you kill Harry?"

Her eyes skittered to the side toward her studio. She wanted to go paint. But she realized that the only way to make him leave, too, was to answer his question.

She looked him squarely in the eyes, chin up. "Yes, I did."

Not a muscle of his body moved, but somehow Herbert's entire countenance changed. Paler, less handsome, and even shorter, he rasped, "Why?"

"Oh, Herbert." She'd totally lost patience with the nincompoop. "He was going to grow up to be a man just like you, marrying some poor woman who didn't so much as like him, and trying to poke at her all the time in the night. I wanted to spare him being hated like that. So, I sent him to God." She pointed skyward and looked up.

Herbert's mouth twitched. His hands balled into fists. His breathing heaved.

"Oh, please, Herbert," she said disgustedly. "It isn't like you didn't know."

Now tears welled in her husband's eyes. Ah, he had known. But he hadn't wanted to admit it to himself.

"May I please go into my studio now?"

"No, Elizabeth. You'll never enter that studio again."

He picked up his hat off the table, put it on, and turned away from her.

"What do you mean? What do you mean I'll never go in there again!" she yelled hysterically as she headed toward the studio.

Herbert walked around the blood on the floor, went to the hallway door, and reached for the handle. Something stopped him. He turned to his wife and said, "Elizabeth, have you ever killed anyone else?"

Taken aback by the question, she slapped her hand to her chest and indignantly said, "Why, no! Of course not.... not yet."

Herbert turned his back on her, opened the door, and walked out. She heard him tell the sheriff to do with her what they must.

The sheriff went to Elizabeth and put his hand under her elbow as if to lead her away. She whipped her elbow up out of his reach. "No! I told you I'm not going anywhere! Go away! All of you, get out of my room!" Her shrill scream echoed off the walls.

The sheriff nodded to two big men in white uniforms who came in from the hallway and grabbed Elizabeth by the arms. Each of them twisted one of her arms behind her and put their other hands under her knees to lift her right off her feet. They attempted to carry her toward the door, doing their best to avoid stepping in the pool of blood.

But Elizabeth wasn't about to go willingly. Twisting and shouting, kicking her feet and flailing her arms with all her might, she flung herself at one of the men and bit his cheek. Blood gushed from the wound.

"Damn!" he yelped. "You bitch!" Dropping his side of her body, his hand went to his face. The cottage supervisor ran back in and whipped off her apron to use as a bandage.

In the meantime, Elizabeth managed to wrangle out of the hold of the other guy, and landed on her hands and knees smack dab in the middle of the big circle of blood on the floor. Trying to stand, she slipped and fell flat on her face. That's when the sheriff grabbed her by the arm, yanked her up, and together with the one remaining uninjured white-coated man strong-armed her into position so they could carry her out of the room.

Her bellowing pierced the night to match the booms of thunder outside as they hauled her down the stairs, out of the building, and across the broad deluged lawn toward the main building, Building 50, where she would be put in a cell with a locked door and bars on the window.

Herbert stood in the hallway without moving, watching and listening to the whole debacle. Judge cautiously came to his side, put a hand on his shoulder, and said, "Let's go home, Herbert."

Herbert Ambrose Sullivan, Jr., left the Northern Michigan Asylum for the Insane, knowing he would never come back.

32

Everyone left at the big house sat at the servants' kitchen table.
All pretenses aside, everyone was so worried about what might
be going on at the asylum they had naturally congregated in one
of the most inviting places in the house. Meg and Jed sat beside each other with Cook at Meg's other side. The older woman looked exhausted, as this was way past her bedtime. Peggy
appeared disheveled, as if she'd been ready for bed and quickly
thrown on a dress to come downstairs. The other servants looked
pretty much the same. Sam came in dressed in jeans and a plaid
shirt, the most casual clothes Meg had ever seen on the man. He
looked stricken, explaining he felt guilty at having gone to bed
instead of being ready in case Mr. Sullivan needed him.

"I should have driven him," he lamented.

"Sam, he was in for the night. You had no way of knowing,"
Hannah soothed. She sat at the head of the table, seeming like a
cross between a matriarch and a mother to everyone here.

They'd already speculated about a dozen things that could
be going on, until Jed suggested they should stop lest they

drive themselves crazy. "Let's just wait until they get home when we can find out the facts. Maybe it isn't as bad as we're imagining."

Cook brought out the German chocolate cake and a few picked at theirs but only Peggy had the appetite to finish off a whole piece.

They drank tea, except for Sam who nipped from a flask in his pocket. For a few minutes, he went outside under the shelter of the back stoop to smoke a cigarette, as Cook wouldn't allow that "rancid smell" in her kitchen, but he quickly finished it off and came back in.

Silent as a menagerie at a museum, no one spoke for a ponderous spell. The only sounds came from the mouth of nature with rain on the roof, wind howling outside, and thunder clapping in the sky. The only living being inside the house to make a peep turned out to be Kitty, who meowed to get up onto Cook's lap, which was, of course, allowed.

When they heard the car pull up outside, Hannah was the first at the front door. Flinging it open, she flew onto the porch to greet Herbert with open arms. Meg and Jed fled out right behind her with everyone else in tow.

Once inside, with hats put up and rainwater shucked off suits, Meg's father looked around at everyone in the room and said, "I need to talk to all of you. However, I'd like to talk to my daughter and Hannah first. Please wait in the kitchen. Meg, Hannah, would you please join me in my study?"

Aghast and afraid, Meg turned to find Jed. His uncle had pulled him aside and seemed to be explaining something to him. Meg followed her father and Hannah into the study, thinking her father looked stricken, walking as straight-legged as a mummy. He closed the door and told them to sit. Wordlessly, they sat.

He poured himself a drink, understandably forgot to offer them one, and then chugged it down before telling them the story of what had happened in Elizabeth's room at the asylum that night. He ended with, "The sheriff has ordered that she be put in a locked room with bars on the windows until he decides what to do. He fears she could still be a danger to others and maybe even to herself. Until this all gets sorted out she'll stay there. He told me he'll probably charge her with self-defense but she's still clearly too mentally unstable to mingle with the general population of the asylum. That's quite a statement, isn't it?"

He spared them the private conversation he'd had with his wife.

Hannah couldn't keep her seat, going to Herbert's side and wrapping her arms around him. He set down his empty glass and returned the embrace. Meg stood, hesitating as to what to do. Hannah looked over at her.

"Meg, come here!" she insisted, stretching out her arm in an invitation to join them.

Meg rushed over and the three of them found solace in the warmth of each other's grasp.

After a few moments, her father pulled away, took out his pocket handkerchief, and wiped at moisture under his eyes.

"You need to tell the others, don't you?" Hannah asked.

"Yes. It'll be the gossip of the town by tomorrow morning, what with so many people from town working at the asylum. They need to know."

Hannah nodded and patted his chest. "Let's go."

They left the study. Meg found Jed and his uncle sitting stiff-backed on a couple of equally stiff-backed chairs in the vestibule. Jed came to her and slowly entwined her in his arms. He kept his arm around her waist as they followed the others into the kitchen.

There her father stood at the head of the table; everyone else took a seat. Her father looked down at them and their expressions told him they already understood that this would be ominous news. "I'm so sorry to have to tell you this," he started, and then he told the crux of the story again. "I wanted you to know so that you won't be caught off guard or embarrassed. It'll be the gossip of the town by morning. If any of you are uncomfortable working here, I understand, although I hope you'll all stay."

Numerous sets of wide eyes stared at him.

"Are you daft, Mr. Sullivan? And you being an Irishman to boot," Peggy piped up. "Now why would we want to be leavin' somebody as good to us as you?"

That broke the depressing spell and everyone smiled, nodding agreement. Sam said, "Here, here!" and raised his flask.

Blushing, Meg's father said, "I'm honored by your loyalty."

Then, as if there hadn't been enough trauma for one night, the most unexpected thing happened. Abby burst through the backdoor.

Everyone jumped in surprise but Hannah almost knocked over her chair, being first to get to her feet. "Abby! Look at you. You're drenched! Come, stand by the fire. Let's get you a dry shawl."

Without being asked, Peggy left the room in search of a warm shawl.

Abby looked at Hannah but her dark glazed eyes didn't seem to see. It was as if she looked through the woman, not recognizing what stood before her. The fortune teller raised the lantern she carried as her gaze scuttled around the room, landing on Herbert Sullivan.

"Come," she said so quietly yet so firmly that he didn't question the command. They seemed to share an unspoken secret that only they could understand. Abby ran back out the door into the festering storm and he followed.

"Abby! Herbert!" Hannah hollered. "At least take umbrellas!" But they were already gone, having vanished into the sodden, black night.

33

Abby tore through the dunes, up one hill, over the gazebo, and down the other side. Wind and rain clawed at her face. Thunder roared in her ears and lightning struck the path ahead, warning her to stay away. She would not be deterred.

Tired of being afraid, tired of living a lie, she carried on with Herbert Sullivan in her wake. He already knew, her spirit guides told her, what would come but he needed to see it in order to overcome the lie himself. He needed closure and healing.

When she reached the cottage, she flung the door open, went straight to the open trapdoor, and descended the ladder. Herbert lagged just far enough behind, having found it difficult to keep up with her pace in the storm, that when he entered the utterly dark cottage he was confused. Where had she gone?

A thick bolt of ravaging lightning struck the bay, casting enough illumination into the room that he could see a faint glimmer of Abby's lantern down a hole in the floor. He followed as a deafening clamor of thunder reverberated throughout the sky and water and earth, bidding him to be aware of what lay beneath the ground.

Herbert didn't flinch at the oddity of a cave underneath the cottage. He had only one objective in mind. Ahead at a bend in the cave, Abby stood with her back to him, head bent, shoulders stooped, and lantern held forlornly at her side. When she heard Herbert's footfall behind her she stepped aside without looking up, her weeping focus on what lay on the ground. Herbert Sullivan stepped over the rubble of rock strewn in all directions and peered into a stone cubby in the cave wall.

His strong, masculine legs gave way as he fell helplessly to his knees and began to wail. Gently touching first one bone and then another and another of the child's skeleton before them, he cried, "Harry. My Harry. Oh, Harry, what did she do to you?"

Abby stood mute for time immemorial before coming to consciousness and stooping to her knees beside him. "Herbert," she said, "let's pray."

Herbert Sullivan grabbed her hand and nodded, hanging on with the grip of a drowning man. Abby held on tight and said the *Lord's Prayer.* "Our Father, who art in heaven…"

They said "Amen" in unison and then one-by-one they gathered the bones, he taking off his jacket to use as a sack and she gathering up the hem of her skirt to do the same. They also took the few remaining pieces of decayed cloth from little Harry's blue suit, his cracked black patent leather shoes, and a lock of black hair. Herbert reverently picked up the skull last and cradled it to his chest.

Solemnly, they left the cave, climbing the ladder up into the cottage.

Meg, Jed, and Hannah, looking dazed and confused, had just come through the door that had been left open to the elements.

Hannah closed the door behind them and they frantically closed their umbrellas and shook off rainwater. Jed carried a lantern that flickered poor light. Some moments passed before they saw Herbert and Abby standing by the fireplace.

"There you are!" Meg said. "We went to Abby's cabin looking for you but when you weren't there we..." She stopped.

Her father ignored them, instead walking over to the chaise lounge and gently spilling his share of the bones onto it. Abby placed hers beside them. They put down the cloth, shoes, and lock of hair. Herbert opened his coat to reveal the small skull he held there, positioning it beside the rest of the skeleton. Two small, black eye sockets set against stark white bone stared up at them.

Hannah gasped, her hand to her mouth. Meg dissolved into sobs. Jed stared in disbelief as his eyes brimmed with tears.

No one needed to say it. Elizabeth Sullivan had murdered her child. They could only pray she'd done so mercifully but knew they would never know. It wouldn't make any difference to know how it had been done.

The child had been dead for fifteen long years.

The storm outside mellowed, with onyx clouds tumbling off into the horizon. Lightening hit miles inland, sending only a murmur of thunder to rumble harmlessly across the bay.

The state of shock induced by the discovery of his child's skeleton ebbed and Herbert eventually spoke. "I want no one else to ever know about this. We'll say the bones were found on our property, which is true. No one needs to know the full extent of my wife's madness. We've suffered enough."

They all stood transfixed as the father gathered his son's remains into his coat with gentleness worthy of handling a sleeping baby.

Hannah hugged him. Jed drew Meg to him in a warm embrace. When Meg saw Abby standing alone staring out the window, her face harrowed with grief, Meg went to her and said, "Abby. Come." Enfolding the Indian woman in her arms, Meg whispered in her ear, "I'll be grateful to you for the rest of my life for finding my little brother." Abby squeezed her eyes shut and stroked Meg's hair as they clung to each other.

So, this was what it felt like to love a child.

34

Elizabeth thought she might go mad.

"Where in hell is that son-of-a-bitch husband of mine?" she screamed for the hundredth time. At first her jailers, who called themselves nurses, had tried to calm her down, talking to her in low tones. Now, after three days, they ignored her.

The cell those horrible men had thrown her into was tiny, only six by nine feet. Oh, they called it a "room," a misnomer as far as she was concerned. The one window had bars and couldn't even be opened. The heavy wooden door remained locked. There was a small bed but they only brought clean white sheets, a pillow, and a blanket at night, and they took them away in the morning. They wouldn't even let her go to a water closet outside the cell; they gave her a stinking chamber pot instead, emptied by a worker three times a day. Twice a day a worker brought a fresh basin of water, a cloth, and a towel for washing but then took them away as soon as she finished. Someone brought her three meals a day, the same food she'd always had, but she refused to eat.

Worst of all, there was no studio so that she could paint. How did they expect her to live without being able to paint?

Deciding to bellow until someone called Herbert, she started screaming again. "Call my husband! He's Herbert Sullivan and he'll have you sacked the minute he discovers how you're treating me, unless you call to get him over here right now! Get me out of here!" She pounded on the door.

Twenty minutes later, her voice hoarse and fists raw, she plunked down on the mattress to think about what to do next. If only she could paint! That always cleared her mind.

Without paint she had nothing to do but think about her past. Her childhood with boring parents. Going to boring schools. Constantly getting into trouble. Being kicked out of school once and for all at age fourteen when the headmaster caught her having intimate relations with a teacher, a woman. The teacher got fired and refused to see Elizabeth, no matter how many times the teenager sent love letters and pleas for a clandestine rendezvous.

Elizabeth remembered a number of liaisons with other women until marriage to Herbert Sullivan. Their wedding night had been her first time having intercourse with a man. She hated it. For one thing, she knew it would lead to having children, something she'd never desired.

Pictures ran through her head at how gentle he'd been, naively assuming her to be a virgin. She'd thought him a total dupe. From then on, making excuses to avoid being intimate with him became a challenge. At first, he truly believed she often had a headache, stomach ache, or toothache. Eventually, however, he realized she simply hated being naked with him and overrode her excuses to insist on intercourse. What did that get her? It got her pregnant, that's what.

Even though every moment of pregnancy disgusted her, at least her husband didn't insist on sharing a connubial bed during that time. But giving birth had been the worst, especially when she'd had to endure it twice. Why on earth any woman would ever actually want to do that she couldn't imagine. It had put ugly stretch marks on her belly, which thankfully faded over time. Her body, she knew, was otherwise flawless and she hated marring it.

Considering the existence she'd led, being at the Northern Michigan Asylum for the Insane had been a good life for her, as long as she had her room and studio, and privileges to roam around. She could secretly meet Abby in the woods for carefree fun. Yes, her time here had been good until being imprisoned in this disgusting cell. When would they let her out? She panicked at the thought they might leave her here.

"Get me out of here," she tried to yell again as she got up and went to the door, but her voice failed her, cracking until broken into silence.

Throwing herself across the bed, fury welled inside of her. How dare they do this to her! So, what if she'd killed a no-good psychiatrist? The asylum should give her a medal for getting rid of the bastard. The place prided itself in being holier than thou. Dr. Charles Whitmore had been the only truly unethical person she'd ever met here. So why would they be angry at her for doing away with him? It made no sense.

Thinking of murder, she found it curious that Herbert asked her if she killed Harry. She'd assumed he knew. Why she'd done it was so obvious. Perhaps she should have told her husband that she did it kindly, merely pressing a pillow to the little boy's face as he slept. The child never felt a thing. So, Herbert had nothing to worry about.

"Why in hell is everyone trying to punish me when I haven't done anything wrong?" she moaned. "And how in hell am I going to get out of this hellhole?"

Her ruminations meandered back to her attraction to women. Sapphism it was called. She remembered her teacher from so long ago telling her that they were Sapphists, called after Sappho, an ancient Greek woman who wrote love poetry to other women. Elizabeth didn't know for sure, but she imagined that back then having erotic desires for a person of the same gender was not a shameful thing like it was now.

Sappho had lived on a beautiful island called Lesbos in the Aegean Sea. Elizabeth had always fantasized about that island. She imagined that artistic talent would have been cherished rather than thought mad. Her need to paint would have been revered. How she wished she could be living then and there rather than here and now.

Lying on the bed staring at the small slice of sky she could see through the asylum's cell window, an idea started to form in her mind. Obviously, she needed to figure a way out of this cell by herself. The window must be the answer. She stood to inspect the bars. Reaching up above her head, the tips of her fingers touched the crossbar that went from side to side. Vertical bars extended up and down from the center crossbar to cover the whole window. Digging with her fingernails into the plaster along the windowsill, she could see that the bars extended deep into the structure, having been build right into the wall.

She sat down on her bed and stared at the window. Yes, that was it. That would be her way out. Never would she let those stupid people cage her in a cell without being able to paint. Come hell or high water she would escape. She had to be free!

35

The Grand Traverse Herald's lead story would no doubt become the talk of the entire region with its bold headline that declared: **Harry's Skeleton Found; Distraught Mother Kills Intruder!** The way the story read was that after fifteen years of no solution to the mystery of what happened to two-year-old Harry Sullivan, his remains had been found in a remote part of the family property. The Sheriff reported that it had obviously been a kidnapping gone wrong, with the child being killed in the struggle to abduct him, the body most likely being left at the point of death. The kidnappers must have abandoned their plan and left the bay area.

The sheriff added that even though fifteen years ago the entire community had scoured the area for days and weeks after the child's disappearance, the point at which the skeleton was found was so obstructed it was a miracle it had ever been uncovered at all. He relayed Mr. Sullivan's gratitude for all the support from the community over all these years regarding this very difficult event in the Sullivan family life.

The newspaper story went on to add that more misfortune

had sadly befallen the Sullivans. Mrs. Sullivan, weakened by the disappearance of her son and residing at the Northern Michigan Asylum with consumption ever since, had been deeply distraught upon learning of the discovery of her son's skeleton. Depressed, she became startled in the night when someone she thought to be an intruder entered her dark room. Without being able to see anything other than the form of a man, she stabbed him to death in defense against impending personal attack. It turned out the man was asylum psychiatrist Dr. Charles Whitmore, who knew of the continued tragedy for the resident and who had gone to her quarters to check on her well-being. Mrs. Sullivan was now sequestered whilst regaining her presence of mind.

Funeral services were listed in the case of each death.

Meg put the newspaper down and wondered how many people in town would believe that intricate fable. She didn't know if her father had wielded influence over his friends, the sheriff and the editor of the paper, or if they'd protected their friend on their own, but in either case it seemed a lot to swallow.

Beyond caring what other people did or did not believe, the facts remained the same for Meg. Her brother was dead. Her mother had murdered him. Her mother was insane. And her father was a good man whose life had been destroyed.

She sat at the dining room table pushing a fried egg, sausage, and toast around on her plate. Not wanting to hurt Cook's feelings, who used food to try to help everyone feel better, Meg had pretended to want breakfast. All she could manage were a few sips of her tea.

Alone at the table, her thoughts naturally turned to Jed, who would be here shortly. She couldn't wait to put her arms around him on this difficult and momentous day.

It was the day of Harry's funeral.

Dressed in a black suit, with a black cloche hat and black gloves at the ready, Meg looked every bit like the mourner she was. The only saving grace was that her father finally knew the whereabouts of his son.

She heard him coming down the stairs. Waiting expectantly, afraid a ruined man would enter the room, Meg was relieved when her father came in looking stalwart but resolved. Wearing a black suit, white shirt, and dark blue tie, he kissed his daughter on the cheek before taking his seat. It struck her that the color of his tie and pocket handkerchief matched the color of the child's suit Harry had worn when he disappeared. It was the color that had faded on the swatches of cloth found with the child's remains.

"Hello, dear. How are you holding up?" her father asked.

"I'm doing as well as can be expected, I guess," she said honestly.

He took her hand and said, "Good. That's all we can do now. Carry on with our lives. You have a good life ahead of you, Meg. It's obvious you and Jed are in love. Don't let this ruin your future."

His words surprised and soothed her. "Thank you, Father. I hope it doesn't ruin your future, either."

He said, "My past has been my torture. I don't intend to spend the rest of my life in misery. We've all known enough of that. It's time that it end. Having you here has given me hope. It's renewed my faith in family. I love you more than I've ever let you know. I hope you know it now."

Meg burst into tears, leapt out of her chair, and threw herself across his lap. "Oh, Father! I love you, too!"

Patting her back, he said, "That's the greatest gift I've ever been given in my life."

When she pulled herself away, she looked up to see tears streaming down her father's face. It made her smile up at him. "Aren't we a mess?" she asked.

He laughed. "Yes, we are. A good mess."

Meg rose and went back to her seat. They both dried their tears with their napkins.

One of the downstairs maids came in with a plate for her father, greeting him kindly. Without asking any questions, she took the crumpled napkins and brought back fresh ones.

"Thank you," he said to the maid. "I do believe I'm hungry this morning." The maid brought him coffee and went back to the kitchen. He dug into his breakfast.

Suddenly Meg felt like she could eat a little, too, and nibbled at her toast.

"Where's Hannah this morning?" she asked.

"The truth is," he said, finishing a bite of sausage, "she wanted to give us some time alone. And she's had a very difficult time with all of this. Oh, she acts brave for my sake, but I know this whole thing has broken her heart, even though she never knew Harry. She loves you, too, you know."

"Yes, I've felt it. She's a wonderful woman, isn't she?"

"Yes. Wonderful."

"Oh, Father, I wish you could marry her."

"So do I. But don't ever think I'm sorry for marrying your mother. Without her I wouldn't have you. So, no matter what, it's all been worth it."

Hannah came in, dressed in black like they were, looking

tired yet becoming. She ran a hand across her lover's shoulders and bent to kiss Meg on the cheek. "Hello, dear," she said.

"Hello, Hannah," Meg greeted her. "I'm glad you could join us. Cook wants us to eat, of course."

Hannah headed for the kitchen. "That's our Cook. But I'm not hungry. I'll go grab a cup of coffee."

Thus, the day began at the Sullivan family home on the day of the son's funeral. Meg and her father had barely finished eating breakfast when the commotion began. Extra motorcars and drivers arrived to take the house staff and all the outdoor workers to the service. Flower deliveries poured in. The priest called to ask if there were any last-minute requests. Neighbors stopped by with gifts of food. Jed and Judge came in and offered help in any way possible.

Jed's hug and kiss were the best help Meg could ask for.

They all went outside and loaded into the cars. Meg, her father, Hannah, Jed, and Judge rode their limousine with Sam driving. It took ten other cars, called in from other towns, to carry the staff and workers. Her father had insisted on providing transportation for them. As they pulled out of the Sullivan property onto the main road, instead of turning left toward town, however, Sam turned their limo right, going north. Meg instantly knew where they were going.

In half a mile, they saw Abby beside Mr. Hollis in the milk cart, headed for town. Sam stopped the limo and Mr. Hollis pulled up on his horse. Meg's father got out and Meg rolled down the window to hear this exchange.

"Hello, Mr. Hollis," he said. "Abby." He tipped his hat. "I'd like you to come with us, if you would. It would please us to have you join the family."

Abby stared at him for a moment. Dressed in a pretty, straight burgundy skirt and black jacket, and a wide-brimmed black hat with a burgundy ribbon, she looked even prettier than usual.

"Yes," she said. "I'd like that."

"Good." Her father took Abby's hand and helped her down. "Mr. Hollis," he said. "Will you be joining us at the church?"

"Of course, Mr. Sullivan. I wouldn't miss the chance to pay my respects after all this time."

"Thank you, Mr. Hollis."

Sam already held the backdoor of the limo open and Abby cautiously stepped inside. She sat beside Meg, who took her hand.

The ride to St. Francis of Assisi Catholic Church in town was a quiet one. When they turned onto South Union Street, they were stunned by the crush of horses and carriages, and motorcars. But the moment anyone set sight on the Sullivan limousine, they somehow managed to move aside enough to let the large motorcar pass until it could park near the church.

As they exited the car, half a dozen lights flashed as photographs were taken. Her father had warned them of this. Harry's disappearance had been such a big story fifteen years ago that the unsolved mystery had drawn interest ever since. Newspapers from around Michigan sent people to cover this final chapter of the story.

Solemnly, the family group filed inside.

Just inside the door, a woman Meg recognized as Jed's sister stood waiting with her husband and two boys. Meg recognized Jed's sister and nephews from the night just a couple of weeks ago when she'd seen them at the train station with Jed and assumed they were his wife and sons. Now Jed offered a quick introduction to his sister Colleen, her husband, and their two boys. Impulsively, Meg hugged Colleen. The woman seemed delightful, and up close Meg could see that Colleen looked like Jed's female twin, even though she knew Jed to be a year older.

"I'm so very glad to meet you," she said quickly as an usher shuffled her along down the aisle of the church with the rest of her entourage.

The Sullivan staff and workers were already there, seated in the third and fourth rows as requested by her father. Walking down the aisle to the first row, Meg recognized many men who worked in her father's businesses, as well as seemingly everyone she'd ever known in Traverse City. Young Louie Sleder, the boy who'd escorted her to the women's room at his parents' tavern, looked miserable in a tight-necked dress shirt and bow tie. But he brightened when he saw Meg, and waved. She offered a little wave back. Passing Patrick McVeigh, Meg nodded. He did likewise in response. The good-looking middle-aged couple next to him must be, she realized, his and Peggy's parents. Their mother dabbed at her tearful eyes with a hanky.

Reaching the first row, Meg curtsied and made the sign of the cross before entering the pew, a practice of all good Catholics. This time, however, instead of looking at the life-size crucifix above the altar, her eyes fell on the small dark blue casket that sat in the center of the front of the aisle. For a moment, she lost her balance at the sight, but Jed offered his arm for her to lean on. Once settled in the pew, she reached down to lower the long, narrow prayer bench and everyone in their row, even Abby who she knew was not Catholic, got down on their knees to silently pray until the funeral mass started.

Seated between her father and Jed throughout the service, she had a chance to observe both men during this heartbreaking ceremony. Her father remained focused, seeming to listen to every word out of the priest's mouth. He nodded from time to time when the father spoke of ascending into heaven and sitting at the hand of God. He knew all the prayers and hymns by heart. Hannah sat on his other side and he held her hand some of the time, when his hands weren't poised for prayer.

Interestingly, Jed did the same. He remained calm. He knew the prayers and hymns by heart. And he held her hand when not in prayer.

The service inspired Meg. She knew for certain that life would go on, as her father had said at breakfast.

When it was over and they filed out of the church, the town mortician had the hearse, an elaborate, black, horse-drawn carriage, at the ready. They didn't have far to transport the casket, as the church cemetery was right next door. Mourners could simply walk to the gravesite in the family section of the graveyard.

Most surprising as they stepped out of the church, however, was that townswomen of all faiths had arranged a huge picnic reception on the church lawn with enough food for an army. The very sight of their generosity warmed Meg's heart.

Walking over to the cemetery, they were constantly stopped by people offering their condolences. The gathering around the gravesite looked as though everyone in the church had come straight here.

The hearse pulled up and Jed, Judge, Patrick McVeigh, and Patrick's father served as pall bearers. Only four were needed with the casket being so small and light. They carried it on their shoulders and gently placed it on the thick straps stretched across the open grave. The straps were secured to hold the casket above ground while final prayers were said.

After a reverent prayer by the priest, everyone with the family took a white rose out of a vase provided for the purpose and placed it on the casket.

The priest then said, "Trusting in God, we have prayed together for Harry and we come to the last farewell." He turned to an altar boy beside him to dip his fingers into the holy water the boy carried in a bowl. The priest sprinkled holy water over the casket. "There is sadness in parting, but we take comfort in the hope that we will see him again." Now the priest turned to another altar boy to take a small incense burner from him, one that hung from a short chain. Swinging the urn back and forth over the casket, the priest continued the final prayer.

Meg could smell the incense from where she stood and closed her eyes to take it in. Harry, the little brother she adored, was at peace. Of that she felt certain.

The priest finished his prayer, reminding everyone about "faith in Jesus Christ." After that, the straps holding the casket were slowly released and the box was lowered into the ground. Sad as that was, it seemed right that Harry finally be put to rest with his ancestors. Meg imagined they would always watch over him.

For a moment the gathering didn't move, even though the ceremony had ended. Then a few at a time, people started to go back to the church lawn.

Jed took Meg's hand as they walked to the picnic. Meg was surprised to find herself ravenously hungry and she couldn't wait to enjoy some of the fabulous food spread out on tables all over the place.

The reception turned out to be a joy. The warmth and camaraderie of the community was overwhelming. Although the funeral of a child had just taken place, a sense of rejuvenation prevailed. It was a beautiful early summer day, and eventually a large gaggle of children cast off their church ties and jackets and shoes and socks, and played tag on the lush green grass. Meg found herself enjoying their antics.

Best of all, Jed's sister and her family joined her family. Meg immediately felt at ease with them. When Jed's two nephews joined the game of tag and ran around like "hooligans," as their uncle called them, she thought of having her own children someday.

"There's nothing like children," she said, "to lighten the mood and remind us to enjoy life."

"That's true," he agreed. "They are the essence of life."

By the time they finally piled back into the cars to return to the house, the sun hung low in the sky, scattering long shadows across the church lawn.

Meg slept well that night, dreaming of her little brother as he'd been when they were children. Harry's adorable little face with its wide smile and lively eyes, and his unruly mop of black hair, would be the image of him she carried in her mind for the rest of her life. He would be happy. Best of all, he would be at peace.

Meg could now sleep in peace, as well.

36

The moment Abby stepped onto the back stoop of the big house, she knew something was amiss. The place was as still as a tomb.

Pausing before touching the handle of the screen door, she said a quick, silent prayer. What could possibly have happened to this family now?

The screen door squeaked as she pulled it open. She knew that door had just been put up, seeing that agreeable early summer weather had arrived. The inner door stood open. Abby tiptoed into the kitchen.

Cook stood at the stove, her back to the room as she stirred a pot. "Hello, Abby," she said without turning around. "Come in and get your tea, dear, and let me tell you what's happened now."

Abby poured herself a cup of tea, sat, and waited, nibbling on a biscuit from a plate already sitting on the table. Cook scooped up a clump of porridge into a bowl and brought it over to Abby. Cream, brown sugar, and a spoon awaited, so Abby fixed up the offering and began to eat, allowing Cook to tell her story in her own way.

The hefty old woman plopped down and explained. "Everyone else already ate. We were all up very early this morning. You see, the sheriff arrived at four o'clock. The sound of his motorcar so early in the morning woke some of us up and the others woke up from our rambling around trying to see why the sheriff had come this time.

"To make a long story short, Elizabeth hung herself in her cell last night. She used a bedsheet, tying it to a high rung of the bars on her window. She'd pulled her bed over to get herself up there, then tied a noose around her neck, and kicked the bed away."

Abby watched as the longtime family cook relayed what had happened. There was no remorse, only sadness. Abby continued to eat her porridge.

"We were all gathered in here by the time the sheriff got done talking to Mr. Sullivan, even Miss Meg. Mr. Sullivan came in and explained it to us. Abby, it's the second time he's had to do that—come in here and explain so we wouldn't be caught off guard. That poor man.

"This family needs for something good to happen, something happy for a change."

Abby finished her porridge. "It will. I know it will. Soon. I don't know exactly what it is, I only know it's coming very soon."

"Oh, Abby! Are you sure?" Cook's eyes lit up.

"Yes. I'm sure."

"Oh, thank you, my friend. You've given an old woman hope."

"There's always hope, Cook. Always." Abby wasn't sure why she said that or predicted what she did. She simply knew from her ancestors that it rang true.

Cook got up and went to work as servants came and went, so Abby rose to leave. As usual, Cook reminded her to take her sack of food. Abby thanked her. She would never leave this offering that Cook prepared for her. It was Cook's way of telling her she was loved. Taking it was Abby's way of returning that sentiment.

Walking across the lawn, sack swinging at her side, she decided to stroll down the beach to get home. She wanted time to think. It came as a bit of a shock to her that she felt no emotion over Lizzie's suicide.

By the time the gazebo came into sight, she realized that she had indeed separated herself from the former object of her blind devotion. Like Cook, she found it incredibly sad that any woman would come to that desperate end. But Elizabeth Sullivan, she now knew without a doubt, had been a violently mentally ill person.

Up ahead she could see Meg lying in the hammock in the gazebo. Perhaps, she reckoned, she should leave the young woman alone. Like herself, Meg might need time to herself to think.

But Meg saw her and waved, and stood up. When Abby reached the gazebo, she put down her sack of food, and she and Meg hugged.

"You know," Meg said.

"Yes."

"I'm so glad to see you. I have a confession and you're the only person I want to tell. I suppose I should confess to my priest, but I'd rather tell you. You won't make me do fifty Hail Mary's."

Meg's thin smile, weak as it was, told Abby that everything would be all right.

"Shall I put up a screen between us," Abby teased, "so you feel more comfortable telling me?"

"Let's sit over here." Meg pointed to the steps leading to the dunes facing the bay. They sat, and Meg pulled up her knees to wrap her arms around them. Looking out at the water she said, "I'm not sorry my mother is dead. Oh, I'm sorry that anyone would come to such a tragic end, but I have no sympathy for my mother.

"Abby, am I a terrible person?" She looked at Abby with a furrowed brow.

Abby said, "If you are, I am, too. I feel exactly the same way."

This time Meg's smile brightened, softening her features into those of a carefree young woman, just what she should be.

"Meg, your mother overshadowed our lives every moment of every day. She was bigger than life itself. She was beautiful, charming, talented, and… insane. In death, we cannot allow her to continue to control our fates. We must move on without her; we cannot let guilt over her bring back that veil of gloom she cast over us. That veil has always kept so many of us here from being happy. We need to step out of that shadow and live in the light!"

Now Meg beamed. Gesturing broadly, she said, "You'll never know how happy I am that you said that. You see, Jed and I have decided to get married. Soon. Just a small family affair. We want you there, of course. And I don't want any lingering remorse to ruin our day. In other words, I don't want the ghost of my mother lurking about in the corner to spoil my happiness."

The ancestor's voice in her head told Abby that would not happen. The woman and her troubled spirit were gone from this earth. Abby told Meg and she was glad.

"Father says he's fine, too," Meg continued. "I think he is. Actually, I think everybody is. Father called me into his study a little while ago and asked if there was anything of my mother's in her cottage or asylum rooms that I might want. He pointed out that she owned expensive clothes and jewelry, and made beautiful paintings. But I couldn't think of one thing of hers I want.

"Isn't that sad? My own mother and I want no mementoes of her."

"I don't think it's sad. I think it makes perfect sense."

"After I told Father I didn't want anything, I heard him call the asylum and tell them to sell everything. They can keep the money. He told them he knew she'd given away many paintings to people there and they were welcome to keep them, of course. In fact, he said that now that her story will make headlines again, the value of her work might even go up. So be it, he said.

"He also told them to cremate her body and bury the ashes in the town cemetery. He doesn't want her around our family in the church cemetery.

"When we talked in his study, I told him I have no compassion for her because of what she did in this life, but I pray to God to relieve her of her madness in the life beyond.

"Father said he prays to God to somehow forgive her because he cannot.

"I think my father is an amazing man." Meg peered out over the bay where a few sailboats had launched to glide along in the early morning sun.

"Yes, and you are an amazing young woman," Abby said, placing an arm around Meg's shoulders and squeezing. Meg patted Abby's knee. Abby lowered her arm and brought her hands together in her lap.

"Meg, I think that Hannah will become your new mother.

She'll be a wonderful mother. But I hope you'll always think of me as a friend, maybe even like an old aunt, or something."

"No, I can't do that. I'll think of you as an aunt, but not old."

Abby snickered. "Thank you for that!"

They sat for a while longer, enjoying the spectacular view.

When they parted, Abby felt renewed. So many secrets had been kept for so many years. Most had now been expunged so that this family could finally live in peace. The only secret she would never reveal was the true nature of her relationship with Lizzie. Abby believed that all sexual relationships should remain private, including her own.

No longer under Lizzie's spell, no longer a prisoner of their web of deceit, Abby wondered if she would ever experience romantic love again. And if she did, would it be with another woman or with a man? She didn't know. She did know she would stay open to all possibilities.

Entering her cabin, she felt lighter, younger, and happier than she had since she'd been a child living a carefree existence here with her parents. There had been happy times in this cabin. There would be happy times again.

To make that happen, there were three things she needed and wanted to do. First of all, she needed to be more appreciative of the loving friends she had amongst the Sullivan family and their household. She had other kind friends around town, too. There was no need for her to feel so lonely.

Next, she wanted to join a church, although she didn't know which one yet. There was her mother's Methodist church, the Sullivan's Catholic church, and many others in town. She would try one out each Sunday until she found one where she felt most welcome.

Lastly, she wanted to see if she could find any relatives from either side of her family, Chippewa and white. She'd never even tried. There might be an aunt, uncle, cousin, or grandparent out there who would like to get to know her. She knew it was possible that they might not even know she existed because her parents had no longer been close to them once they married. But that didn't mean everyone in those families would reject Abby. If they did, she'd always know she tried.

Her enjoyment of her newfound freedom suddenly allowed her to make one more decision, this an astonishingly madcap one.

Living so frugally all these years, she'd saved an enormous amount of money. She wanted to buy a Model T Runabout motorcar. In all honesty, she could afford ten Runabouts, what with all those metal boxes of cash buried in her yard. But one car, maybe even a burgundy one with a cloth top, would do.

She'd been utterly fascinated by her first ride in a motorcar, the Sullivan limousine, on the day of Harry's funeral. Sam would teach her to drive. And she'd heard that Mr. Sullivan and the judge were opening a Ford store in town within a week. She could be their first customer.

It was time to move on with her life and a car was perfect for trying something new.

She couldn't wait to move out of the veil of Elizabeth Sullivan's shadow herself, and get on with her life.

37

Meg leapt out of bed. Smoke! She smelled smoke! Holy moly, the house is on fire! What else can possibly go wrong? her mind screamed.

Without taking time to grab her robe, she fled out of her room in her nightgown, colliding with Hannah outside their doors.

"The house is on fire!" Meg bellowed.

Hannah grabbed her by the shoulders. "No! It's not the house. He said he wanted to do it, but I never thought he would!"

Meg heard her but didn't comprehend, still heading for the stairs. "Do what?" she shouted behind her.

"Come," Hannah said, grabbing her arm. "I'll show you."

They scampered down the stairs. The maids and Cook showed up in the vestibule, everyone rushing about in their nightwear for fear of being burned alive.

"Jesus, Mary, Mother of God!" Peggy hollered. "The house is afire!"

"It's not the house," Hannah reassured them. "It's out here."

They ran out the front door and looked toward the bay, where there was no mistaking what was going on. A towering inferno stabbed the night sky from the location of Elizabeth Sullivan's cottage.

Hannah grabbed Meg's hand and they ran toward the blaze.

Coming over the rise of the knoll, Meg could see her father, calm and composed, standing outside the reach of the flames. An empty kerosene can lay on its side at his feet. Reflections from the fire dappled his face with a flickering glow, an image Meg would have thought sinister except that his countenance was one not of a man possessed but rather of a man on a mission.

She and Hannah halted abruptly, staring at the wild flames that shot thirty feet into the air with black furls of smoke billowing into the heavens. Golden sparks showered out in all directions to float around in the sky, competing with the stars for sparkle and brilliance.

Slowly, they walked up to Herbert Sullivan. He put an arm around each of them, one on each side of him. The heat assaulted her face, but Meg refused to leave her father's side. He needed this. They all needed this.

Her mother needed to be exorcised from this place, too.

Pinpricks of light appeared around the bay as people awoke from their dreams to investigate what had roused them in the dark of night. Lighting their lanterns and candles, they no doubt stood transfixed by the spectacle across the water.

It didn't take long for the sheriff to arrive. He came running over the hill but stopped when he saw what was burning down. After assessing the situation, with no fear of the fire spreading, seeing that the knoll where the cottage stood was surrounded by acres of sand dunes on three sides and a large body of water on the other side, he merely sat down in the sand and lit a cigarette to watch the show.

Workers and volunteer firefighters started showing up, but no one objected or tried to put out the flames when they realized what had happened.

Elizabeth Sullivan's cottage sanctum along with all her paintings was being burned to the ground by her husband. No reminders that she ever existed were to remain on Sullivan property.

Jed and Judge appeared. As he approached, the judge whistled and said, "Hot damn! That's one hell of a fire!"

Jed put his arm around Meg and stared in wonder at the display in front of them.

Meg thought she saw Abby way up north on the beach, but the dark silhouette disappeared. After some time, however, the silhouette appeared again, this time dragging some kind of large object behind it. Closer and closer it came. Curious, Meg broke away from Jed to go see what on earth Abby was doing. Meg's movement made her father notice Abby for the first time and he headed in that direction, passing his daughter and reaching the woman first. Meg could now see that Abby had lugged the large painting from above her fireplace all the way down the beach.

Of course, Meg now understood, the painting had been the work of her mother.

Her father unburdened the Indian woman by taking the painting from her. Tall enough to carry it unfettered, he marched to the edge of the fire and pitched the canvas with all his might.

A flurry of flames engulfed it within moments.

By the time the blaze waned into nothing more than husky hunks of cinder, the promise of dawn painted the eastern sky in glorious shades of pastel.

They'd all sat down in the sand, Meg's head on Jed's shoulder as she dozed. Throughout the night, a hundred people had come and gone, one declaring, "This is the most exciting thing I've ever seen! Better than fireworks on the Fourth of July!" The sheriff had disappeared an hour earlier.

"It's over," Meg's father said. "Let's go home."

They got up, said drowsy good-byes, and everyone went to their respective residences for some welcome slumber.

Meg crawled into her bed, curled into a ball, and slept like a baby.

38

Abby pulled up in front of the big house in Rosie — that was what she named her new burgundy Roadster — and hopped out. She had a lot to do.

Sam waited for her on the porch and came hustling down the steps, tossing his cigarette into the dirt. "Abby, you're doing a fine job of driving that motorcar," he declared as he grabbed two baskets of flowers out of the backseat. Abby had the top down and the entire car looked like a giant flower basket, it was so full of lush arrangements.

"I'm a good driver," Abby contended, picking up two baskets of her own, "because I had the best teacher on earth."

Sam grinned from ear to ear. "May I add," he said as they went up the steps, "that you look particularly fetching today?"

"Why thank you, Sam."

They took the flowers inside and Sam insisted on bringing the rest in himself so she wouldn't muss her dress.

She did feel becoming for the first time in her adult life. When Meg had insisted that Abby join her, Hannah, and Jed's sister Colleen to shop for dresses to wear to the wedding, Abby thought her young friend daft. When they'd talked her into trying on this elegant "tea gown," as they called it, she thought herself daft. But when she put it on and looked in the mirror she'd been stunned. She knew she'd never looked so good.

The dark rose color, she had to admit, accentuated her smooth, tan skin. The delicate pleats down the top of the dress, the sash across her hips, and the mid-calf length graced her form with ease.

Those women even somehow managed to talk her into a pair of garters and silk stockings, which felt dreamy on her legs. But she said no to those horribly uncomfortable high-heeled shoes that felt like wedging her feet into a meat grinder and instead got a nice comfortable pair of pretty, flat ones. To finish her new look, she left her long hair unbraided and loose to cascade down her back.

All four of the shoppers bought lovey tea gowns that day for this day, Hannah's silver gray, Colleen's lavender, and Meg's the most beautiful ivory-colored lace dress Abby had ever laid eyes on. And Mr. Sullivan had insisted on paying for all of it.

Sam brought in basket after basket of flowers and Abby put him to work helping her twine the long garlands around the length of the vestibule staircase banister, all the way up both sides.

When they finished, they stood back and looked at their creation. The pastel iris, bluebell, and primrose blooms interspersed with green leaves looked fantastic. The fragrances they brought into the space were a bonus.

"Abby, that's beautiful. Miss Meg will be so pleased," Sam said. "You could start a flower business."

Abby tucked that suggestion away for future consideration.

"Well, I'd better get into town to pick up the O'Neills," Sam said. "They need an extra car what with Jed's parents and grand-parents in from Detroit on the train yesterday."

They said their goodbyes and Abby went back to concentrating on her task, setting baskets around the room. Chairs had been set up in a few rows of semi-circles facing the center of the room with an aisle down the middle. Meg would walk down the stairs; the priest and Jed would be standing at the end of the aisle, with Colleen and her husband standing as witnesses.

Abby thought the large vestibule with its grand staircase and two-story ceiling was a perfect setting for the occasion. The piano had been rolled in from the parlor so Hannah could play.

Abby picked up a table centerpiece and opened the door to the dining room. The aroma of Cook's scrumptious wedding feast made her nostrils flare in delight. The long dining table had been set with the Sullivan's best china, crystal, and silver. A three-tiered wedding cake sat on the buffet side table. Going back and forth until all three centerpieces were in just the right places on the table, Abby finally felt satisfied that her work was done.

She left the dining room and reclosed the door, just as Hannah appeared at the railing above. "Abby! Oh my! This looks wonderful! It couldn't possibly be any better than this. Come! Come!" She held a hand out over the railing. "Come join us."

Abby hesitated. She'd never been deep into the belly of this elegant house. Or any elegant house.

"Come on," Hannah insisted, waving her on.

Abby picked up the bridal bouquet and went to the stairs, cautiously taking each step as if she might hurt it if her footfall struck too hard. When she reached the top, she followed Hannah into what turned out to be Meg's room.

What she saw before her took her breath away. Meg turned away from a full-length mirror and faced Abby. "What do you think?" she asked.

There she stood in her ivory lace tea gown with a sheer veil edged in lace, attached to a pearl headpiece on top of her head, flowing to the floor at her back. She wore the earrings, one pearl in each ear, that Abby knew Jed had given her as a wedding gift.

"You're the most beautiful bride I've ever seen." Abby felt herself tearing up, she felt so happy. She handed Meg the bouquet.

Meg beamed. "Oh, thank you! The flowers are perfect. And look at this veil! I love it so much. It's handmade Irish lace. Jed's grandmother gave it to me last night. She wore it at her wedding, and so did his mother. It's one of the few things his grandmother was able to bring when they came here from Ireland." She gave Abby a quick hug.

A knock on the door pulled them apart and Hannah opened the door to Herbert.

"Father, you look so handsome," Meg said. "I love that new black suit."

"And you... you..." he said, "are the most gorgeous young woman alive!"

"Oh, Father, you're prejudiced. It's your job to think I'm gorgeous, remember?"

"But with you it's true. And I have one more thing to add to your ensemble." He handed her an old, tattered, blue bandana.

Meg took it, turning it over. "Is this what I think it is?"

"Yes, it belonged to your grandfather. I know you never knew

LINDA HUGHES

him, but I think he'd love for you to have his 'something blue' on your wedding day. It's from his days as a shanty boy."

"Oh, my goodness. This is such a treasure." She pressed it to her chest. "I'll tie it around my leg." She pointed to just above her knee. "Thank you so much. It's a perfect wedding gift."

"I've been thinking of him on this day," her father said, "because neither he nor I chose well when we married. You are the Sullivan who is breaking that spell. I think he's smiling on you from above. And I'm smiling on you from right here."

Father and daughter embraced for a long, quiet moment as Abby and Hannah slipped out of the room.

39

Mendelssohn's "Wedding March," played by Hannah at the pi-
ano, filtered up the stairs, letting Meg know it was time. Taking
her father's arm, they left her room and walked down the open
hallway. Below in the vestibule, all heads tilted back to see the
bride at the top of the stairs.

How it warmed Meg's heart to see Cook, Sam, and the
maids; all dressed in their Sunday best; here to be part of this momentous day. Judge sat with Jed's two nephews, doing his best to
keep the rambunctious boys quiet. Jed's parents and grandparents
looked radiantly happy. The women, of course, wore jaunty hats.
Abby sat next to the chair where Meg's father would be seated
when finished with his duties. The priest stood at the ready, with
the witnesses, Colleen and her husband, on either side of him.

When Meg and her father reached the landing, she glanced
up at Angela, her angel in the stained-glass window. Angela's
raised hand surely offered a blessing as a beam of sunlight shone
through to make the angel's hand glow.

The bride and her father turned to walk down the rest of the stairs, and it was then that Meg's gaze landed on Jed, "the handsome man." With wide eyes and a dropped jaw, he stared at her. When they made eye contact, he regained enough presence of mind to close his mouth, which quickly morphed into a huge grin.

The ceremony was lovely, with alternating tears, laughter, and a big kiss at the end. When it was over, Hannah played a few bars of the "Cannon in D Major" by Pachelbel that Meg and she had agreed upon, but quickly broke into "For Me and My Gal," the lively popular tune Meg and Jed had danced to in the parlor. Delighted, the newlyweds danced down the center aisle as everyone clapped.

Meg had never been so happy in her life.

The priest escorted them to a side table to sign the marriage certificate. Jed took his spectacles out of his pocket to sign and when the witnesses had to sign, his sister did the same thing. When finished, they both stuck their eyeglasses back in their pockets.

In that moment of looking at the license, an idea sprouted in Meg's mind.

"Father," she said to the priest, "why don't you marry my father and Hannah, too?"

"Now?" he asked, flabbergasted.

"Yes, now." Everyone had heard what she said and turned to look at Herbert and Hannah. Meg had never seen them look so flummoxed.

Her father said, "Dear, this is your day, not ours."

"But it could be all of ours!" Jed chimed in.

The priest said, "I don't have a marriage license for them."

"Oh, Father, I'm sure you can take care of that tomorrow. I'd bet my last dollar that's been done before."

The priest cleared his throat. "Well, it's possible…."

"Oh, yes! Mr. Sullivan and Miss Hannah, ya need to get married so ya won't be livin' in sin anymore," Peggy offered.

Meg saw Jed's grandparents titter behind their hands. Everyone looked on in anticipation. Meg handed her bouquet to Hannah.

Herbert took Hannah's hand and said, "Hannah, will you marry me?"

She paused. Necks all over the room stretched forward like ostriches to catch her response. "Yes," she said, "I believe I will."

The priest married them right then and there.

The joy in the room, already at a fever pitch, heightened and continued as Cook diverted everyone's attention by announcing that dinner would be served in fifteen minutes. Once she opened the dining room door and the smells of her feast wafted into the room, everyone's thoughts turned to food.

Meg grabbed Jed's hand and pulled him out the door. "Come with me," she insisted.

Galloping down the front porch steps, she dashed toward the path that led to the gazebo, her long veil billowing out behind her like angel's wings in the warm breeze. Jed took off after her.

Once at the gazebo they fell into each other's arms and kissed.

"Oh, Jed," she said when they came up for air, "I'm the happiest woman on earth."

"And I'm the happiest man.

"Meg, you know I'll probably never be able to give you everything your father can. But I promise to do my upmost to take care of you and our family in every way possible. I may never be rich as a small-town lawyer, but I can honor your family's legacy by serving this community well. I promise to make you proud."

"I am proud of you, Jed. I don't care about the money. What I want doesn't call for a fortune. All I want is to be your wife and the mother of our children. No, that isn't *all* I want. It's *everything* to me."

He offered one of his irresistible grins. "I think we should start on the family right away. What do you think?"

"I think we already have."

"Oh, well, yes, that vow of chastity of yours only lasted forty-eight hours." He chuckled.

"And we both know," she added, "it would have been twenty-four hours if you hadn't needed to go to Detroit for a day."

"So, let's keep working at it."

"Jed, when I said, 'we already have,' that's why I pulled you out here. I'm late."

"Late for wha…? Oh! Ohhh! La-a-ate!"

"Ah huh. A week. I'm never late."

"You mean…. Hail Mary! Already? Oh lordy, do you need to sit down or something?"

She chortled. "No! I'm fine. I just wanted you to know. Our secret for now until another month has gone by and we know for sure."

Meg glanced in the direction where her mother's cottage had stood. Once the ashes from the fire had cooled, her father had workers shovel the debris into the cave to close it up. The blackened foundation that remained had been covered with sand from the dunes. Not one sign lingered to suggest anything had ever been there. Turning her gaze to the bay shimmering in the sunshine, Meg knew that the insanity her mother, Elizabeth Antoinette Wolcott Sullivan, had brought to this family had died with her in the asylum.

"Jed, if it's a boy, may we call our baby Harry?" She looked at her husband, knowing he would understand.

"Of course, sweetheart. And if it's a girl, let's call her Harriet."

"Oh, yes!" She flung her arms around his neck and squeezed.

When they parted, she nodded toward the big house. "Can you imagine how much love this child is going to feel with all of those people in that house?"

"That's the way it should be," Jed said. "That's the way it will be for all our children."

"'All our children.' I like the sound of that."

The newlyweds held hands as they strolled back to the big house. They knew that no matter what came their way in the years ahead, they would be surrounded by people who would be there for them and their family.

THE END... AND A BEGINNING...

Acknowledgements

Thank you to my sister Karene Hughes for a great editing job; my friend since seventh grade Cheryl Reed for teaching me about farming, flowers, and the geology of the northwest region of Michigan's lower peninsula; my many Michigan Facebook friends who offered advice on blossoming fruit trees; my cousins John Shoemaker and Michael Bodus for their hospitality, especially the boat rides, every time I visit Traverse City; and Sue O'Connor, the best yoga instructor ever, whose savasanas gave my mind the space to conjure up this story. Also, thanks to Bob, Jan, and Mark Babcock of Deeds Publishing for their continued support, talent, and good cheer; and my husband Joe Martin for listening to my stories for thirty years.

And, finally, to my readers. Without you, I would go insane myself!

About the Author

When award-winning author thor Linda Hughes toured the former Traverse City State Hospital, once known as the Northern Michigan Asylum for the Insane and today known as The Village at Grand Traverse Commons, she couldn't help but be enthralled by the notion that so many secrets must be hidden within its grand facade. This story is the result of her musings and research about those possibilities. Visit Linda's website at www.lindahughes.com